The Fringes

a novel by
ALEX CLEMENTE

Raw Earth Ink

2025

For my love, Jose

First paperback edition October 2025

ISBN 978-1-960991-52-2 (paperback)

Published by Raw Earth Ink
PO Box 2
Humboldt, IA 50548
www.raw-earth-ink.com

CONTENTS

If you want me
You can find me
Left of center
Off of the strip
In the outskirts
In the fringes
In the corner
Out of the grip

"Left of Center" by Suzanne Vega

PROLOGUE

I woke up and remembered the screaming, it was a warm night in June, it was the senior prom. We were all dressed up. We just didn't see it coming. The accident happened, and I was angry. Or maybe it was everyone, they were all pissed off. Each for the same fucking reason.

"We went too far," said my good friend Tommy. He had his hand on my shoulder and I was shaking uncontrollably. "We have to call the police."

"That is out of the fucking question," I barked. "We'll think of something."

"Like what?" whispered my other friend, Anthony.

"I don't know," I replied. "But he slipped." I looked at Tommy and Anthony. They didn't say a word. They just stood there paralyzed, gazing down at the body under the shining streetlight. "That's the story. That's the fiction."

"You really going to be able to make that fly?"

"What other fucking choice do we have?"

"I'm not prepared for prison."

"None of us fucking are."

The body was cold and staring up at the lights in the sky. There were sirens in the background. We stood there motionless and breathing heavily. His left arm was severed. The car was stationary, hot and metallic; we smelled the metal. It was our fault, but somehow it didn't feel that way. Sometimes we get what we ask for, sometimes we don't. They say the lord works in mysterious fucking ways, sometimes they're not mysterious at all. They're intentional.

"What are we going to tell Terrance's family?" Anthony asked as he stared at the body in the street. This whole situation had unraveled in seconds. My face was still throbbing from when he cracked me in the face, I just used more strength. More than I should have. They told me to stop snorting coke, to stop drinking.

I had good cause. He was a bully.

For the first time that night, I had nothing to say. We waited for the sirens to stop wailing in the still darkness. It was nearly 3 am. My friends and I just stood there. Everything changed so quickly. We did our best to cover our asses the best way we knew how, it bound us together and it was a sensible explanation. He slipped; it did begin to rain pretty heavily. There was a struggle, we fought, and it was violent, blood splattered on our faces, there was nothing left to salvage, he pushed me to the brink. Terrance pushed all of us to the brink, this is what we get in return for our benevolence. Just insults, rumors, and violence.

No good deed goes unpunished does it, you sniveling fuck?

Sometimes it's better to sit in the dark, reality is darker. Complete absence of light. The forest with the absence of the moon, it can never be the same. The moon is its ancestor to the birth of Christ, or something like that. Lucifer's only companion. In high school all I did was get high as fuck, just to make it through the fucking day. It was all I could do to have some kind of control. It was unbearable at times. Insufferable torment with the workload, spending time with my girl, Deanna, whom I still see every now and then. But more of her later, trust me it's a whole thing. I want you to hear it from beginning to end. It's not exactly cinematic.

I have been depressed for a total of two years, each day and minute more debilitating than the previous one, it was as if it just happened; it didn't bleed normally. It would flow endlessly, and I wouldn't feel too much, numb, anesthetized from any kind of cathartic thrill: sex, drugs, music, movies, nightclubs, smoking, alcohol, it all went out the window. I almost felt as if I was dragging a huge weight behind me, pulling it, struggling with trying to handle myself when I was around people, while the feeling of loneliness and isolation tightened around my neck.

When I'm alone I feel better, I feel calmer. Of course, I wanted to someone to talk too but I was fine, for the most part. I glance at my phone, and I don't see any replies or anything, and then I remember what I'm capable of handling, but it just goes to show you some people are alone for a reason. They don't need anyone or anything, they just need what they are passionate about and in my case, it's writing short stories or poetry. I was always the creative person in high school, the person who made everything feel better because I could whip up a poem on the spot and lighten someone's day, even if it was just three stanzas or just a few lines, or a sentence. I could visually see the elation on their faces, relieved, at peace, content. It made me happy. It still does.

But I guess people have changed too, there are no loyal people anymore. It's a sad commentary but it happens to be true, I would rather live on the fringes of life than have to be suffocated by the vapidness of other people. They just bring me down, they're envious old fucks, thieves of joy, because they can't get laid, or they're alone and miserable.

Maybe I feel too much. Maybe I don't feel anything. I just want a release, a kind of orgasm perhaps? Feelings are messengers from beyond, but I figured I left everything behind. I abandoned by better self. I live in luxury, my parents are never around, I'm popping pills all the time, specifically benzodiazepines (Xanax, Lexapro, Klonopin) it was all in the medicine cabinet in my room, usually popping one for every time of the day, breakfast lunch and dinner, one of those pills would be waiting for me to swallow it with some water or Vodka, or just dry swallowing perhaps. I would smoke a joint, usually all day long, I would turn my phone off and just slip into the void. It was so quiet in the backyard, it was completely cut off from people and noise and distractions, my own private Idaho. It was just grand, life could be bizarre sometimes, but it was comforting to know when my parents were on vacation, usually half the year, I had this palace to myself, nothing could touch me.

I would smoke and smoke all day long. It didn't matter, depression is a motherfucker, but that doesn't mean anesthetization was out of the question either. And it usually took time for it to come back to me again, the waves of blue depression, that dark undertow that dragged me under and through a rabbit hole out the other side. It was a thrill to be seeing the undercurrent of Hell from a lounge chair facing the pool.

For the first time in forever, I glanced at my phone and it was riven with calls and messages. I placed my phone back down. Fuck it, they can wait. It wasn't meant to be responded to; the world had nothing to say anyway. I felt fine laying here, and now the drugs were kicking in. I was above the clouds in my head, not bombarded with trivial bullshit, just taking in the scenery and the quiet, walking alone was common for me.

Going to the movies, out to dinner, to a coffee shop, or just driving my car, I was constantly perpetually alone. Maybe it's better. It's safer, you're not judged, you're not being critiqued, you're not expected to listen to anyone. Nobody gives a fuck about me, not really. They're fine without me. I'm just that invisible man who shows up when people need something, when people need my advice. It was better to just blend into the background and not answer anyone.

My heart was broken several times, a wounded animal will strike at the heart of another, and it seldom misses, and the wound is invariably fatal, we don't mean to cast evil spells on others, it's human fucking nature. We are all guilty. Nobody is innocent in this fucking game. Even with all my money, I can't seem to shake the feeling that I will never be able to love again. He broke my heart, she broke it even worse than he did, it's wounded, done, my cold soul is dead. Numb. I will always be fucking numb.

All these tumbling fucking thoughts in my head, I just want them to stop. I light a joint and take a giant hit and exhale slowly, consciously, removing them, there is no pain, not for me anymore. I just want to get laid three or four times a week, one quick satisfying fuck after another, kick them out of bed and never speak to them again.

And yeah, I'm bi, men, women, sometimes both but my body and cock work in tandem so I prefer men. Sex numbs you, it's the ultimate pain reliever, far more potent than any synthetic pharmaceutical. Men fucking need it, it's unbearable dealing with what I deal with, I need to ejaculate it, explode on some hot guy's chest, and have him lick it off, or on some beautiful woman's tits. Sometimes they would call me and ask about me, needing more but I don't sell myself short, my dick needs a break. Why have me surrender to them? Why not play them? Always leave them wanting more, always. Make yourself the prize, make them want you.

Trouble is, I don't want them; I find people disgusting and selfish and petty. There is always something wrong, no matter what you do to make life better for them—no good deed goes unpunished. My pain was real no matter what I did, or who I fucked or what pills I took, it was a real fucking animal. Unbearable though it was, it had a kind of existence that was terrifying. When I felt nothing, it crept inside of me and burrowed there for months.

I isolated myself for weeks, never answering my phone, kept myself quiet in front of the pool, I had plenty of weed and I just rolled and rolled and rolled. I ordered food, grabbed it, slamming the door behind me, tipped generously of course. Since I didn't have much of a relationship with my family anyway, I may as well have one with their money, their cold hard cash from God knows where. I would call my dealer and friend, Shift, his real name was Steve but when doing deals, he was always Shift, don't ask me why, but his shrooms and herb and psychedelics were always fantastic, so I had to oblige him. I would drop $200 without batting a hair and be set for a few months. Stoned and tripping balls by the pool, the water became a kind of cylindrical wave going up and down, in and out, breathing, pulsing it had an uncanny vibration to it, dazzling, wild, magnificent.

"That's a lot of potent mushrooms there Hugo, be careful."

"It's nothing that some fine herb can't cure, I know what I'm doing."

"Didn't you say that you saw the clouds dancing?"

"I don't control the fucking weather Shift; I just watch it."

"True. Use wisely."

"Thanks."

A pursuit of expensive happiness always makes me a happier man. They always made me think I would never buy from anyone else; I could be getting a blow job in France, and I would still take a flight to Brooklyn, on Nostrand Avenue and walk up to his apartment. Maybe one day. Maybe. And I would eat them, swallow them down and an hour later when the sun was just beginning to set it would hit, and I would be on another plane. Sometimes we just needed to do that, as human beings, reality is destructive enough, we needed a break, a distraction. Mushrooms were just what the fucking doctor ordered. And my entire backyard was in this curious vibration, moving in sync with the universe, in this sensuous fashion, it was mesmerizing, and I would trip all day and night, completely untethered from reality. I remember I mixed it one night with MDMA, and Jesus, I never felt so light in my life. It was as if my pool formed waves big enough to swallow me.

The trees appeared to be speaking in vowels to me, the wind picked up and felt heavy flexing its muscle, I waved my hand in front of my face and there was this long vivid trail of light behind it, almost like the light sabers in *Star Wars*. There was no force on earth that could make me feel this calm, this present. Absolutely fucking surreal. I also felt it sedating me as I went into this strange trance, falling through the voids of space, passing by galaxies, witnessing my own mortality in the ether. From whence we came, I went back.

I was lying down reading *The Dead Zone* by Stephen King, I always loved his works. His books are fucking terrifying, yet they all have some kind of common thread. Desensitization, the removal of humanity from others. It's a terrifying premise to imagine. My phone rang, for the first time that morning, despite the messages that flooded the screen. It was Deanna, my old girlfriend. My on and off fuck buddy.

"You missed your daddy huh?"

"If I could smack you I would..."

"Yeah, I'm sure you would, you sexy freak."

"I don't know who you insult more Hugo, me or all those hot guys you get?"

"Probably you. You're more pliable. It's more delicious that way."

"It was always nice with you"

"Yes, it was, you did pretty well yourself. What can I do you for Deanna?"

"I'm not sure if it's my place to ask but I thought maybe... some mushrooms?"

"You're looking to go on vacation?"

"Yes, I'm just not sure where yet."

"I'll see what I can do." Her friends were in the car, jabbering away on their phones no doubt. Deanna was driving, she was always calmest when she drove, when she was in control, but when we fucked, she was out of control, wild, untamed, magnificent. I never came so hard or so frequently in my life. It was a thrill to be with her. Not bad for a woman. She was something different maybe, something better. I'm not always so fucking cynical and mean, I just have a difficult time loving others for who they are, they constantly disappoint me.

"I saw Brad the other night at a bar... I—I know you two aren't..."

"That fucking prick?"

"He said for me to tell you he's... sorry."

"Yeah, that really makes it better. Thanks. I uh—"

"Hugo just—"

"Should I go over and smoke a joint with him?"

"Well he may—"

"Maybe blow him..."

"I have to go."

"You called me."

Neither one of us hung up.

"Thank you for helping me with this." I was silent.

She hung up. Arguing with her is no aphrodisiac, I never used to listen to her anyway. You tend to block that shit from happening. Was hoping for something else though, I was hoping it would actually be a longer conversation, but it wasn't. It was brief and it doesn't mean anything.

Part I
Beneath the Surface

"Every man is guilty of all the good he did not do."
— VOLTAIRE

"Mankind is poised halfway between the gods and the beasts."
— PLOTINUS

"Things without all remedy should be without regard.
What's done is done."
— WILLIAM SHAKESPEARE
The Tragedy of Macbeth

CHAPTER 1
When Push Comes to Shove

I stared at my phone, hoping it was this delicious guy I met at the museum the other day, he had no idea I had taken MDMA, a small quantity, and was admiring art in a new way. He was truly divine, a body that I wanted to be on and under forever. I didn't see anything from him, sometimes these things take time, but he was so beautiful.

"I've been wanting you to ask for my number all night... I'm Frankie."

"Hugo. I couldn't help but look. You're so fucking hot."

"I try. But I'm also not just gay, I'm bisexual."

"Meet your new competition."

"You too?"

"Isn't it great?"

"Powerful. What do you do, Hugo?"

"I lay concrete. All night long sometimes..."

"That sounds promising."

"You have no idea, but I actually don't have a job. I was laid off from this art gallery, apparently blowing the security guard isn't considered appropriate."

"Get out of here man... you did?"

"Oh my god I appropriated him for a good hour. He didn't want me to make him cum—which, I mean, what the fuck is that about? You live in a freezer? Jesus. But oh god he was so hot... so fucking luxurious. I didn't mind feeling him all over me, all the time."

"And then what happened? Did he cum then?"

"No. Almost finished the job but he almost lost it." Frankie looked sexy as hell standing there with a drink in his hand. "But fuck it. Do you want me to make *you* cum?"

"Oh, I don't know, I have to think about it..."

"You fucking serious..."

"What are you? Fucking high?"

"Now this is promising..."

"Oh my god. Oh. Oh. Sweet god. Yeah—yeah... I'm—I'm—" And yeah. "That security guard doesn't know what he's missing."

"Believe me it was the handcuffs... it's always the handcuffs, Christ oh mighty. Frankie... come here. Come here." Frankie got under my arm, we split a joint, and lay in silence.

"I like how you sound right before you cum," he said.

"Yeah, that turns you on..."

"A lot of things turn me on, Hugo... it just made it such a hot fucking moment you know."

"I do know. Trust me."

"This is a gorgeous home you have."

I lay there, smoking heavily, hoping the ceiling would collapse on us. We didn't speak another word. It was comforting. Frankie was erotic to me, he had really gorgeous pecs, muscular arms, a tanned fit physique it all fit the mold. And I was grateful for it too, I just needed someone gorgeous to fuck me, it's all I wanted right now. I didn't want a friend or my family. *What family?*

I didn't need any of it, no tears, nothing. Fuck it all. Don't hug me, don't touch me. I'm not a man of sentimentality; I can't fucking stand it. And above all, don't fucking lie to me. I just wanted something hard in me.

"That was some blow job, baby."

"I'm your baby now?"

"Don't get it twisted. You made me cum that's all."

"Fucking right I did, so what's the problem?"

"Nothing."

We lay there in silence again, smoking and gazing out the window. I couldn't stand talking to people, it was hollow and unnecessary. I had my convictions, I loved poetry, I still do. Sometimes. I did and do enjoy writing it from time to time, but it feels as if I'm always leaving a piece of me there on the page.

In the morning of course I barely spoke to the guy. It was just a blow job, nothing to write home about.

"So... you want to meet up sometime, Hugo?"

I had rolled myself a joint, probably the fifth one in the last four hours. And as I slowly exhaled, I looked at my guest in the eye.

"Maybe, right now things are a little haywire with me. So, I just have to take it easy. But last night, well you definitely took my mind off it."

"It's why I'm here."

An hour before he left; we kissed but I didn't enjoy it. I just wanted him to leave. I kept his number in my phone. Just in case a booty call was necessary. Get my rocks off.

I sat in my backyard, laying down on the lounge chair overlooking the pool.

He slipped, that's what happened. That's the fiction—

I took a deep breath and didn't allow anything to fuck with me. I thought about snorting some coke but the herb in me thought differently, I needed something else. I just wasn't sure what it was, everything felt easy for me, getting drugs, when I wanted to fuck a man or a woman, it didn't matter, but it was the hardship I had known before, the battlelines were drawn that night...

He slipped. That's the fiction. That's what happened—

Hugo, it can't work.

ANTHONY! IT WILL WORK!

It will... it has too.

Cops, lights, questions. Ambulances

It was all too surreal now. And it kept coming back to me, that horrific memory. A memory that has discovered a way to replay in my head over and over, like some demented broken record.

Is Terrance a friend of yours?

I never answered the question the cop asked me. I was standing there over Terrance's body, and I saw for myself, just how far things had gone. And how there was no fucking way to un-ring the bell. Anthony, Bobby, Tommy, and I all stood over Terrance's body. Out of breath and not knowing what to do. Things happened so quickly, but we all do bad things. Right? I just didn't see it coming, and when it did. It changed everything. Fuck it—

My phone was blaring. I stood, glancing at the trees and the sky. And the fuck was it this time? Can't people just fucking leave me alone? And to my surprise, it was somebody I actually enjoy speaking to.

"Tony bag of donuts... how the fuck are you?"

"Hugo. I'm well man, I wanted to call. It's been a while. brother." He sounded as if he were in traffic, driving down a highway.

"Yeah, I've uh, I've been doing alright, better than alright actually."

"That's a relief, brother; I'm actually on my way to work but I was thinking maybe we can meet up soon. Get some dinner or something."

"Yeah, I would like that, Tony. Just a lot happening right now."

"It's understandable, you were always on your feet, even in high school..."

"It hasn't changed; I just can't stay too long in one place."

"Motherfucka! Move cocksucker!" Tony shouted into the phone, navigating the traffic. "Sorry bro. People here really test my patience."

"I always thought I did that."

"Yeah, but you I can just as easily drown in a fucking pool."

"Just as long as you blow me beforehand, I mean really make me cum like a fire fighter..."

"That sounds so fucking hot."

"Oh, it's so hot Tony... it's so hot. Oh my god..."

"I would do it for free, Hugo."

"Even better."

"Listen, I have to go. I'm almost at the office. I just wanted to drop you a line, I'm glad we're doing this. I was thinking Yellowtail Sushi for dinner. You know where it is, right?"

"Sure, yeah let's go there. We can smoke first if you want."

"I will never turn that down. Does this Saturday work for you?"

"That will be fine man. Thanks. It'll be interesting to see you, I can't imagine you're getting any."

"Speak for yourself.

"Oh, you are?"

"Yeah plenty. Your mom *and* your sister."

"Ohhh, see *that* was well-planned."

"I'll see you then, brother. Saturday. Yellowtail."

"Take care, Tony."

That was unexpected, Anthony and I had not spoken since that night... the night of the accident with Terrance. I figured it wasn't much to talk about anyway. What happened, happened. We all stood there, and we all supported each other, covered for each other. That's friendship to me. That was what bound us together, all of us lost touch as a matter of fact. Bobby, Tommy, Anthony, and I, but maybe this was the time to reconvene.

All for one, one for all. That was our saying. Corny, but it meant something then and I'm sure it means something now. I decided to text Anthony, about asking Bobby and Tommy. Making a night out of it, why the fuck not.

Ok. Let's do that. Sounds good. Tony wrote back, almost immediately.

Cool. I'll put us in a group chat. The MotherFuckas.

I always thought you were the only one.

True, your mom called me that when I walked out on her. Your girl too.

Touché bro. I love this I've always loved it.

All of us busted balls all fucking night long. Speaking of which, I needed some dick in my life, I would flip back and forth between men and women all night, but it was in the arms of a man where I felt the most alive, the most exhilarated, the most passionate, it was different with a man, they have more emotional intuition than women fucking realize, they just don't give them the chance they deserve, maybe it's different with women, more complexity, more of a firmer grip on their emotions than men. As much as I respected women, and loved being with them, on or under them, loved by them, it was heaven with men. They love differently, deeper.

And the sex was an affirmation of life all on its own, it changed me. It changed my perceptions of everyone and everything. It was just something I wanted to have constantly in my life, which wasn't as comfortable as people believed it to be.

My family is going to Europe every fucking month, not inviting me, but they wanted me to sit with them at dinner, or during breakfast, or when they were in the foyer reading, or perhaps when they decided to take me for dinner in Manhattan, we normally just sit and not speak to anyone. But the alcohol, that was something else entirely, if they drank then yes all of that affection and unassailable attention poured out of them, just a violent outburst of parental instinct gradually taking control. It was astonishing, truly the moment of my life. Especially when my father wanted to do a line with me in the men's room... yeah that went well. He finished it all, just gave me a bump. Anything worse than being with my parents, is dealing with them when they're inebriated. I'm not one to turn down cocaine, or marijuana, or any drug thereof, but that was the night... that was the night it happened. Terrance.

I remember my mood that night as well, quiet, and pale. And they didn't notice a thing, but the waitress did. She actually pointed it out to them. That I looked pale, they barely looked up. I could shoot heroin into my arm at the dinner table at home and they wouldn't notice. But not show up for a fucking dinner? Well, I can't let that happen. It might concern them. I would hate for them to become normal fucking parents, who showed me some slight attention, but no, I can't do that. With everything I have and could ever have, why rock the boat? It would be too much for them, I can't have the fuckers believe I'm ungrateful now, can I?

"And you're feeling guilty about this?" My psychologist, Jason Kelly, thirty-five years old. I've been going to him since before the incident with Terrance, since I graduated high school. I don't know how he is able to maintain a certain level of patience and restraint around me; I have this effect on people sometimes; I can't control what comes out of my mouth. Fortunately, I don't really have to talk too much, he is able to assess the damage even before I realize what I'm dealing with or sit in the chair near the fireplace in his apartment. He lets me smoke weed in his office, which is interesting but it's fucking weed. What else can I say? It's a plant for fuck's sake. As I said earlier, Jason didn't mind when I spoke or didn't speak, he knows what he is doing when I'm there, venting, crucifying everyone to a fucking cross, we had an extra-long session today. It went a little overtime, we spoke for forty minutes, nothing important, and then well... my time was up. His patient had to wait. I was paying him extra for overtime anyway.

"I needed this so fucking b-bad... so b-badly." I was getting vocal, loud, obnoxious and then I came. All over everything.

"Oh YEAH! You see it's worth the money... always worth it."

"I think we've just had a breakthrough, Hugo."

"I'll say. Oh, fuck you really know how to make me feel better..."

"You're paying me, remember."

"I'm paying you extra, daddy."

"Fuckin' right I'm your daddy."

"I thought you were just my sexy therapist."

"What's the difference?"

"Touché. Nice touch."

We got dressed, I wiped the jizz off my still-stiff cock, and held it in my hand.

"You want some of this?"

"Yeah, I'll put under my tongue."

"Wouldn't be the first time."

"And hopefully not my last."

"That will never happen." I finished getting dressed. Grabbed my phone and keys. "Time is definitely up."

"I can see that." Jason looked at my hard-on. He turns me on in ways nobody will ever understand.

"Yeah, it happens..." I took a few more pulls of my joint and put it out. Jason sprayed Febreze all over his office, it was a nice ocean scent, but it was overpowering.

"I sent you today's bill via Venmo."

"I hate this shit, thank you."

"Until next week's blow job."

"Until then..."

I couldn't believe how fantastic that blow job felt, he really goes in for the kill, he never disappoints. Mr. Kelly can blow. Without question. Jesus. I would smoke when I get home, I feel depleted after ejaculation, my fall from enlightenment but I didn't mind. Smoking helped my body to cope, as exhilarating as it is, it does affect me, and not always for the better. I left the office and saw people in the waiting room, one of the women gave me a look but I admired it. More of a sneer than a look, she must've heard me...

Walking back to my apartment, I just wanted to hear the sounds in the street, the passersby engaging in meaningless conversation and gossip, exchanging experiences about the different kinds of weddings they've gone too, the new shoes, where to have brunch. It was a collective effort for them, to sound even mildly interesting. People are so boring; I would never subject myself to that. But I do need to hear it. I need to hear it all, I'm a writer, so sometimes it helps to hear conversations, the verbalizations, the detailed account of what they did over the weekend, chit-chat. There was nothing more excruciating than chit-chat. I'd rather be deaf. Maybe there was a safety in being unable to hear, it can be remedied too.

I had to appreciate, however, the beautiful day; I think we

take it for granted. We never acknowledge the idea that if the sun is out, we have to keep it company. A forever being, bringing life, giving life, helping life to grow and thrive.

Sometimes I'm so angry, I forget. Perhaps it's what happened with Terrance, that night, of all nights. It's been replaying in my head over and over, but it happened too. There was nothing anyone can do now; we made our decision. Perhaps it wasn't the best one, but it was one that needed to be made. It practically demanded it of us. And I couldn't shake the feeling of waking up in the middle of night, constantly wondering why the fuck we didn't make a better choice.

However, at the very least, we were bullied by Terrance, it's just nobody knew the little thing we had in high school. I wasn't even an established bisexual than, and he captivated me entirely. He interested me, there was something different about him, and his body was a winner, in my eyes. Those dark eyes of his that were soft and understanding, his touch, the way his skin felt on mine. It was everything.

I get hard when I think about one night when we were hanging out and there was a blizzard outside and we got it on in his bedroom. His family was on vacation. We fucked in nearly every room in the house. And it made me want him so much more every day. We had to keep our distance a bit in school, but to keep it repressed, there is a certain erotic sensation to that as well. It means that it can be a heavier release, a greater sexual thrill. Sometimes I just jacked off in the bathroom. He was so built, so jacked, it was hard to not get it out of me before dismissal. I just couldn't help myself.

One day he was getting some water after playing some basketball, I walked out of class to use the bathroom and saw him, sweat all down his shirt and arms, bent over the water fountain, those gorgeous succulent lips. I thought I would've cum in my pants right there. At the time, I was banging this chick I met at a house party, her name was Daniella, and I was all over her too. She lived in a gorgeous house in New Jersey, her parents had more money than they knew what to do with, and well, we fucked constantly. Walked around the house almost naked, sometimes naked, we were a duke and duchess, living a life many people will never understand. The house was ours; the world was ours. We had a staff waiting on us hand and foot, we did every kind of psychotropic drug there was, and we bought it wholesale to boot. It was nice, it felt different to me each time, my family had money, plenty of it, but not this kind of money. Daniella grew up comfortably, and so did I. There was an electric current going through us every time we had sex, or watched tv, or were in the pool, or when she blew me in the cabana shower.

Romance, tragedy, pleasure, everything. She confided in me, her father was never emotionally available to her, but gave her anything she wanted, anything her cold heart desired. It would explain her moodiness, when she was in a dark mood, or was cold to everyone around her, including me, when she would ignore me entirely. Not even look up when I kissed her on the forehead. She was angry, seething with a rage she couldn't ignore but repressed, almost like a wire that was about to explode. She did explain to me once how she was able to cope with all of the darkness in her life.

"We are constantly being educated, Hugo. I've practiced detachment. I have learned how to look happy, while under the table I stuck a fork into the back of my hand. Perhaps it may be best if you did the same." And I knew, almost immediately, that she was absolutely fucking right. I admired her independence, I never resented her, I was living in a fucking palace rent free. What man wouldn't love it here; it was fucking gorgeous.

She respected me for being bi and never admonished me about not being out of the closet about it already, these things need to happen on your own time, on your own terms. Something so incredibly personal is never simple to deal with and can be nerve-wracking. That's my advice for anyone fearing coming out or explaining your sexuality to somebody.

I think she was the one who really understood me, not even Terrance was able to determine my depression, or what causes it, it just happens. You can't explain it. You never can, it's a numb feeling. No excitement, no fear, no anxiety, nothing. No joy, it's that lonely and blue section of Hell, the coldest depths. It wasn't even just darkness; it was something different. Something far more terrifying. It was emptiness, pure unmitigated emptiness. It doesn't just go away. You have to be a fucking moron; you have to have your head wedged so far up your ass to even believe that would ever be true. And we bonded with this. despite all we had, it was just never enough. It was never enough. We would fuck constantly, take plenty of Molly's, drink Vodka sodas all the time, and somehow, with everything at our fingertips, it was a far more potent entity.

Infinite in its superiority. Most mornings I don't want to be around a fucking soul, sometimes I can just lose altogether and then it becomes harder, more difficult, challenging, and it doesn't stop fucking with me. Luckily for me, I had a great cocaine dealer, that helped to smooth it to help me get myself through the day. Just a line, one long white line that I snorted in one go.

I never completely understood why people insist that drugs are something illicit or corrupt, such a subjective term. Drugs. If someone was on the verge of suicide and the doctor gave them a script for Xanax or Lexapro and they felt moderately better, what's wrong with that? Yes, people become addicted, just the way I'm addicted to helping myself to be better, addicted to cock, a hot sexy guy in my bed, clothes on the floor, rumbling in the sheets, or a beautiful woman, her sweet cunt to my desperate lips, that crevice of truth. Now I need to smoke.

I was sitting on a lounge-chair near the pool smoking a pre-roll and wondering what Deanna was up to now. We haven't spoken since... since *that night.* But I know she always made me feel good, happy, relaxed; she was the female equivalent of marijuana. All you needed was to be around her, to have her hand on yours, on your face, dick, anywhere, and she had this miraculous ability to cure whatever ailed you, whatever was bringing you down, dragging you into nothing. She casts that spell, man, that delicious woman. Those hard-ons weren't wasted, and I made use of them every chance I got, and it was often, even when she was seeing Paul. We banged every weekend almost, and it was great every time. He bullied me, so I decided banging his girl would even the score completely. And it did, and the best part about it was he never found out, even when they fucked, she never told him, and he never suspected a thing. Below the radar, I'm a mastermind. Maybe it was a little selfish of me, maybe it was rather manipulative too but when you're bullied and insulted and some unnecessary second-rate prick is the one who is instilling that anger, is it really such a terrible act? The way I see it, I was off the hook: he bullied me. I didn't have any kind respect or appreciation for him, nothing, I was just the guy who fucked his girl because he couldn't do the wet work himself. Over time, the relationship faded anyway, slowly collapsing, becoming undone, mission accomplished.

And here's the best part, she still calls me, she still wants me, even when he almost hit the roof with his anger over Deanna's fading love for her precious loving Paul, that man-child she was so in love with, or was she?

I stuck a fork into the back of my hand.

A wrecking ball, that is love to me. Who needs it? Overrated. Large quantities of chocolate work better. Especially with extra caramel, heavy cream. Deanna desired that as well, I had to bring the heat with her. However, she had her moments too. Hot and cold, happy and sad, angry and tolerant, envious and grateful, constant fucking contradictions, head games shit. And as that happened, I desired men to be with me, I wanted that steel, that tropical beat, that heat, that power, being with a man is about the transfer of power, a current of electricity flowing through, plugged in, charged up. It was a nice flow, and it had the propensity to make me even stronger than I thought I was. Unlike the bargaining and drama of a woman, men are different, there is little to no room for the games, just fun, it was about sex, it was about making fantastic love, it was about having the bedframe nearly break in half.

Frankie was my go-to fuckboy, he was a cop. And I was the happiest man on the face of the earth, Christ we fucked constantly, the neighbors complained of the noise. An exuberant wild sexy, even slightly bizarre night of straight sex, nothing more nothing less. It's how we wanted it to be, keep it simple in life.

The woman who lived across from me would knock on the door each time Frankie and I came home after a date.

"I can hear every word you two are making, and just constant banging. It can cause damage."

"Damage? I barely started."

"Why isn't he out protecting us?"

"He is, he's serving and protecting me."

"Oh hey... yeah, it's alright miss. I'm off duty," the cop said as he looked up from the couch in my living room. "Now if you don't mind... I'd like to read him his rights."

"You heard him."

She rolled her eyes and walked away.

"You have the right to start shouting as loud as you can, anything you say or do will be used against you in a court of law, if you can't find a condom one will be provided for you..."

"OH FRANKIE!"

"Resisting arrest that's five years minimum..."

"Cuff me, baby..."

Most nights she didn't complain but it was a thrill to get her to do so, she hated me ever since I moved in, always scowling. After another half hour we both came so hard at the same time. GLORY!

"If that's resisting arrest, what does murder get me?"

"You'll have to wait and see."

"I'll wait all fucking year if gets me another night with you." We shared a joint and as he exhaled the smoke into my room, I wanted to go another round.

"You're fucking gorgeous Frankie, God. Fucking love machine."

"And I work for nobody but you."

"That's right daddy... we just fuck. It's a good life."

He glanced at me and smiled ruefully. "It's not often I get into bed with a man, but it's nice. It's wild, thrilling. The handcuffs probably help, right?"

"The handcuffs, the way you put your hands on your belt, the gun, the loaded fucking gun, you keep it cocked all day long..."

"Exactly and I pop off some rounds with you, Hugo."

"Women... women are complicated."

"Draining."

"Yeah, dramatic, needy, emotional. I don't need that shit. I'm none of those things, people underestimate me."

"I'm not that way either, thank god." We finished the joint and I rubbed Frankie's cock in my hand.

"Weak in the knees and now I want to fuck again..."

"This time it's possession with intent to distribute..."

"Time for me to show you what happens in the showers..."

"Come to daddy."

The next morning, we had coffee, and he went off to work. In his uniform. Sweet baby Jesus, he looks even hotter in uniform, the gun by his side, that toolbelt. The slicked back hair, the tattoos. God bless America. He can make me cum in my pants the minute I see him, all he has to do is grin the way he does and Jesus, I'm at the cleaners again.

"Keep your dick hard."

"Don't make yourself cum, Hugo."

"You're worth it. I may murder someone, Frankie."

"That's twenty to life."

"I know. I've done it before, remember."

"Yeah, I do... I'll tie you down now. Make sure it never happens again."

I stood there in the kitchen sipping fresh hot coffee I'd made for us, and his presence lingered there unwavering. His cologne, the feel of his hands on my body, it was exhilarating. But it was his voice that I found to be the sexiest characteristic. Soft, mellow, relaxing, and strong. It was a voice that had been used in several police shootouts, screaming, bellowing, howling but it was controlled, of course, with me. But when we were hitting it from the back, I finally understood why most of the thug trash on this island listened to him.

I remembered my therapy appointment with my other fuck buddy, my psychologist Jason. Sex is therapy to me, and we usually go at it for a while and then stop, orgasm or no orgasm, he wasn't as irresistible as Frankie but I find it cathartic, nevertheless. I still haven't spoken a word about what happened on *that night*, and the more I think about it, obsess over it the more I need to say something.

He fell. No, he slipped... he just slipped and fell into traffic. That's the fiction.

He fell. He didn't have to fall; he didn't have to meet such a dark end. Things went down that night, it got out of hand, we were all drinking, heavily, all smoking heavily, passing around psychedelics, we were all dazed, confused, stoned, drunk. It was a fucking disaster. Nothing could have made me believe that it was meant to happen for a reason, I certainly fucking hope not. Words were exchanged, harsh mean words, quips that usually began as jokes or mild ball breaking. Sprinkle in some Molly, some marijuana, Jack Daniels, Vodka cranberries, arguments that became heated, a slow fucking burn, another burn, another drink, another bump... ticking time bomb. Tick, tick...

HE SLIPPED.
BOOM!

And then I don't remember much. It was all just a fucking blur, but the sirens, the cops, the questions, the people surrounding the street, Terrance in the street barely breathing... well those things I remember. Just fine. I can't say the pain hasn't remained. It's just been years since it's come to my attention, I suppose I changed after high school. I suppose we all did, there was nothing we could do about it, it happened, and for the life of me I wish it hadn't. Hindsight being twenty-

twenty, it just—the way his body flew in the air hitting the pavement. The wound is there, and it bleeds and bleeds when it wants to. It's been cauterized for years but the bandages are loose and unraveling, I wonder if my friends have the same problem.

I remember going home after that and sitting in the chair in the living room near the piano. The tv was on but the volume was completely down. My father asleep with my mom under his arm. The paintings on the walls seemed to stare at me in unison and wouldn't change. It was a horrifying feeling that this would never go away either. It was pouring, so I was soaked and I just sat there in the chair, staring out the window, in complete disbelief, nearly fucking catatonic. My parents woke up, looked at me, said goodnight and went upstairs to bed. They didn't even ask what happened or if I was alright, and I guess now it made sense. I sat in that chair for a solid two hours, not moving, shaking uncontrollably, sobbing at times thinking of smoking to ease the fear of what I felt, convincing myself that it would somehow evaporate overtime. Wishful thinking, it never works out. The guy was a fucking bully. I tried convincing myself of that too.

He slipped! That's the fiction.

The guy who hit him didn't stop. He just kept driving. And never came back. I couldn't sleep that night after tossing and turning for hours. And once that memory revealed itself, I fell into a deep sleep, and never thought about it again. Let sleeping dogs lie.

The car didn't come back. It sped off into the dark summer night.

When all the skies blacken
There is a ray of light beyond me
I can find myself there.
In a meadow, where the sun never sets
And the clouds disappear
Where life can be life
Where love can one day heal the world
Where pain dies
And we can all sit together
Forgiven of our misdeeds
Dreams you dream of
Now lullabies we whisper to ourselves

Blue heaven, oh my beautiful heaven
Wake up every day and let the sun in

I wrote that down on paper, I left it on the kitchen table in my house. I don't think anyone read it. But I saw it on the fridge the next day when I woke up, with my eyes sore from crying all night. I just wanted that world so badly. Things just got so fucked up. And fast. I remember not feeling anything, just numb, cold, alone. I can handle that shit, what I wasn't able to determine was how fucking scared I was. Even though I slept, I had a horrible feeling inside of me.

"Oh. Oh. Oh, good god. I'm going to—" His cum tasted better than usual.

"Looks like you had a breakthrough there," I uttered when I sat next to him on the couch.

"Yeah, it's about time too, switch it up, daddy needed that."

"It's my pleasure." I said as I lit up a joint. Jason was sitting up and using a cloth, cleaning the cum off his cock.

"Let me just take care of something first."

I rocked out with him on his desk and in just three little itty-bitty minutes, I had another breakthrough.

"You are worth every penny. I just needed to take care of that." I took the joint that I carefully placed in the ashtray and walked out.

Another patient stood and stared incredulously as they walked in. I made a face, rolled my eyes and left without saying anything. I was so detached anyway, I didn't see the value in talking to anyone for the rest of the day, I did that with Jason, more or less. He looked delicious in his new shirt and the suspenders. Jesus. Those alone made me want to jizz all over the rug.

With Frankie perhaps it was different, there were no extra concessions made, we both understood the parameters and we fucked, we fucked so hard and for so long it put Jason on the backburner most times.

Plus, I was in love with Deanna and she made me feel beautiful, I was bisexual, it's what we do. I consider myself to be blessed from God. Except Deanna didn't know I was banging Officer Frankie Condo of the NYPD, and Dr. Jason Gervasi, M.D., at the same time. A cop and a doctor. I'm a fucking genius.

CHAPTER 2
Lost Kingdoms

I had dinner with friends from high school; we lost touch as the years rushed by but we decided to meet tonight. Tonight of all nights. We thought maybe it was best, we had plenty to talk about, and what happened must have been sticking in their craws as well. I never really believed something like that ever went away; it just got easier to deal with. Lighter in a way, like carrying a brick in your pocket, you know it's there, sometimes you don't. But you reach in, and oh, yeah. That. We just got used to it; we didn't let it stop us. Perhaps it was a comfort to know we had a collective guilt about it all, at least I hoped so.

Get off HIM HUGO!

Terrance, you piece of shit!

Hugo! Stop bro! STOP!

"HUH YOU WANT SOME MORE FUCKER?! HUH! GET THE FUCK OFF ME!

"NOOO!" And it happened so quickly.

It's been surfacing so hard lately, but I didn't want it to make everything spiral out of control either. I just needed to remember who the fuck I was. I just had to remember what came off that horrible night, friends with three guys who supported me, who had my back, and I theirs. And without that I would be fucked.

The family cleaning lady, Maria was leaving for the day. I was standing in the kitchen having some red wine and scrolling through my phone. I saw her as she came down the stairs with her coat over her arm.

"You finished for the day?"

"Yes Mr. Hugo, I go home now."

"Thank you. I love this house when it's clean."

"You okay?"

I rubbed my face and tried to pretend as if it was just fine. "Yeah, just dealing with some shit. I'll see you next week."

"Okay Mr. Hugo, have a nice day."

"You too Maria."

She left and as she did, I felt stricken with a slight sense of loneliness. Just having her here cleaning and making my family's home feel comfortable and clean was a blessing. I wasn't aware of all I had growing up because I could have everything I ever wanted. Anything. People are at your feet when they know you have plenty of money to burn. And personally, I wish it really would fucking burn, because I don't think I would be so fucked up if it was, if somehow I was fucking liberated from this fucking cold museum I lived in since birth. Jesus! My parents... we didn't celebrate anything when it came to me, a birthday, a graduation, a good grade on a school project, nothing. It was merely a slap on the back and $1,000 to do whatever I wanted. That was the fucking reward. Money. I got hooked on drugs because of it, I had depression and felt deep loneliness because of money, how the fuck is any of this shit acceptable?

I had to call Deanna soon. I had to talk to her about what happened, I don't think she ever really showed much emotion when it came to the aftermath and what it meant, what it meant for the rest of our lives. I remember I stopped drinking and had nightmares for years, night tremors, sleepwalking. It was unbelievable. Not sure why I even bothered, but I wanted to go over there and just confront her. What she thought happened, what was her take? Did she even think about it anymore?

Knowing her, probably not. She was gorgeous, and classy, and driven, always in control, but she was cold, angry, even selfish at times. She had her cross to bear. Her own parents pretended she didn't exist, living in a mansion. Completely cut-off. I felt for her. We were nearly the same person. That could explain the on and off relationship we had. It was maddening. Not for the weak. The sex was spectacular though, oh Jesus she was amazing, athletic, sexy struts, she made me nuts. How do you end a relationship when the sex is great? If it's bad, then you have one more date. You know, just to be sure.

But I had plans with the boys tonight. I can't back out now. Maybe she'll text me, when she wasn't in a mood. She'll wake up, do a workout, drink a smoothie, lay on the couch flick on *American Horror Story* and drool over Evan Peters. I did that too. I still do that. He is gorgeous. Perhaps that is what drew me to her in the first place. She wasn't like other girls when I knew her in high school. She was different. Detached, removed, outwardly self-assured, and likeable too, engaging, she can make you feel like the only man in the world, over and over. I think when my parents were fighting or just sitting at the dinner table not saying a fucking word me walking on eggshells when I needed the bread, it just became too much. All that money and what has it gotten them? What has *it* really changed? It changed me. Maybe it was hate in my heart and it grew exponentially over the years.

I remember making dinner one night because my parents were screaming at each other for hours, I mean fucking hours. I cooked a nice dinner, salad, lamb chops, some leftover pasta, fucking warm bread.

"You going to come and eat? I figured you guys were having a bad day, so I wanted to do something nice." I sat down and got ready to eat and they just stood there, confused, and angry. Just wouldn't fucking move. They shot each other a look and walked out of the room, went upstairs, and slammed the door. I poured a full glass of wine and downed it in one fucking gulp. I stared at the glass in my hands and flung it hard against the wall, watching it shatter in hundreds of unfixable pieces on the hardwood kitchen floor. I had some dinner, and looking at the table with the unlit candles, all the best forks and spoons and glasses laid out properly, two glasses on each place setting like my mother taught me. And they didn't even say a fucking word.

Next time I'll just make some fucking ravioli.

"I'm so sorry—"

"Deanna please... don't. Alright just fucking don't!"

"You're right. I don't mean to sound like I'm pitying you. Obviously, you're in pain..."

"Yeah obviously!" I snapped. "Fucking unbelievable." I was smoking a cigarette, which I rarely did only in hours of great stress and contentment, that's what I told Deanna.

"Which one is this?" she asked, that snide bitch.

"You're a fucking comedian. That's really good of you."

"He had it comin', he had it comin'. Listen, if you want to stay here tonight, you can. *Mi casa* and all..."

"*Que Pasa*, baby. *Que Pasa*. You would love that if I did."

"I haven't been able to get you out of my mind all day."

"I know." I took a drag of the cigarette, slowly exhaling. God she was stunning.

"I actually need a bath."

"I'm wearing shorts."

"I should just fucking stab you right now."

"Well, I mean you said you needed a bath. So, you know, it's really up to you. I know you can't resist a cum bath."

"I can't. It's perfect for my hair. All shiny."

"You are one kinky bitch you know that."

"Oh, I do. I mean I know you like men and women so..."

"Does that turn you on."

"I'm turned on by it turning you on."

"The thought of me getting head from a man doesn't get you hot?

"It might."

"What if I was pitching not catching?"

"Hotter, much hotter, I just find it erotic."

"It's good you do. It's nice to explore right."

"I think so. I always wonder if I'm bi? Maybe it's easier for women?"

I took another pull and exhaled quicker this time. "Fuck that. The right people will love you. But you are right about it being easier for women, when it comes to the feminine mystique. Being bisexual. Men don't wear those flashy rose-colored glasses. Ever. I was just fortunate to be friends with Anthony and Tommy, and it all worked out.

"Anthony is the one who got you into smoking in the first place."

"And the framus intersects with the ramastan." I hit the cigarette, exhaling slowly, and just sat there for a moment.

"And what the fuck is that supposed to mean?"

"There are worst things. And for all the poverty and drug trafficking and general horrible shit in the world you devote your protection to the dignity of Justin Timberlake.

"That is so misdirected Hugo. We both come from aloof parents. Only children, nevertheless, doesn't it stand to reason that maybe we're more alike than we seem?"

"I suppose so." I took a final hit of the cigarette. And sat there listening to *Concierto de Aranjuez* as it mended my broken soul, piece by piece.

"I'm just broken, Deanna. I'm so—" I fought back the tears as much as I could. It just kept coming. I was crying into my hands, and I moved her hand away from me. I didn't want anyone fucking touching me.

I saw my phone blowing up with texts from the boys. Getting myself together, I did a little cocaine and locked the door behind me.

CHAPTER 3
Memories of Prom Night

I arrived at Yellowtail Sushi about twenty minutes later and waited in my car, took half of an edible, and stuck the bag into my North Face jacket. I saw Tommy get out of his car heading to the restaurant. I got out of mine, locked it, and glanced at him.

"The French are glad to die forrrr.... Love." He turned around and had the biggest smile on his face. Sly, secretive, an inside joke only we understood.

"Only if they were to die first. JESUS HUGO!" We rushed up to each other and hugged like it was high school again. He was my boy in high school; we pulled some heavy shit in our time.

"I can't fucking believe it man, Hugo Gold."

"It's great to see you man, so great to fucking see you."

"You getting some action from the boys up at Rykers?"

"Yeah, and your mom told me to let them know her address."

"Oh, you're not enough for her anymore?"

"No, I just remember her birthday is next week so..."

"It's like we never left."

"Never brother. So where are the rest of the fucking scumbags?

"You know Anthony, always wanting to make an appearance."

"Probably dressing his mistress up right now."

"He always did look the most presentable."

"And Bobby, forget about it."

"Fucking guy always rolling in three hours later. Stoned and drunk."

"He was a fucking trip."

"He should fucking take one."

We stood there in silence, Tommy whipped out a spliff which we shared, I was so gloriously stoned. I felt lightheaded but I knew a beer would pull me back down to earth. It was just something we all did in high school and those of us who went to college, popping a Molly when it was raining out and swimming in the pool, taking mushrooms a few hours later, sitting around after it stopped and going in to a dazed and warm confusion. It was a relief, we all just tripped out and got so quiet we could hear the crickets as if they were beside us. It was uncanny. I'll never forget it, the trees, the bushes, the wind. How it felt on our skin, the rain, the mist, the fire from the candles. It all felt shattering to me.

"I was just thinking of that day the four of us taking mushrooms." We were sitting at the bar and having drinks. Still waiting for Anthony and Bobby.

"Oh yeah and it was raining; we went swimming."

"Wait we did molly then we did shrooms."

"Yes, that was the order. That was some fucking night man. The power went out..."

"Yeah, and the dark felt as if we were in a nightclub, smooth glass it felt like. Bizarre."

"Absolutely. I've been hearing from Deanna, talking with her. Hanging out..."

Tommy sipped his drink and looked around the bar and restaurant. "She was never my favorite person."

"You guys never got along, which I never understood."

"She's troubled Hugo. There is no telling what she's capable of." He ordered us another drink and there was a noticeable beat between us. People coming and going from the bar, the music was hip-hop, rock, alternative and it all had a relaxing feel to it. "She was there you know."

I looked at Tommy and his face didn't change, maybe even a little harder to me. "On that night. If it wasn't for sure it would've—"

"It spun out of control, but she didn't..." I lowered my voice to a whisper and leaned in close to Tommy. "Push him. She didn't."

"He slipped."

"Exactly. We made a pact. I think we were all fucked up that night, no?"

"For sure. I could barely see."

"See?"

"He was a bully, Terrance. He just didn't know when to stop."

"Part of me thinks he had it coming... in a way. We all have some blood on our hands but he's not exactly a fucking pariah."

"Well... hey, here they are!"

"Oh! The Flying Gavone brothers." I shouted in the restaurant. Space-time was different here.

We all sat down to dinner and as the drinks flowed and conversation was lubricated, I felt as if we never really parted company, any of us. Tommy, Anthony, Bobby, and myself. I think we just knew we would be friends, the kind of friends who keep you up and make sure you don't fuck it all up. The kind of friends who keep your head above water and your feet on the ground even when you're so baked you can barely see. I was just blessed to have three of them.

"Tony. How's the Scotch treating you?" I asked as I finished the last of the fried calamari and chugged down the rest of my red wine.

"Better than your girl has treated me over the years."

"Oh, I'm glad, I figured all those years banging my sister, you needed a change."

"I did. Glad I did. Jesus. The Fridge-Air corporation."

"Hey!"

"Never gets old," Tommy replied as he sipped his beer.

"Not as old as you Tommy," I said.

"Well, you always enjoyed the hot teachers."

"I did."

"You never thought maybe trying some of the women?"

"What makes you think I didn't?"

"Oh, see I knew it. He goes for it, Bobby," Anthony remarked.

"Damn right I do."

"You do, Hugo. I love you for it, brother."

We all clinked glasses.

"I just wonder if many of them just wanted to run away from you."

"Well, you did. We had some sleepovers remember?"

I raised up my hands with a big smile on my face. "Every weekend, the two of us in the basement. Dropping the soap, playing hide the cannoli. The closet, the bed, the couch, behind the fuckin piano. Yeah, we made music that night, bitch."

We were all loud and laughing, the last time I did that I was in high school, really truly laughed to the point of tears coming out of my eyes, losing my breath. That feeling of exhilarating and powerful relief. Anthony nearly spit out his beer all over the table. I needed this. I really fucking needed this.

The waitress came and placed our food on the table, and we ate like kings. Memories of times past flooded back to us in waves; it was surrounding us the need to reconnect and pick up from where we left off.

We spoke about Deanna. My friends never liked her and part of me understood why. She almost died of pneumonia, suffice it to say my boys and I were announcing the updates for the weekend on the loudspeaker, and we played "Ding Dong the Witch Is Dead" to the entire school.

"This one goes out to Deanna. Our best wishes!"

We almost got suspended. It was hilarious, so many people were singing it all day long, I even remember our Social Studies teacher participating, she was crushed. I remember tears coming down her flawless porcelain face. I think it was a long time before she forgave us, maybe she never did. Her father left when she was ten years old, and her mother drank all the time to the point where she had to be rushed to the hospital, after that night Deanna was never the same, her mother needed rehabilitation and for years she kept leaving and turning back to the bottle. I understood the context why she was the way she was and still is. Nothing much has changed since then. I think I felt a modicum of pity for her. Her unlovable, mean, bitter self. Lonely and scared.

She confronted us the next day. I never knew somebody to be so cruel all the time, and then I remembered what she told me in confidence about her crumbling family. It didn't give her the right to sabotage people, their life and relationship maybe something just died inside of her, her inability to really love.

"Anthony, tell me something: is it your opinion that I'm a slutty twat? Or is that just your mother talking?" Deana had asked.

"I think your father would know more about that, than I would, no?" he snapped back.

I had to bite my lip, I had my own bone to pick with this awful human being, but I knew keeping my mouth shut in front of my boys was a wise choice.

"You know what's interesting is that I don't know where my father is, he left when I was ten. But you, that charming family of yours. That young mom, so soft and respected."

"Don't you talk about her." His voice went cold and firm. Just like him most of the time.

"I think it's time we did. Your mother left too and after that well, I guess your father who's just a little older than my mother, wanted something a little younger, better, hotter."

Anthony sat there on the stairs of his apartment; we split a joint between us. And he kept smoking it slowly, and he had a look in his eyes that meant something darker, his anger had a boiling point reaction to it. We usually knew when the meter was up with his rage, and it wasn't imminently explosive either, it was more implosive. Having these small explosions within his bones, until a nuclear reactor was triggered, and all hell would break loose.

"Your ignorance is astounding, Deanna. Maybe he did. Who wouldn't, she is beautiful. But perhaps it would be better if you quit while you're ahead, you sick cunt."

"Tony," I whispered to him. Only he heard me and glanced in my direction. I didn't want to make it worse.

"No, it's alright Hugo. I got this. Unfortunately, my mother left. I deal with it every day. There's nothing I can do. But right now, for example, I can do something, it's worth doing some time for right Hugo? Wouldn't you say?"

"Maybe he finally found something he liked." Deanna remarked and smiled, as she walked away. He ran up to her and shoved her on the ground into a puddle. Her face was covered in blood from the impact, and her clothes were soaked. After that, that's why we got over the loudspeaker and announced the wicked witch is dead. She didn't move for a good minute, and he was standing over her looking down, I had my hands on my forehead unsure of what to do.

"What do you have to say now?! You fucking slut!" He walked away and back inside as I stood there frozen. I went to help her stand up; she pushed my hand away.

She nearly ran after him I held her back, but I almost couldn't anymore. I think it all unraveled badly. I can't remember too much after that, for some reason it was bound to happen though, the fact that someone finally shoved Deanna into a puddle is understandable. She was never loved by anyone, people respected her because they knew she was *trouble, but she was never truly loved, and admired, and wanted. But they feared her, were suspicious of her, she had no love in her heart, just pain and misery and isolation. But love? Not likely, not even a little. I always felt bad for her. Maybe I'm an anomaly. I'm sure Anthony wasn't the only guy in our school who wanted to deck Deanna Rinaldi. Plenty of girls wanted to get a bucket of pig's blood and make her the prom queen.*

"Look at me, you fucking asshole! YOU FUCKING ASSHOLE!" She kept whacking Anthony and as I held her back, she was biting my arm and kicked me in the balls. I screamed so loud, I passed out a second later.

"You're a fucking mean bitch, you know that! WHO DO YOU THINK YOU ARE?! You're a fucking bully, and I can't respect a bully!" Anthony was shouting, practically screeching at Deanna and it became a whole thing once again.

I never laid a hand on a woman, but I have to say in this case she had it coming. Anthony had been dealing with his parents' disintegrating marriage for years and out of all of us, I was the one he spoke to, opened up to, especially about Deanna. I think we were the only two people on the planet who actually saw through her bullshit, and despite us hooking up a few times, I really didn't have feelings for her at all. I don't think I ever did. She was unbearable. I did however sympathize with her; her pain was justified, and I couldn't shake the feeling that we were more alike than I cared to admit. I just never admitted that to anyone, why should I? She's a horrible despicable creature, somebody I have extreme revulsion for, someone I enjoy fucking, it was just sex. I went back and forth. And so did she.

"That woman has issues." I said as we finished our dinner and sipped our drinks, I was feeling a little buzzed by now. The weed and the alcohol. Beautiful.

"Yes, she does, she was beautiful though, what a prized piece."

"Absolutely. Great ass."

We made small talk for another half hour, shared some dessert and some drinks, and left for the night. It felt familiar, the way we interacted. How little life changes between us. Anthony, Bobby, and Tommy were, and are, my boys, great friends that I would never have again.

As we said our goodbyes, I got back into my car and felt a wave come over me, a painful pull of my body down towards something else, something dark. That sense of hovering, that intense dispelling of anxiety as it transitions into depression. It's been happening more and more lately, and I can't seem to get through an entire day without it happening. I have been making myself cum a lot lately, having sex with Jason, Deanna, Frankie... as if I was a savage beast that was going a hundred miles an hour in the wrong direction. Something had to fucking give.

CHAPTER 4
Sex, Lies, and Breakfast

"Wow Jason. Pretty soon I guess I'll have to start paying you in installments, huh? My poor dick. It just goes wherever I want it to."

"It's your cock, I just make it sing."

We got dressed in a hurry and sat back down.

"So why don't you tell me what's been bothering you."

"I love therapy. It's like a talk show where I'm the special guest."

"I thought we spoke about your narcissism."

"We did but then I had some Scotch."

Jason sat there for a minute and took a deep breath.

I did enjoy antagonizing him. "Alright I'm sorry. I was out with the boys last night. I got back int my car at the end of the night and boom... it just hits me. That feeling."

"What feeling?"

"Jesus, *you* are the psychologist, Jason. I mean you obviously know!"

"I don't. The meaning is elicited through verbalization."

"And the framus intersects with the ramastan. I'm talking about being pulled down, that intense anxiety almost like a fucking panic attack or some shit." I took a spliff out of my pocket and a lighter.

"I can't let you smoke in here, Hugo. You know the rules."

"Right, it can be a brothel, I just can't smoke. Got it." I rubbed my head and took a few deep breaths before putting my feet on the table.

"Come on Hugo, just give me something."

"I thought I just did, on the desk."

Jason stood and closed his notebook. "This is fucking ridiculous Hugo, if you're just going to make jokes."

"Alright I'm sorry... I'm sorry. I just—I'm not good at this."

He sat back down, crossed his legs, and stared at me intently.

"I've just been feeling lonely, even with people, and it's worse when I'm alone. For the most part I can deal with it, and I have."

"Does this happen often?"

"More times than I care to think about."

"I see."

"Oh, do you? Well, for your information, it's been almost every day. I just have nobody else to talk to about this. And I fucking hate it."

"I understand that, but I'm glad we are discussing it."

"It's a constant numb feeling and then it just *turns*... and it gets worse before it even gets better. I don't know what to do anymore, what happened back—"

"What? Go on."

I stood abruptly and walked out.

"Hugo," he called after me.

I walked out his office, got into my car, and drove away. I can't face it with Jason. I can't. Not now. Not ever.

As I drove home, it began to rain heavily. I felt those feelings coming at me again from all angles. I felt the tightness in my throat, a hard constriction in my lungs, and I almost lost control of my car as I drove through traffic. I pulled over as my vision began to blur and I was sitting there flipping out in the car, slamming my fist into the passenger seat and screaming at the top of my lungs.

After about five minutes of the nervous breakdown, I tried to calm myself down and took a few deep breaths. My heartbeat was racing, and my anxiety was demonic. Everyone was able to move on after what happened to Terrance on that night and I can't. I just can't fucking do it. It's eroding me.

He slipped. That's the fiction. I remember saying to all of them and later to Deanna. Everyone kept their fucking mouths shut. But do I know that for sure. It was hard to tell, the entire night was a hazy memory that was just now beginning to thaw, as if it were a fragment of a memory that comes and goes depending on the day. I remember the silence though. I couldn't hear anything after it happened, no voices, sirens, screams... nothing. It was the sound of never being able to un-ring the bell. And then the rain, light at first, then a heavy downpour. The rain changed, and until tonight, until this dark unfriendly night began, I never knew a rain like it.

I wanted to go home and begin punching holes in the fucking wall, to destroy everything, to have a fucking nervous breakdown, because I never fucking had one before and I wanted one now! This was something sex would not be able to heal, or weed or mushrooms, this was just pure anger, rage, hatred, the black lashing out of my pain, and the numb anesthetizing effects of being heartbroken. A lightning flash cracking open my heart, the deep regions of my own hell, I walk it blindly every day, even in my dreams. And they come and go so frequently, melodic waves of darkness to me, I can't determine if they will end or just repeat and start again from the other direction, but I feel their pulse when I'm awake, I can remember the cars that went soaring by on that night. That night.

I knew what I needed. I'm not the kind of person who just reaches out to people. I need something far more gratifying.

"Yeah Frankie."

"OH GOD! THAT'S RIGHT BITCH!"

Sometimes it's just the easiest answer of all, that release that finds itself all over his face, as he takes a wet rag and cleans himself up.

"You really cum like a boss, don't you?" Frankie asked as he got back in bed with me, sharing a joint, and staring at the ceiling as Francis Albert played lightly on the radio.

"Would you want it any other way?"

"Probably not. How's it been going with you? You're quiet."

"A lot on my mind."

"Like what?"

I pulled on the joint and didn't answer him, I just wanted to relax and not have to think about anything at all. Nor did I want to talk, it was a burden to me. However, he did suck my cock very well, so I think I owed it to him.

"Just my friends, drama, non-stop fucking drama. But that all changed when I busted the way I did all over you, and I have to change the sheets."

"Yeah, they're fucked now, but I think you're keeping something from me."

"Jesus Frankie, please not now."

"I just fucking blew you, like I always do when you need

something. Which I don't mind but at least talk to me, I don't just want to lay here."

I took a deep breath and exhaled loudly. Of all the fucking times to ask me he does it now.

"What do you want to know Frankie? Talk to me, tell me what you need to know. Ask me anything, I'm a free fucking agent. And it's 2021, what do I have to hide?"

"I just think— you seem different. Not your usual self, tense, nervous. Like you have something on your mind."

"It's not worth talking about alright, I just got into a fight with my boys last night at dinner, it's bullshit."

"Why do I feel like you're taking me for a fucking idiot. I'm a detective."

"Is this an interrogation now?"

"Do you feel that way?"

I stared at Frankie; this whole night took a dark turn. Was he playing me here? Was he interrogating me or was he truly just asking me?

"Feel what?"

"That you're being interrogated... sometimes people don't like it."

"I'm an anomaly."

Frankie grinned in that way he does and I felt my anxiety increase. "I don't believe that to be true, Hugo. I don't buy it. And I still think you're hiding something from me, you're next to me in bed but... I don't like the vibe here." He rushed out of bed and got dressed in a hurry. He grabbed his pants from my desk, knocking over a lamp.

"Hey Frankie, easy bro!"

"You're fucking lying to me, you know that. Lying to me, a *detective*."

"What is it that you think I'm keeping from you, Frankie? I wouldn't lie to you!"

"I don't know what you're keeping from me. I just know it's not good, something happened to you, I don't give a fuck what it is, I just—I can't help but think it would cause problems for you and for me. And I have to watch my ass; I had that coke issue a year ago. I can't fuck up again, I'm on thin ice as it is with my ex-wife."

"I'm sorry you're having fucking problems, but I didn't tell. You *do* have an issue with coke."

"No shit, Hugo. I fucked up. And if you're deliberately

hiding something from me, a crime or something worse... it can put me in jeopardy. You can lose everything. It would unravel in ways you can't imagine, especially if you tried to cover something up. If you had accomplices, it's even worse. And I don't mean to suggest that you did but if it's true, I can't protect you. One thing you can never say that you haven't been told. The decision's yours. I have to go."

Frankie left with the door slamming behind him. I stared at the ceiling and the fan that kept whirring above me. I didn't move from that position for the rest of the night.

Part II
Cloak & Dagger

"Well, you may throw your rock and hide your hand
Workin' in the dark against your fellow man
But as sure as God made black and white
What's down in the dark will be brought to the light"
—JOHNNY CASH
God's Gonna Cut You Down

"Ha, ha, what a fool honesty is !
And trust, his sworn brother, a very simple gentleman."
—WILLIAM SHAKESPEARE
The Winter's Tale

"I met him out for dinner on a Friday night
He really got me working up an appetite
He had tattoos up and down his arm
There's nothing more dangerous than a boy with a charm."
—CHRISTINA AGUILERA
Candyman

CHAPTER 5
A Slight Case of Depression

It's that blue section of hell that you can never leave. I remember Stephen King describing it that way and it always stuck with me. After Frankie stormed off last night, I woke up and it all came back to me, seized me with immunity. I didn't feel much, it's more like a numbness, anesthetized, all the pain and sorrow and anger, it turns to mist and fades into every cell of my body. Something shuts down. You don't feel anger, or sadness. You're in a void and it's so hard to get out of it. The numbness cradles you or it thinks its cradling you, but it isn't and you see the hell you have created for yourself. And the demons that come along with it, the contract you signed, and they know what torments you, and they use it until they become bored.

You get up out of bed, or you try too, and you go use the bathroom, brush your teeth, put your contacts in, and lay on the couch, and just stare at the fucking wall for hours. Or you decide to put the tv on and it just fills the void in a way, takes you away, zones you out, and sometimes that's not that bad actually. It helps.

Maybe it's healthier to just disconnect. To sit back and smoke all day watching reruns of *The Sopranos,* the greatest thing since sliced bread. I had a book by my bedside table that I haven't pick up in a few days, it was *The Amsterdam Experiment* by my friend Jesse Gallo, and I couldn't stop turning pages, Christ what a narrative and the characters are so damaged, violent, cruel. I could feel their pain, especially Hugo's but Hector did assure me, it wasn't about me. Just maybe me on a good day.

Thanks a lot asshole! I understood however, I loved his humor and that character from what I've read, is quite an amusing character, what a fuck up but what a thrilling energy he has, almost a character as evil and engaging and untouchable as Richard III. To me, he was my favorite out of all of them, Isabelle, Carlo, and Victor were and are as wholly human as anyone on this planet, and I'll never forget what he said to me when we were up 'til two in the morning talking about it. He said *I didn't write them as villains, Hugo. I wrote them as human beings.*

I think I related most to Hugo and Isabelle, and not because a character my friend wrote is named after me, I immediately was drawn to him. He struck me as someone you would want to talk to. And as dark and formidable as he was and he is, it felt electrifying just to be in his presence, such a powerful personality. I think I can really relate to how lonely he was growing up. It hits differently. Sometimes that's worse than depression. I was lucky enough to have friends like the ones I have now when I was in high school. But sometimes I wasn't always invited and that could hurt, I felt that every time and yeah, I'd cry. I'd get into a really bad depression because of it but sometimes that's how people are, I guess. They're not awful they're human. I'll always be different and I know they respected me and sometimes that's enough. Especially nowadays.

Self-medicating helps. People disappoint, that's all they do. They don't fucking care and that's the whole fucking problem from the beginning. There is a lack of concern in people that I find to be quite disturbing. They have this innate ability to let you down. And if something can be done about it, it would make this fucking world better, a little more stable.

For instance, when I was in high school, I did some crazy shit, I took acid at my friend's pool and had the music blasting from speakers he bought and hooked up, from my house. It was surreal and we dropped acid. I remember banging my English teacher, that was always a cherished time in my life. The idea of rebirthing yourself, is stimulating. And I found a kinship in that. I wish I could say it was all fun and games, and I suppose it was... but after what happened on prom night, we all knew the party was fucking over.

Accidents happen every day, and ever since it did happen on that night, one to go down in history, I felt as if I have been reliving it ever since. In my dreams, I can't wake up quietly or gently; it's always in surprise, or shock. A jolt, a nightmare reliving that night, or some kind of variation of what happened. Sometimes it's in a club and he's knocked down by a car that comes barreling through the club. I'm terrified of that dream and when my stress is really high, it happens.

These dreams and night terrors happened for years after the accident. I couldn't let go, I nearly lost myself keeping it between my friends, and I guess through years of being numb and plenty of sex, drugs, and alcohol, it almost evaporated. I repressed it, as far down as it could go. And now it's found its way out, clawing itself out of me, reaching for light, for release. It's found its power once again, imbued with a ray of hope and locomotive determination.

Perhaps it was my subconscious making me realize the gravity of what happened, the entire night, from beginning to end. Terrance was a bully, a mean, abusive prick. My boys and I busted balls of course, but we weren't bullies and we didn't associate with them on any level, the ones who fucked with people we would vouch for, let's just say we didn't take kindly to it. And at one point before all of this other drama happened, Terrance and I were friends. And it didn't take much to know that he could be the most charismatic motherfucker on the planet, likeable, personable, good-looking and someone that could make anyone feel better, even fantastic at times. Nothing more dangerous than a man with charm. I always saw charm as a vice, something to be jettisoned eventually, I liked when people had balls and could stand their ground with me, someone who could be an individual. To me that was the ultimate prize.

And, one night we were on the couch watching *Goodfellas*. We had been smoking weed all night long, four hours on end, and we would fuck. And it was grand, so powerful, so incredible, engaging, everything. We knew back then we were bisexual, we both had beautiful women in our lives, we knew how to handle it. Both of us were so into each other, it was so passionate we would be sweating like crazy and take so many mushrooms and smoke so much weed, one night I felt as if I was in a video game being controlled by God and every time we came, we would be laying in a tower made out of diamonds. I loved how we both felt when we were so gloriously stoned and baked. I mean baked, like fucking clams at a seafood restaurant, like baked ziti on your birthday. And I remember what we spoke about one night, a conversation that changed everything.

"Fantastic Terrance, that was fantastic. Jesus, god bless you. Goddam." I lay back on the bed staring at the ceiling. He was under my arm, and we just lay there, looking at the speed of the ceiling fan on high, it was the middle of June and the AC in Terrance's house broke down. We fucked in his bedroom, and the windows were wide open. I was so erect.

"Anytime Hugo, you know that. Everyone at the fucking school is a fucking disaster. I'm not even going to consider it."

"You got that right, just stick with me. I'll show you how things work."

"I'm sure you would. What's with Anthony?" He went over the window and lit a cigarette the smoke gracefully flew through the screen. "Why doesn't he like me?"

"He doesn't like anyone, much less someone like you."

"Someone like me?"

"You know, different. You're fucking gorgeous, I didn't live in a freezer before I met you."

"I never would've thought you were bi," Terrance replied as he took another drag of the cigarette and handed it to me.

"Well, you do now. Deanna and I have an arrangement anyway. She says it makes it easier for her to see other guys."

"Seems fair."

"Yeah, absolutely. No strings attached." I took a nice pull and let the smoke linger above me.

"What about with me? Are there strings attached?"

"No. I love our arrangement. Believe me. You're the kind of guy who just does things, rather than talk about it. You have great balls. Finally. I get to bang an actual man."

"You may be right, I take control."

"I'll say you do." I uttered before finishing the cigarette, which I handed back to him. "I mean who wouldn't want to fuck you?"

"A lot of people would love it."

"I know they would. It's what they love about you."

"What do you mean?"

"No just that you're great in bed, and you have this hot delicious body and people feel obliged to be in bed with you getting down and dirty, I'm glad I had this privilege."

"So, you're saying that people only like me because they want to fuck me? Or want me to fuck them?"

"I mean, yes, I suppose. In a way, I mean what's wrong with

that?"

"Plenty actually, Hugo. Why would they want to just have sex with me? Don't I have other virtues? Like you?"

I paused before answering Terrance's question.

He continued, "I mean, I would like to think I'm respected not somebody's fucking boy toy or some shit."

"I think you're taking it completely wrong."

"No, I'm not. I'm actually taking this at face value."

"Well, then it was more of a lip service."

"So, you do mean it? That people only want to talk to me because they want to fuck me?"

"I think we both understand what men and women want and how they behave."

"And you have the market cornered on human sexuality?"

"I could. Yes, I've been with men and women and will continue to do that 'til I die, so I think I have a dog in this fight that you're starting."

"I'm starting?! You make this ignorant fucking crack..."

"Terrance, I didn't mean it to be insulting! I meant that people love you because you're awesome and sexy and they can be themselves around you."

"You're reinventing the wheel now?"

"Alright put it in fucking second gear. I'm not doing anything."

"Yes, you are. You just refuse to see it. Given your enormous wealth."

"Oh, you know what... fuck you man! That's my family not me!"

"Since when?"

"Since they went to fucking Europe for six months, that's since when, you fucking arrogant prick! Six months Terrance! You think I'm banging some sexy Italian guy on a gondolier in Venice; no, I'm here with you!

Terrance stood there in disbelief. He didn't move, but he didn't blink either. "Clearly you fucking resent me. It shows." And out of nowhere, he breaks down laughing, a loud boisterous laugh that ran like venom in my veins, my anger reaching a new and frightening level. He laughed until he nearly couldn't speak.

"Do you think that's funny, Terrance?"

He was laughing so hard he couldn't breathe and as he pointed his finger at me, I felt it boiling over.

"Great, fuck you!" I took a glass that was on the table and flung it across the room, and it smashed against the wall and shattered, not even that action stopped the laughing, it only added fuel to a fire. Finally, he regained some composure and he sat up near the radiator. Lighting a joint now. Casually hitting it and handing it to me.

"Did I—have I ever told you about Florida?"

"No. Why?"

"I didn't tell you about the cop who pulled me over for a speeding ticket?"

"No."

"Well, one night I was going out for some drinks, had about two at this bar in Miami, and my friends and I went to a nightclub, a placed called The Crescent. On our way there, I was driving a little too fast, and a cop pulled me over. He was, I don't know, thirty-five or so. He walked up to me, asked for my license and registration, I gave it to him, and he looked them over. Handing them back to me, I saw a card with his number on it. I considered it and put it in my wallet, I didn't want my friends knowing. He let me go with a warning. That night I went home, called him up and we went for dinner. Nothing fancy, just some sushi. And when I saw him in that shirt, that black t-shirt, I couldn't believe how sexy he was, it was gratifying to actually be in the company of a real man, not just some casual illusion of one, you know? We go back to his place, and we fuck, so hard, so long, so nice. It made me forget just how common a night in bed with you is sometimes, how depressingly boring, how rote. I think I nearly melted in his hands when he mounted me that night, I could barely keep up. We finish, we get dressed and as we walk down to the lobby of his apartment, we say our goodbyes. And I was relieved."

I sat there, frozen. The pain has maneuvered its way through my veins, and I felt it rise within me, with such force and power. It was the first time I ever experienced heartbreak. Real crushing heartbreak. Beyond painful. I nearly went fucking numb.

"You...," I began.

Terrance looked at me and grinned in way that almost made me bash his face in.

"You *cheated*... on me?" I whispered. I was shaking.

"All I know is, I had to travel south more than once."

I jumped out of bed and stood there in the middle of the

room above him, breathing heavily. I backed away from him and saw the glass on the floor, all shattered into a million pieces. It made me think of my own life, how delicate it was, how wounded I really am and now in the midst of all of the chaos, I was this cold hard-bitten prick. That's what happens. When you think love is a solution, that it will somehow alleviate the envy and resentment and that stored demonic energy you keep within you.

"You know something, Terrance... the next time I hear my friends ripping you apart I'll know why... you really *are* a fucking bully. I think your father dying left you feeling completely fucking alone in this world. You're so hateful and mean and all of that hateful bile has become the only thing you could hang onto because it's the only part of you that makes you feel alive, one cheap thrill after another. You are a manipulative prick; it's probably the only thing you've ever known. And to be perfectly honest, the reason Anthony doesn't like you is because you never learned how to be a man, you're a lost cause, a cheat, a motherfucking liar.

By then I was putting my shoes on. And as I got them on and headed for the door, I turned around and stared him right in the eye.

"In the end, it doesn't matter, anyway. You are who you are. Once a man to be reckoned with, now a small-minded bully with nothing to offer. Nothing real, nothing meaningful. Just a mess. Have a nice life. And I really hope one day you get hit by a car and die, that way the rest of us can live in peace. It would be great."

And from that point on, when he and I called it quits, when I left him there, wounded and alone, he was out for blood. I bested him. I beat him to the punch, I took command. I had the courage to leave that bullshit relationship, as I said before. There is nothing more dangerous than a man with charm. I knew he would be vindictive, I just never suspected it would end in bloodshed. Blood on all of our hands, and we washed it off every day. It just wouldn't leave. It wouldn't disappear; it kept coming back. In our dreams, our memories, everything. It would come and stay for a while without the intention of leaving.

When would it? My depression was a part of me since birth, I've always struggled with it, always felt the tumultuous effects of it within me, ensnaring me, wrapping its tentacles into my body, and squeezing tighter every time I woke up. I was lucky though; depression makes you feel absolutely nothing. So, no matter what I did, I was constantly anesthetized. I would do lines constantly, every day when I woke up, or when I was making the bed, or cleaning the house, or when I would fuck a guy or a woman, when I went out to lay by the pool. It was my Achille's heel in a way, a quick refuge for me that was never in short supply. When I went to school, my boys and I did it after lunch, or before gym.

Nobody seemed to see anything, and we had a ball. It was easier back then; we didn't worry about anything or anyone. We had ourselves to look out for and even with all my family's money, my friends Tony, Bobby, and Tommy were my *real* family. Terrance was a dissatisfied bullying prick who resented everyone. And yet during our time together, he never once drew blood from me or my friends.

I do miss banging him, I have to admit. Sex with Terrance was passionate and wild and even a little weird. It was so hot so fevered, he couldn't always make me cum but when he did, I would moan his name so loud. But then I hated how I felt so depleted after ejaculating and Tony once told me to always smoke a quick one right after you orgasmed: men can't deal with feeling empty. I preferred weed but every now and then I needed a cigarette. So we would play Radiohead or Biggie on the radio and sit there staring out into the darkness of the night devoid of stars.

CHAPTER 6
Prophylactic Measures

Brooklyn. July 1999.

Gorgeous day out that day and my friends and I decided to see *Eyes Wide Shut* at Regal Theater in Bensonhurst. We had a pocket full of goodies, plenty of weed and some mushrooms, enough to pass around. I had always been a fan of Kubrick; may god rest his fucking soul because he is missed by me dearly. *Clockwork, 2001, Strangelove, The Shining.* Unbelievable filmmaker, and here my friends and I are seeing the last movie he would ever make. And it made me believe that escape through a movie and some psychedelics was the answer, even if we *were* underage... how can you deny the public their right to see it? The trailer was exquisite. It didn't betray any of its secrets, that's what drew me to it. We all took the shrooms and enjoyed a fatty before heading in and buying massive amounts of snacks and drinks. Luckily, Bobby was the tallest of all of us and he got us tickets to see the movie. It was great.

We stayed way in the back row, sitting down and enjoying the fact that there were almost no people here at all. And then before we knew it, Terrance walked in with a woman we had never seen before.

"Yeah, let's sit here. Quiet." They sat down and didn't to notice us. We were so stoned and the shrooms were beginning their magic on us now even before the coming attractions started. I don't think we cared though, we were too fucking excited to see this movie and to see the sexy Nicole Kidman undressed in the first two seconds of the movie. Yeah, that's reason enough for any man, bi, straight, or gay. She is a fucking goddess.

"Jesus you always fucking bring this drama its insane."

Terrance shouted in the quiet theater, and we all looked down at them. "I just— oh fuck. Yo." He waved when he noticed us and we all shot each other a look.

I didn't move from my seat, Tony, Bobby, and Tom walked down. They exchanged pleasantries and he introduced his woman who was named Miranda. He saw me and we nodded to each other. They came back up asked me if I was okay. I didn't respond, just sipped my soda.

"Everyone shut the fuck up now," I murmured instead.

The last coming attraction ended, and the lights went dim. The movie was starting. You could hear a fuckin' pin drop in that theater it was so quiet.

When it was over and the credits loomed over the screen, my friends and I couldn't move or speak. It was unbelievable; that movie fucking slapped.

"Am I the only one who can't think right now?" I asked through my mushroom haze. All of the lights slowly came back to life again, whirling around me.

"That was fucking incredible, Hugo!" Tony remarked. We looked at each other and couldn't stop grinning. "That orgy scene... oh my GOD!"

"I may need to stay here," Tom added.

"Bro, the movie is over," I replied as we all started to get up.

"What did you do? Wet your pants, man?" Anthony quipped.

"I—uh not exactly... but..." Tom trailed off.

"BRO."

"Yeah, the orgy scene and all..."

"You fucking serious?! You came in a movie theater?" I howled, nearly laughing myself into hysterics.

"Those women, Hugo, come on..."

"No bro, I hear you... oh dear Jesus."

"I can't with this guy! I fucking can't!"

"Do you want to just maybe make a run..." I started laughing again and none of us could stop.

"What do you fellas want me to do? I mean..." Tom tried again.

Twenty minutes later, we left and nobody saw a thing.

We were hanging out in Tom's backyard and having something to eat, it had been hours since we did the mushrooms and, for me, they really came alive when Cruise goes to the party, and you see all those naked beautiful men and women having the times of their lives.

"So how about we invite Terrance and Miranda? I just spoke to him online and I think he needs to be with his friends."

"Is THAT really necessary Tom?"

"I know how you feel about him, Hugo. I'm just trying to be a good friend."

"To all the wrong people, homie."

"So, is that a no?"

We all looked at each other and acquiesced.

"If you want to bring them, that's fine, but any drama... I can't promise anything won't happen." Anthony said this candidly, realistically, firmly. When he spoke, people listened. Including me.

"I get it. Trust me. Okay I'll let him know."

"One day he's going to go too far and say something... I don't trust Terrance too much."

"I don't trust him at all, Hugo. I don't."

"If we can be civil, I'm sure it'll be fine. But we're no longer dating."

"What do you mean? What happened?" Bobby said with exasperation. Totally dumbfounded, completely. At one point I may have told him, but I can't remember now.

"You can probably guess," I responded coldly. I was lighting another joint and was staring at the stars while I took the long leisurely pull. I held onto it for a while; nobody seemed to notice anyway.

"I'm sorry—"

"Please, Bobby. I love you but please..."

"Alright."

We sat there in the quiet, taking in the beauty of the night and hearing the cars coming and going in the long-abandoned street.

I felt as if I had just slipped and was plummeting down towards earth. As if I was walking on the sun and I slipped off. It was beautiful with Terrance, but my wound bled again, and all those emotions came back to me, almost reliving the experience each day at different times, in different frequencies. Most of the time I didn't care, and it was temporary of course, a kind of prophylactic measure.

"I don't want to talk about it. At all. To anyone. Ever."

They didn't say a fucking word, but their silence was their understanding.

"Is he coming or what?" I asked as Tom came out of the house to sit down with us. "I really hope not," I added.

"He is but just for a little while."

"Wonderful." I didn't hide the sarcasm.

"Everything alright?"

I shot Bobby a look and he kept quiet.

"Fuck it. I'm leaving."

"Hugo, come on man, stay here. We're really stoned anyway."

"I can't be in the room with him; something is bound to happen." It was something I felt inside my bones, something crawling, looking for release. Something that made me feel the unbearable tension all over again. Just to be in Terrance's company was awful enough, now I had to deal with him again.

No.

"If you knew what happened..." I started.

"I don't bro, tell us. Come on, we're friends. All of us."

I thought about it and remembered the yelling, the throwing of objects across the room, the glass shattering, the slamming of the front door, the dead silence. I felt the familiar anger again, only this time it was a kind of rage I was not used to, a heartbreak in disguise.

"I just can't do it tonight, boys. I'll talk to you later."

I left and felt lighter, better, but deep within there was a part of me that wanted to confront Terrance and talk about what happened, but I knew his stubbornness and mood swings. I drove away, content in my decision.

I arrived home around midnight, went to take a nice leisurely shower; my parents were already asleep. They had another getaway planned, Asia this time. Maybe they wouldn't come back, maybe they would just start another family there. I was the only child anyway. They just weren't a real part of my life, plenty of food in the fridge and over $4,000 in the wallet. Another prophylactic measure. Ensuring the well-being of my existence while jettisoning around the world for a month. I fell asleep reading *Hamlet* by Shakespeare and the next morning around eight am I woke up and heard the door opening and closing. I walked downstairs and saw my parents gathering their luggage and heading for the front door.

"Hey, you guys are going to Asia?"

"Yes. There's food in the fridge and money in the drawer," my father said as he opened the door. A taxi driver already stood there, waiting to take their luggage to the car.

"Okay thank you, how, uh long will you guys be there?"

"We don't know. A while. Enjoy," my mother replied, checking her pockets and then her designer purse.

And before I knew it, they were out the door.

"Yeah, have a good time guys. Love you too."

I stood there in the living room a few moments before sitting down on the couch and lighting a joint. I opened the side windows and smoked the entire morning away. Nobody around me, nobody to interface with, it was just pure silence and sometimes we really fucking need that.

Even if the fucking house burned down, they would be getting hammered in China or something anyway; they didn't live here, it was just a place to hang their hats. It was beautiful out too, an ideal morning: the sun coming through the windows, the pool peaceful and free, the birds singing. I made some coffee and sat outside. The memories of the shroom trip yesterday, watching *Eyes Wide Shut* with my friends; it was an experience. Despite Terrance showing up with another victim, her hand on his cock, it was a great day. I felt closer to them now than I ever did before, maybe it was the bonding, maybe it was Kubrick, or the shrooms, I just knew that they would be there for me when the chips were way down. I could handle some chaos, but sometimes we needed more.

The phone rang twenty minutes and in my haze I answered wearily.

"Hugo, *como stai*?" It was Anthony, and I was relieved. I didn't want to talk to anyone else.

"*Que Pasa* Tony. That was some day yesterday."

"Yes, it was, I almost want to go and watch it again. Blew me away."

"Agreed, definitely agreed. I think we will be watching that one for years to come. How was Terrance last night?"

"It's why I'm calling. He and Tommy got into it last night, just some mild ball-breaking and Terrance lost it."

"Why did he lose it?"

"Tommy kept busting his balls over how clingy his girl was. I guess he just didn't like it."

"Oh no. Alright I'll be there in ten minutes."

"Where? My place?"

"Yeah. Tell everyone to meet so we can talk about this."

I went in to my room, put on some shorts and a t-shirt and

my shoes, brushed my teeth, and ran out of the house. I picked up a coffee at the deli down the street and headed over to Anthony's. It was better face-to-face whenever someone had a problem. We came together as a group and tried to figure out a way to resolve it. Considering this was between my boy and a past fuckboy of mine who I am already in hot water with, it was a delicate situation. Sticky. And not in a good way. It really—

New York. Present Day.

"What?" Jason asked calmly. He was listening intently to everything I told him.

"Nothing. It doesn't matter."

"I see," said Jason.

I told him everything. And sat back in the chair. We didn't fuck this time. I was not in the mood. But he looked beautiful, hot, it wasn't easy to resist.

"And how did it turn out? Did you talk to Terrance?"

"Yeah, we did. It's all water under the bridge now of course, that was over twelve years ago. We've moved on since then."

"What was the outcome of your meeting with Terrance and the guys?"

"I told you I would rather not talk about it."

"I see we are at one of our favorite junctures."

"I'm not being difficult. I just can't discuss it right now. I— it would lead to..."

Jason sat there crossing his legs again and weaving his pen between his fingers. Christ, he turned me on so much. "To what?"

"If I told you. Would something happen to me because somebody got hurt?"

"If you're completely honest with me, Hugo... no. But I need you to tell me. I need you to tell me exactly what happened."

— — —

"So fellas, I think we need to talk about this. Obviously, Terrance is feeling guilty. About what he did to Tommy, so I've organized a sit-down to help clear the air and hopefully make amends between the two parties."

"What is this? *Goodfellas*?" Terrance quipped, the more he

spoke the more I understood Tommy's position here.

"It can be," Anthony remarked. "Very easily bro."

"Exactly," I added. "Show some respect, Terrance. It's because of you that we're here anyway. Now Tommy, I understand you busted Terrance's balls about his woman?"

"Yes, and now we have to be his wet rag."

"I always thought that was your job," Terrance came back.

"Terrance," I said evenly.

"Next time I'll just take your girl out for dinner. Or something else."

"I don't think leg-breaking is the answer here," Terrance responded. "I mean we can come to an agreement without violence, right?"

I looked at Tommy and I saw nothing but violence in his eyes. When he was angry, things got really quiet really quick. I didn't hear crickets. Anywhere.

"What do you want to say, Terrance?" Tommy exhaled his cigar smoke and his voice was dangerously low and even. I felt a slight chill come over me. I've known Tommy since elementary school, and he was the guy looking out for me. Nobody would ever cross him. Not even the teachers. These sit-downs can be fickle. Sometimes they worked, sometimes it was of no use; it depends on the mood of my friends and the offending person. And in this case, it was ill tempers all around. Terrance sets people off constantly, a real fucking mean streak with mouth. We had a mean streak too; we just preferred to beat the shit out people.

"I just want to say that it wasn't necessary to bust my balls about my lady, it's private, our relationship."

"Well, you were making it abundantly clear to us all the time. But maybe I shouldn't have said what I said. I apologize."

"Thanks. I guess."

"You guess?' I said shocked and disgusted.

"Yeah, I just... well. My girl isn't here to defend herself, she's home. Making dinner and I'm here with you all and I think I should be the one who deserves a real apology. Wasting a tank of gas for this half-assed *sit-down*. She was upset but she spoke to me about a lot that happened that night; it's interesting. You consider yourselves the good guys, and I will always be labeled the motherfucking villain because that's just the kind of prick I am, but you, Tommy. You. You are the injured party here, what? Because I defend my girl's honor?"

"I don't consider myself a victim. I apologized."

"Yes, you did."

"You know what? Fuck this. Fuck you." He got up and nearly left the sit-down.

"Tommy, come on, just..." I tried.

"What, Hugo? What? Sit?"

"Yeah, just please, just come on. Please."

Tommy rubbed his face and took another long hit of the cigar.

"Terrance," I looked toward him, "You say one more thing to Tommy, I will let *Tommy* take care of it. And then you'll just have medical bills to worry about. You fucking hear me?"

Terrance nodded his head. Tommy sat there, behind his dark sunglasses there was an anger I could feel, it was coming off of him like a strong vibrating heat. It was the sticking post for me when it came to Tommy: he could flip a switch so fast, and without warning.

"It is so decreed. I apologize too. Hugo, I'm going to leave now."

"Fine."

"Are you busy later?" Terrance asked.

"Yes."

Tommy passed his cigar to me, and I enjoyed smoking it and staring Terrance down. He wanted to fuck me now. Not likely. Let him sweat a little. Let that fucker sweat a lot. He wants me badly; my friends knew I was bi-sexual, and they all loved me more for it.

— — —

"Terrance never really had the kind of friends I did and his loneliness and isolation were something I felt bad about. And if he wasn't so crass and mean I would let him into my circle, but every day, *every* day he is just a mean motherfucker who brings everyone around him down. Down below him. Sometimes people are born with tragedy in their blood and their pain is stronger than their spirit and they are crushed below and as it turns back to its original state it turns again and we are all bound on its wheel of fire, forever burning. Heartbreaking life and terrifying. Love can be dangerous, but I have my friends here with me. And it seems a little better to stare it in the face." I paused, in thought and memory. "I think that's it though, for today, Jason, I'm fucking tired."

"Alright. Alright that's fine. I'll see you next week, Hugo."

I walked out. I had to leave, it's unbearable and I'm not ready yet. I'm not ready to tell him... everything.

Crash. Terrance's body...

Sirens.

"Hugo... what just fucking happened."

"I don't know..."

"What the fuck just fucking happened.'

"I think he's dead."

Heavy rainfall, sirens, people screaming, complete fucking pandemonium.

"He had it coming though, I mean he just wouldn't stop." *Tommy's voice.*

Oh fuck. This isn't happening.

"Jesus!"

"NO. Listen, listen, there was a struggle. it was a struggle. He slipped."

"Yeah. He slipped. Bobby?"

"Slipped, he fucking slipped."

"Fucking A he did," Tommy replied.

I heard a loud crackling of thunder outside my window, and I woke with a start. Heavy rain now. And in that heavy silence, my heart was beating so wildly I thought it was an anxiety attack.

CHAPTER 7
Drugs & Wildflowers

"I'm taking fucking mushrooms today, Tommy. If you want to come you can, I really need a day to just not do anything. And to sit outside in my backyard looking up at the sky. And I'm thinking of smashing my fucking phone with a hammer."

"Bro I'm in. I'll bring some party favors too. I was actually thinking of taking a fucking bat to mine."

"Bring the hammer, the bat, your phone, and the party favors. I have the kryptonite."

"Hugo Metaphysic shit is dope Gold."

He rang my doorbell, and we hugged it out like we always did, for me Tommy was the kind of friend who can love you and drag you across the coals at the same time. He was always bold, a little unfeeling, but deeply loyal. And that's precisely the kind of friend I needed right now.

"This is just what the doctor ordered."

"Absolutely man I'm glad you're here."

"Oh, by the way, our prescription."

"Oh, look at this. It's Easter Sunday again." I took the bag filled with edibles and pre-rolls and I knew right away we were going to have the kind of day you dream of having with your best friend. Just Tommy and I and some food deliveries. We left our phones in the tv room on airplane mode.

Tommy and I sat by the pool under the warm blistering sun. We took the mushrooms in a tea and were sipping it gently. But after a few minutes we started taking bigger gulps. We both lay back on the lounge chairs overlooking the sky we weren't feeling it quite yet, but we had a strong feeling that it would be triggered any minute now. They were always more potent when we put them in tea and easier to digest too, no matter how many times I've done them they are still the most disgusting things

I've ever eaten.

We didn't say much for a little while, I was feeling relaxed, and Tommy did too, I could tell. We both wore sunglasses and the sun beamed through them it seemed, that blurred line between reality and fantasy is thin, almost unheard of, invisible. A thin string that binds two worlds together, the glue begins to loosen and before you know it those strings are crossed and spun around a spindle, weaved into a complex comforter you lay on for your come-up and you see roses burning and turning into violets, you feel the heavy hand of God on your body lifting you up having you touch the stars and rearrange the universe, and those dreams people claim you have about who you dream to be, happen. They fucking happen. And nobody can fucking stop you. Nobody. Not even yourself. Those limitations you are cursed with, those shackles society and educators have bounded around you burn off and that is your potential. Teachers are brainwashers, Tupac couldn't have said it better. Or more clearly. As clearly as he could.

"You alright there, brother?" I asked him.

"Yeah Hugo, it's beginning to work now," Tom uttered.

"Good, brother. Good. Same here. We drank it at the same time."

"We couldn't have timed it any better, Hugo. That was fucking perfect."

And for a whole uninterrupted three hours, we lay under the vivid blue sky, tripping on shroom tea and allowing the sun to sail away with us. Astral projection at its finest.

Hundreds of songs played during those three hours on my Spotify, and they all seem to connect flawlessly with the vibration of the moment, and with mushrooms you had all kinds of feelings, memories, ideas, feelings, everything. It's a cathartic and funky experience every time, sometimes in different frequencies. And those come up when you see the colors running into each other, seeing the changes of the sky, the way the clouds danced yet remained the same, the way the trees and leaves swayed in the summer wind.

"These are pretty great, Tom. I think I needed to just escape for a little while."

"I know, it's been turbulent with me too. That night came back to me."

"When?" I asked coldly. I knew this was bound to come up

eventually.

"When we were all hanging out at your house and..."

"Look Tom I really... I don't want to keep fucking reliving this thing that happened years ago, it's almost twenty fucking years, man."

"I know. I just—it just keeps resurfacing."

"Can't we just fucking enjoy our fucking mushroom trip?"

We sat there quietly looking into the distance of my backyard and as the sun hid behind clouds, so did my understanding that everyone around me is a fucking coward. I just wanted to take shrooms and forget about life, I should do them alone from now on. For some reason, being in solitude for me is better, it's quieter. Nothing can compare, just to be myself and not be subjected to a fucking inquisition every fucking time.

I saw Tom taking off his sunglasses and closing his eyes. I did the same, but I kept my sunglasses on. Glancing at the sun didn't feel as difficult as it does when I'm not 'shrooming; shrooms simplify things in life that people aren't capable of doing. Sometimes even jumping a fucking puddle is a fucking issue for them, never mind being able to properly construct a narrative for me. Why bother? Why should I even fucking bother with Tom or Anthony or Bobby, I think it's better if we didn't have fucking contact.

And let's be fucking honest here, I'm a loner. The majority of my life is spent alone, so friendships mean something else to me, something profound and meaningful. That's what I look for because people aren't fucking earnest and they believe their lies, their stories, everything. The fucking fictional glass castle they've constructed, the view must be fucking great from there. Their ego is a cathedral, and they pray to St. Peter every night, I'll say that.

I loved Tom. I did. He was and continues to be a wonderful friend, that kind that most people would be honored to have but there were times where he was unbearable, always having second thoughts, tripping over his own wires all the time. It got to me for some reason.

But we all have our schtick, our habits and ways of managing stress and anxiety. I could be fucking aloof, unaware of other people's feelings, perhaps even more difficult than Tom would ever be, and there were times when I felt the resentment of other's success, choking on their own ego; it gave me fucking nightmares, they couldn't bust a nut if they fucking tried, they are not bulletproof, they can't walk on water either.

People are a virus and I kept breathing it in. If they didn't make me fucking sick, I would be a little nicer, a little more gracious despite how much I try. But what do you fucking expect in life? To me, all they do is cling to you like a spider, sting you and leave, I wish they would drop dead, but they will always touch the wound, fuck letting it heal.

Before my job went belly up, I worked with some fucking maniacs, it was as if a Roman Polanski thriller was happening, and everybody is in it but me. Completely out of touch with who they really are. It was surreal, they did not look like normal people. They appeared to be freaks with a passion for Vincent Van Gogh's ear rather than his art. That is probably the best way for me to describe them. I just could not connect with them, the fucking island of lost freaks. Sometimes I think that it was safer living and working with the fucking Manson family. At least I would know and understand my place.

Tom woke up after a lengthy nap on the lounge chair, I hadn't moved from my spot in hours just staring aimlessly into the horizon, the gold blue firmament above me and the masterful stroke of heaven behind the evergreens, a glistening window of solid glass, where stones are refined into spears to be harpooned into the enemy's spine. It's a funny thing being taken under the wing of a dragon, it's warmer than you think.

"These are potent, bro," he uttered.

I didn't say a word; I was sick of hearing my voice and I'm sure Tom was lost in his fucking haze anyway. It was irrelevant. I rolled myself a fatty and sat up and smoked, listening for the elves in the woods beyond the pines of my imagination. I also thought of Frankie, Det. Condo, that sexy godsend piece of ass, that Cuban Adonis. I just wanted him on me, under me, all around me, making me cum so hard with that well-packed 9-inch anaconda of his, with that fantastic body, that hard-chest, everything. He was everything. My dick sings Madame Butterfly every time he passes through my mind. Total abandon while I was lying next to him in bed, late at night splitting a fat one and staring at the ceiling, we never really spoke after we fucked, it was better to just be, and let everything sink in. Majestic elements of Sinatra on the MacBook, playing softly.

Frankie never had a suspicious nature and for that I was

grateful. He made me feel better just to be with him in his arms, untethered from chaos. We would usually just chat about how good the sex was, how attracted to him I was, and still am. It was hard to erase what happened with him the other day. How can I tell him of all fucking people? It would be the fucking end of everything for me, Tom, Anthony, and Bobby.

This was bad, and I had no clue what I was going to do to repair the damage. Maybe women were different. Deanna certainly was, so much resentment in that woman, because I was the one man who would never fall in love with her, with every fiber of being I resolutely fought every urge to call her even when I needed to have sex with a woman this time, it shifted like tectonic plates under the earth's core.

All of these thoughts passed intermittently in my mind, a giant pendulum with tentacles breaking free from its shackles. Silky pure cologne on my face and under my nose, I sucked it up. His beloved scent and I wanted him so badly, so desperately, daydreaming about him was seductive and he always made me fucking laugh. He had such a sexy voice, body, face, everything but it would never go beyond our established line in the sand. I suppose most relationships I have been involved in had a contract we all blithely sign without reading the terms and before we know it our tongues and hands are tied, we do what we can to get through it.

I left all of my issues at the door where I hung my coat. He was my bliss, a heaven I never discovered in any man before or since, a fevered deliberate obsessed attraction. Electrifying in bed, nothing short of fucking remarkable. He wasn't faking it. One does not applaud the tenor for clearing his throat. What I loved was how raw it felt, how invigorating it was to be on top of him sweating, perspiring the lust generated viciously from our bodies, our compatibility a succulent lust we swooned for.

Despite our causal disagreements transforming into bitter arguments, it was luxurious to be loved by him, and he by me, which I love. I made him feel better and more exhilarated than half the pudgy, balding, middle-management riffraff he typically fucked on a weekly basis. If I wanted a man I had him, if he wants to tell he finds that he can't. That's my story. That's my life. I'm not a fucking idiot, nor was I born in a fucking freezer there were plenty of men and women in the course of my life, but I succeeded with the one who would make my heartbeat quicker, who got my blood pumping, my dick harder.

Perhaps Deanna was right, detachment is a solution. Frankie is a wild card and I envied it, envied his recklessness, an absence of introspection and insight. I have no intention of tearing myself away from the arms of someone so astonishing.

I enjoyed a cigarette by myself by the pool hours after the mushrooms wore off. Tom had gone home and I was relieved. I just did not have the propensity or stomach for other people. Things seemed to be crumbling around me, unraveling was my life, quicker and faster down this unstoppable slope, the depth expanding. Nightmares, anxiety during the day, hyperventilating and I knew the cure for it all: opening up to Jason about what happened... *that night*. Which perhaps may help me come clean with Frankie too.

I stubbed out my cigarette in the ashtray on the table and stared at the black velvet sky. Hoping a meteor would hit the earth's stratosphere, devouring us whole. I soon fell asleep, and I dreamed of the car. And the sound it made when the man drove away. And then nothing. Nothing at all.

CHAPTER 8
A Cool, Dry Place

I woke up again in a panic, nothing but fear running through my veins as if it were a demonic synthetic energy, this black matter, coursing through my body like a malicious amphetamine. I had cold sweat dripping from my forehead, my t-shirt was drenched. I saw my hand lightly convulsing, as if I had just come off a narcotic and running headlong into withdrawal, the ugly demented side effects of addiction but I knew that was not the case.

I was addicted to me, even on my worst days, I still outshined everyone. Including Frankie. He was sexy but he wasn't interesting and worst of all, like most intellectuals, he's intensely stupid. He didn't need help, he needed hindrances. If he has to climb over enough men, he might inadvertently fall on top of him. Perhaps this recent disagreement has led us to a more comprehensive understanding of just where our sexual complicity stood. At the moment it stood in a cold shower with the water on high. No need for him to pull my trigger any time soon. I can do that standing on my head.

Useless dramatic fuck.

I shook it off, got dressed and texted Tom.

Let's meet. Libertine Coffee House. Broadway and 12th St.

Now? Tom wrote back.

No next month figured I would let you know ahead of time. Yes now. Please.

Okay. I have some time.

I brushed my teeth, splashed some cologne on, and walked to the coffee shop. I smoked a joint before heading in. I ordered a cappuccino and left it on the table to cool down. Upon awakening, I found I could not handle anything too hot or cold or intense. Everything seemed heavily amplified for the past few weeks, a violent turbulence I have never known before.

I waited for a few minutes attempting to relax myself and take a few deep breaths before seeing Tom walk in. Calm as usual, in control of everything within him; something else I greatly resented him about. It was this sneaking pathetic emotion that crept up on me like cancer.

He ordered an iced coffee, came to the table. We said our hello's and as he sat down, I felt my mind twist and spin around in my head stumbling back and forth with accelerating speed.

"What's up man, you alright? Those mushrooms were intense. I'm fucking relieved I was able to handle it."

"I know. That was fun, right? Chilling by the pool."

"Yeah man, we have to do that again soon."

I rubbed my hands against the cup and glanced out the window, seeing people coming and going, distracting themselves with their various concerns, not a care in the fucking world. I looked at Tom again and down at my coffee.

"Possibly man. Look Tom, the reason I thought we should meet here is I wanted to talk about... about that night. The prom."

Tom smiled briefly and rubbed his head, shaking his hand through his hair in exasperation. "You called me down here for that?" he said tightly.

"I know it's a sensitive issue I just—I haven't been sleeping. I keep having nightmares, and irregular heartbeats. I keep waking up in a cold sweat... I don't eat very much... it's the lie—"

"Hugo, the fucking lie—" he nearly shouted in the moderately packed coffee house. He looked around and waved in his sarcastic way. "It wasn't exactly a lie. Terrance *slipped,* Hugo."

"That's what we agreed on, but that's not... That's not what happened."

"What the fuck are you trying to say?"

"I don't know if I can live with this any longer. I don't know what that means for our friendship, I just—I can't deny that it doesn't exist. Running away from it, pretending that it was all an accident, lying to myself to other people to my doctor... it's wrong Tom."

"It may be fucking wrong... I have been struggling myself, but what's our recourse? Huh? It would mean the end of everything. *Everything.* For me, you, Tony, Bobby...

everybody. Please, Hugo."

The rage inside of me was boiling over. The nightmares took on a new and dangerous shape, an unending loop of fury and murder, constantly reinventing itself. I tried to remember what our lives were before that night, we weren't reckless, but we had a liberated sense of self, an identity, a purpose, and significance, I also wondered how many high schoolers would be able to speak those words in any given situation, the possibilities seemed to be a far-fetched fairy tale. I suppose as you get older, you become a philistine, a nihilist, a lost fucking cause.

"I don't know what to fucking do anymore, but there's this part of me that won't let me go through with it. I would never betray our friendship."

"I know that, Hugo. I wouldn't do it either, I couldn't live with myself, never mind looking at myself in the mirror, your reflection always looks you right in the eye. So, what do you think?"

"Frankly, maybe I'll just go home, get my handgun, and put a bullet in my brain. Problem solved."

Tom inhaled breath, wiped his eyes, and looked at me. "Don't fucking joke about that."

"Who the fuck says I'm joking?"

"I don't know how to help you."

"Imagine my fucking surprise."

"Fuck you. You bitter little fuck. *You* called *me,* brother."

"What is this, Tom? Huh? A farewell speech, a sermon on the fucking mount? Are you at least going to be my boy or what?"

"Since I am, and I always will be, I'm not going to fucking sit here and have you threaten me with something like that. You think coming clean about something like this would help anything?"

"It's eroding me. I don't know what the fuck it's doing to you, though."

Tom looked out the window and sipped his coffee and glanced back at me. Then looked down and rubbed his face.

I think the reason we had such a contentious friendship was because we were more alike than we cared to admit.

"What about Tony and Bobby?" he finally asked.

"I didn't meet with them yet. I figured you would be my first stop."

"You mentioned nightmares; to be honest, I get them too, night terrors too. Just... waking up, screaming. Right before the car... and seeing Terrance, I wake up and for a minute I'm screaming." He stopped abruptly, fighting the urge to cry and a tear rode down his delicate skin. We didn't move from our seats until the coffee house announced they were closing.

We split a cigarette by my car and made small talk about the moon and other things, trying to think of how it used to be before we drifted apart before what happened on prom night changed everything.

"Honestly Tom, I don't know what the fuck to do." I smoked the rest of the cigarette and tossed it in the gutter; I rubbed my hands over my head.

"I'm with you, brother, I don't know either. These night terrors..."

"I can't fucking live like this, the nightmares the memory, the lies... I just... How can we live with it? How? I'm lying to everyone, to J—" I immediately stopped myself.

"Huh?"

"Nothing. I—I don't know what I'm saying."

Tom stood there and looked at me for a good minute. He checked his phone, and I did the same.

"Listen, I have to go, brother."

"Me too. Call me tomorrow or something bro. We'll meet up."

"Sure. Sure, brother." Tom got into his car, told me to have a good night and drove away into the late-night traffic.

I never felt more alone than I did standing in the parking lot of a closed coffeeshop with nobody around me. It was as if the world had gone cold, silent, detached, and my wounded body began to crumble even further within me. No refuge. Nobody to hear my torment, my nightmares however, they felt lighter and less frightening. There is beauty in a breakdown when you're all alone.

As I had my head in my hands, I cried it out. All of it. Swallowing me whole. It was entrapment from the beginning! From the beginning! If I hadn't listened to Anthony if I had just walked the fuck away, if I just walked away and not pushed—if I just stopped myself, and not used so much strength, he never would have— it would be different now. Everything would be different, and I knew the only way out of this was by talking to Jason. I had to. I can't do this any longer, it's too much. I wanted to wake up calmly, I didn't want the nightmares, the anger, the moodiness, the feeling of guilt wrapping around my gut like a fucking wire, I had to tell him. That was my pound of flesh, eventually I would be paying interest when it comes to my friends. More than I care to think about.

I ran out of cigarettes, and I had a little blow in the car, in the glove compartment. I did a line on my hand and snorted it fast. The most meaningful way to not feel is to just do a little coke, blast some music, and drive into the desolate black night.

I searched within myself for that cool dry place I remember as a child, where I went to the Jersey Shore in the summer because my family had rented a house. I remember the rooms: they were huge, spacious, and beautiful, but the house felt cold to me, lacking in comfort, the real kind where you felt welcomed.

So, I would just spend my time at the beach with a towel on the sand and my hands behind my head looking up at the sky. It was a heatwave I think, this day that I'm remembering, and the beach was packed. I was eating ice cream and I had Anthony with me. It was simpler back then whatever we did was peripheral, we were punished but it faded into the background and the repercussions were small, almost null and void. My parents were never around anyway, even when I was fucking ten years old, they were going around Europe for the summer or spending time in The Hamptons or shopping, who the fuck knew.

But they had time to take me to the Jersey Shore and I loved it; I had my own private Idaho on that beach. Perhaps this isn't the life for me. The softness of the sand was soothing, and just being with Anthony, a wild child yes but awesome just the same, a great friend. I didn't need my family, and I knew they did not need me either, it didn't take much to know something that's been there in front of my face for years. Even at the tender age of ten. Anthony definitely realized too. We had ice cream, hot dogs, burgers, we went in the ocean and lay under the sun watching the clouds move in that vivid blue firmament.

Time moves on and it makes you feel as though it's another concept developed by men to send us over the edge. It does not heal all, whatever tragedy might have befallen you. It numbs you, disorients your thinking that if enough years have been surpassed you can never face it again, but you do. Except you can't go back and change it because it's too late. Years too late.

I wanted to be free of it, emancipated from the burden of it but I was shackled inside of my own prison. Locked by my fear of the truth. Caged though it was, it was close, it was very close to me, and I could feel the pressure of it each day. The weight, the sound of him contacting the car, and how everything went quiet; eerily, deafeningly quiet. A pin dropping could be heard a mile away. He was shaking as blood covered his face and his left foot was lying by the gutter. Everyone in complete shock, a chilling sense of darkness overcoming me as the moon went silent and moved behind an oncoming cloud. And Terrance lying there on the ground, the look in his eyes, a longing I never knew, but it was the longing that made me feel a little nervous. It appeared as if he was happy.

Pain can be unbearable, and too much of it is toxic. I knew what I had to do...

My phone rang. "Hugo. It's Frankie."

"Frankie, what's up?"

"Listen why don't we go somewhere and talk. I just want to talk."

"Frankie..."

"You're not in any danger, I just need some answers here. I can come pick you up."

I thought about this for a minute before answering. I knew he was telling the truth. I told him where I was, and he was there ten minutes later.

We sat in Frankie's car, and I didn't say anything for a few minutes. We kissed of course, and fuck me, he smelled so nice, it was the Calvin Klein up his shirt, and I wanted my hand down his pants.

"You seem a little better, Hugo." Frankie began. "Are you?"

"Handcuff me and let's get it on in the back seat," I stalled.

"We will. I just need some information... because you haven't been yourself and I think I'm entitled to know. Did something happen to you?"

"What do you mean?"

"You always look so distracted Hugo, as if something is on your mind."

"I just—I don't know, it was a long time ago, Frankie... Alright. What do you want to know? What exactly are you asking me?"

"It's something back in high school, right? An accident of

some kind?" He asked as gently as he could, I never knew him to be this way, he was usually so full of guile and sarcasm, but not tonight he seemed different, cold, detached, something had changed. "If it was an accident, that's a different story. I just want to know..."

"How do you fucking know about that?" I asked with tears in my eyes. Now I was fucked. He didn't answer me.

"I... it was just an accident, Frankie. It happened so fast."

"How did it happen?"

"I. I can't tell you. I can't do that Frankie. I—I want to, and I don't want to lie, I just, I don't, I don't know what will happen to my friends and I, if I do."

"Listen... nothing will happen. Alright? But you have to tell me what actually happened, Hugo."

I sat there in my car. Hoping something would happen. Something permanent.

I went home and did about four lines of cocaine and finished a half a bottle of Jack Daniels mixing it with diet coke. I smoked so many cigarettes I was fucking dizzy. I was watched *A Clockwork Orange* and *2001: A Space Odyssey* on HBO Max. I put it on mute and watched myself float down the Jupiter worm hole at the end. Breaking apart, being stretched like taffy, and turned into a monkey by the end.

"Hugo? You're still up? It's after four in the morning."

"I'll be right in, Frankie. Making some tea."

I sat there and drank my hot ginger tea and looked into the face of the monolith. It seemed to me that this dark world I lived in could be changed, switched, and removed. If I could just find a spaceship, a wormhole. I wanted to be in that room, lying on the bed, pointing towards the blanket of stars and the rising moon.

A half hour later I stripped down to nothing, got into bed with Frankie, and we fucked. I wanted to be numb for a while, numb to the fucking bone.

"Hugo. That was incredible. But I still need to know."

"And then what happens?"

"Nothing. But something will if you *don't* tell me."

I closed my eyes and I turned on my side, facing the wall. I told him everything, everything I believed happened. And then I passed out.

Part III
Hit & Run

"Those friends thou hast, and their adoption tried,
Grapple them to thy soul with hoops of steel."
—WILLIAM SHAKESPEARE
The Tragedy of Hamlet

"And the rain is brain-colored.
And the thunder sounds like something remembering something."
—STAN RICE

"And the cloud that took the form
(When the rest of Heaven was blue)
Of a demon in my view—"
—EDGAR ALLEN POE
Alone

CHAPTER 9
A Dark Matter

The next morning, I felt as if weeks had flown by. I passed out and had lost all concept of time, all moments where my anxiety was so great I thought I would become something else, a ghost, a futile entity in this cracked universe. I was between a rock and a hard place; Frankie and I sat in the living room not saying a word. I rubbed my face and braced myself for whatever happened next. It was becoming something unbelievable, the crumbling of a castle I worked steadfastly to build, a glass castle, where stones are thrown through plate glass windows and I'm ducking each one. We all have our survival tactics. As hot and gorgeous and wonderful as Frankie was, and he always was and will be, I just couldn't face the idea of telling him the whole truth. The guy is fucking dead after all. What difference did it make now?!

"He drove you to the breaking point, didn't he?" Frankie uttered into the still morning of my living room. "Hard to believe it isn't anything worse than that."

"It was an accident. I didn't mean for it to happen, Frankie... but it did. He kept bullying my boy, how can— how can I let that slide? He was a bully. A piece of shit. Just antagonizing everyone all the time, he called my girlfriend at the time a whore. See some of what I think I remember is a fucking haze, but Terrance calling my lady a whore, well... that part is clear. That part I remember. Just fine. I think that alone is justified."

"Who is this girl?"

"Deanna Soprano."

"Okay." He wrote her name down. "I think him calling her that is reason enough..."

"No fucking kidding. He's lucky this is all that fucking

happened to him. Bitter little shit."

"He must have really resented you for a reason. Did something happen between you two that may have triggered him in some way?"

"So now *I'm* in the wrong?"

"I didn't say that Hugo, I'm just asking questions. Not pointing fingers."

"We were in a relationship for a little while; we would meet, fuck like crazy, not talk for a while, get into another stupid fucking argument, then come back together again. It was a little ridiculous and I have no idea why I pushed to keep it going with him. He was exhausting, he was just really nice in bed, so I kept it going and going...." I trailed off and rubbed my eyes, which were filling with tears.

"Listen Hugo, I'm not taking this to a higher authority here, mum is the word. We know each other, we know how we think, I—I honestly don't know what to make of it. But. Looks like Terrance had some blood on his hands too, technically. I have zero tolerance when it comes to bullying."

"Okay, Frankie."

"It's alright. Okay? It's alright. I'm just relieved you told me everything because it's hopeless to think anyone in your shoes would have the balls to do it. I commend you. You're a good man. I enjoy fucking you."

"You're the only cop who did."

"I think I'm the only cop who would."

"Yeah okay... you want to see my fucking payroll?"

"What a jib," Frankie replied. He got up, opened the window, and started smoking a bowl, holding it out for me.

"You really believe it was an accident?"

"A very unpleasant one. Perhaps the kind that didn't necessarily have to happen, but an accident, nevertheless."

"Last night, though. You were hotter than usual."

"I was reading you your rights the kind you want to hear."

Frankie air kissed me with that smirk that I found to be pure sexual energy. Frankie was porn. Frankie was walking porn.

"You were the one who turned on *Love Machine*."

"Listen I saw it in a movie, and I was inspired. You sexy thing."

"I always love when you moan my name, Hugo."

"I know. I love it too. It's hot."

"You feeling the need to fuck before I go?"

"You mean you?"

"I should just arrest you right now"

"Read my rights."

"You're one snide prick, you know that, Hugo?"

"Believe me I know." We kissed passionately and the volume for once in my life was turned down. It usually is when I'm with Frankie. Something about him, something calming and reassuring.

"To be honest I'm craving..."

"A woman. Happens to the best of us."

"So... it's all going to be alright?"

"Yeah. You told me what happened. I need to process it but, nobody needs to know. I just hope that your friends are on the same page."

"Frankie, they have no fucking clue that I told you. Please, if they find out..."

"Told me what? I got you. Alright?"

"I did kind of mention that I had a difficult time holding it together to my boy Tom but he's my guy. He understood."

"Did he give you any impression that he was against this?"

"He was having the same fucking issues that I am. Nightmares, trauma, etc."

"Alright. Make sure. Talk to him."

"I will."

"Okay. I have to go alright. You okay?"

"Yeah. I think so."

He rubbed my lip with his thumb, and I wanted to pin him down on the floor and cum all over his hard chest. He was just so sexy, it was unbelievable.

"Call you later. Let me know what happens with Tom."

"I'll keep you posted."

"Have a good day Hugo, get some sleep."

"Hugo... Huuugo. Hugo. HUGO." And we were looking and listening to the whirring fan above us. No pre-rolls or cigarettes. We just stared, making small talk.

"I missed you, Deanna," I whispered into her ear.

"I wish I could say the same."

"Oh, wait a minute I think it was you who texted me. Because you wanted my cock in you."

"Yes, you may be right. But I wanted something firm too,

something familiar. And you are familiar..."

"Something about a fork being plunged into the back of your hand."

"I never allow anyone to get the best of me."

"I know that."

"Hugo. That night with Terrance and the accident...."

"Yes."

"Well, it's been sticking with me. Terrance was a wild card, not entirely made to hang in our circle but still I believed there was something else that was missing, something darker something strange. And it makes me think..."

"You're doing that now?"

"Well, I learn from the best. For some years now this whole incident has been buried along with this memory and I feel it's about time we did something about that, but perhaps somebody else beat me to it."

"I can't live with it anymore alright."

"Hugo! You can UNDO everything!"

"It's making me fucking crazy. It's driving me fucking crazy keeping this a secret... I. He died. And he didn't need to. It just didn't need to happen that way. Horrible fucking night."

"Hugo, we made an agreement, we can still see each other but you have to let this go. It happened and it was a tragedy; we all have our demons but this. This can never see the light."

"You were barely fucking involved Deanna."

"I was there! I could've—"

"It happened so fucking fast, there was nothing anyone could do."

"I don't know about that," Deanna's voice was the animated iciness it usually was, today was different something was off, perhaps it was this need to feel sorrow or pain but keeping it contained at all costs. A wrath that was masked by beauty and glamour.

"So because I'm feeling guilt, immense fucking— do you have any clue what has been happening with me?"

"No."

"I've been having nightmares, losing sleep, it's not normal alright? Something is wrong here, Deanna. Something dark, I don't know what exactly, but the fucking wizard of oz doesn't exist here Deanna, this shit is real. Between me and you, I haven't told the entire truth."

"I know you're being honest with me, Hugo."

"I'm not a fucking monkey Deanna, alright? Trust me. I know what the fuck I'm doing."

"Very well, then."

We lay in each other's arms, allowing time to pass through satellites.

"What about Tom?"

"What *about* Tom?" I uttered as I began to drift off to sleep. "It's the usual routine, isn't it?"

"Well, he was the one who—"

"Watch your fucking mouth. He slipped, remember? Nobody shoved anyone. And that's the fiction."

"Is that what you told Frankie?"

"Yes, as a matter of fact, it is. It's all a blur."

"Everyone was so drunk and stoned."

"Who remembers what? That's my alibi. I just keep hearing him hit the fucking car."

"I do too from time to time. It was a long time ago baby, let's just move on."

"I've tried to do that. Clearly, it's not working for me. these nightmares, these crazy fucking dreams I have."

"Hugo, they are just dreams baby, just dreams."

"You're a dream to me, too; you just happen to *come* true every night."

"So have you. Surprisingly. How is Frankie?"

"He's doing alright."

"He is one beautiful man, Hugo."

"I know, amazing in bed. Amazing out of bed. Men like him do not happen often, when he pulled me over for passing a stop sign... well he's been pulling me over and over almost every day for a year."

"Is he better than I am?" Deanna slipped her hand under the blanket massaging my cock that was already partially erect and kept rocking it back and forth.

"Well, he doesn't use his hands all the time."

"I do."

"You are fucking gorgeous, you know that. I am not kidding, you fucking Helen of Troy. Just deliciously sexy."

"Keep it up, Hugo."

"I mean it."

"I know you do, that's not what I mean."

"It isn't?"

"No."

"I see." I exhaled in passionate euphoria. Her left hand was where it was at, in high school, college and beyond it never lost its uncanny ability to make me explode.

"Just let me do the work."

"By all means, Deanna." I sat back and closed my eyes. Her hand thrusting quickly and then slowly, and back again. I lay there in peace. Feeling the ejaculating anticipation through my body and veins, but I made myself not cum for her too quickly. Ten minutes later she was wiping her hand on the blanket and we fell asleep each wreathed in each other's arms, our pastimes done as the firmament above possesses a golden slumber, lulling us to sleep.

CHAPTER 10
Erosion

The earth swallows you whole, but you don't hear it. You feel its crushing weight when you wake up, having your morning coffee, listening to the symphony of chirping birds, smoking your first pre-roll of the day, staring into a void of space you would trade anything for, to be able to slip in and never come back. The castles of everlasting fire come down, and you see how complex they were for they are the castles of your better self, as a car comes plummeting to your death. Locomotive speed in a split second.

I had an appointment with Jason today and it was the last fucking thing I wanted to do. Why can't life just move on after tragedy? Why can't I just get better? It's terrifying. I sat there by the pool enjoying a cigarette with my sunglasses on as the sun worked its way from behind the white vapor clouds, hitting my skin. I took a deep breath and exhaled the smoke slowly. The cleaning lady came in through the back gate, waved, and I waved back. I watched as she used her key to get into the house and start her day. I had a completely different life, one of privilege and abandon, money, and frivolity but what was missing was love, peace. Perhaps that was her life. I would trade up in a fucking minute. Smoking was a relief for me, usually I just smoked after sex but now it's becoming a habit and a dependency that I need. I loved them in the morning.

I had no fucking clue what I was going to tell Jason. All I knew was that I had to tell him what I told Frankie and keep it consistent. People bend the truth to their will all the fucking time, who am I to disabuse it? If everyone was happy, what is the big fucking deal? I'm not a fucking anomaly either. I banged my own therapist, is bending the truth a crime too?

My parents were expected to come back from their month-long trek through Europe, not that I hoped it would make a big difference with me but not much existed with us anyway. We came and went and never saw each other. Never spoke, never had dinner together. That was my life growing up. I was not invited to Europe; I know I mentioned this earlier. The fruits of their labor, minimal though it was. They barely worked: they barely did anything. My father went to work for a couple of hours a week and made millions.

My mother... *pffttt*. Not a day in her life. She usually just left the house, came back with bags from Barney's and Bergdorf's. She would get me shirts, shoes, ties, jackets, anything, and I never asked for it nor did I wear them too frequently either, but the colognes I wore every time I had a date with a man or woman or both. It's why I would get laid so smoothly, it was never something I struggled with.

I could come downstairs - reeking of weed, still stoned from MDMA, or cocaine or mushrooms - making myself some French toast at two in the morning and nobody said or did a thing. I would have my friends over for a barbecue and they would turn it into a house party, drugs everywhere, every beautiful woman you can imagine, everyone smoking weed, the house a mess, the kitchen a disaster, music blasting. They never said... one. fucking. word.

Ever. And that to me was the trifecta, I was the invisible fucking man. Just their vanity project, their putrid child, their ward, in a way. I lived there for free, I ate for free, they never even said a word about what happened with Terrance on that night, they never asked me why my face was covered in blood, smeared in dirt, why my suit was torn to shreds, why I was shaking and convulsing when I came through the door and threw my shoes on the carpet near the front door.

Sometimes I would swallow three-and-a-half grams of mushrooms and lock myself in the basement, which had a full kitchen, a stocked fridge, and a master bath. It was my haven. My second office to fuck around and do nothing. It would smell of marijuana every day, I would be so blessedly powerfully stoned, and would watch *Star Wars* and *Kubrick* all day every day. The volume on my tv was so loud, the house shook. I would be fucking women, men, and still not a word. There was a door from the yard that led into the basement. Especially the men who moaned so loud and so long, and me, forget about me, they knew how emotional I got when I had a nice fuck, I always welcomed it, god I kept them coming back and back and back. And that's where I met Frankie, I had a traffic ticket, I blew him in my car and from that point on every ticket I got was expunged. I asked him why he had to give me this ticket; he told me because I was driving recklessly, and I quipped: *How about we get reckless?* I'll never forget how fucking sexy he was in that uniform, Jesus Fucking Christ. With the belt, and the gun, and the baton, forget about it. We were rocking out in no time. The rest is history.

I remember Frankie and I fucked on the living room couch watching *Cruel Intentions* and my father walked in with some packages, I was cumming as the door opened and we didn't flinch. He didn't either.

"Jesus, Frankie... get off me," I quipped.

I will never forget how hard he and I laughed. It was those fires I lit everyday just to see their reaction, to see how far I could fucking push them to their limit, and they never budged, fucking human statue syndrome or something. The same expressionless looks on their faces, it was surreal. And from that point on, we just sat on the couch, not saying a word.

On my way to Jason's, the music played quietly from the speakers. On Spotify I had my playlists all set up, and this time I wanted to just go with Radiohead. It didn't matter what I was feeling but they usually helped me to manage my feelings better. Their atmospheric tones made me relax in my car while driving, and I usually had the most anxiety whenever I had to be out in public, it was never desirable with me.

I kept remembering the sound Terrance made when it happened, the tragic accident, and it never left my brain. I just wanted to be free of it. But it appeared as though this meticulous world of mine was a cleverly constructed prison, where a key was swallowed up by greed and pride. Sinking below the ocean, at the very bottom, where no light escapes. Gardens no longer grew beautiful flowers, the women were weeds now, and their eyes lost their electrical black velvet, those secret quiet lightning storms, now just a gray cloud of nothing. With a man, it was, of course, a hurricane. And their currents flowed through me, that was the world I was divided in, pulled apart by an invisible enemy with their claws sticking into me, as my body tensed and the blood poured forth in a black stream. Hypnotic, dancing, sensuous jellyfish that flowed effortlessly through the quiet and abandoned ocean. And I never saw them again; they flowed into an abyss. One that I never felt or experienced. The opening embrace of silence.

I was at another red light now; it was pouring out now. I needed a coffee to go with the second cigarette of my day, I rubbed my face and as my foot was coming off the break, I almost nipped the guy in front of me. I quickly slammed down and just missed the car ahead of me, by the skin of my ass. I rubbed my temple as the cigarette in my hand dangled precariously and hyperventilated. I longed for release.

"What have I done?" I whispered. "What in the fucking name of God did I do?"

"That's not for me to say, Hugo. You have to tell me."

"What good are you, Jason?"

"The meaning is elicited through verbalization."

"And the—"

"Hugo, please. That's what happens in therapy. I'm more interested in your perceptions."

"And just last week I was blowing you."

"Can't say that I didn't enjoy it. But now it's time we spoke about why you're really here."

I sat there, quiet and motionless. I stared blankly at Jason, without flinching. Quietly observing the subtle changes of his face, the way he communicated a need to know what was happening within. I couldn't tell him what was really happening, underneath.

As much as Jason and I enjoyed each other's presence on the sofa or on his desk, I had a surprising feeling of revulsion towards him now. Contempt is a fiend for which we have no recourse, a terror fills our hearts and lives, our existences are thereby called into question. And we never find those pieces again. We lose who we once were and come to embrace who we believe we should be. Condemned to a life of hindsight, as the car came plummeting towards Terrance, and that sound, that thundering sound we heard when—

"What is it, Hugo? You have to tell me."

"I want to, Jason, I just—"

"You feel you can't. Don't you?" he asked gently.

I rubbed my temple again, and I couldn't sit still. I felt the tightening of my stomach clench my intestines, and it pulled harder and harder, like a sharp wire around my bones. There had to be better life than this one, and it was waiting for me, on the other side of paranoia. That glowing rainbow where darkness is absorbed by the sun, and madness is muted. The technicolor of our dreams are streamed in glistening yellow dandelions. The sound and fury signifying release under a wing of a broken angel, soaring through the clouds in freedom, hope springs eternal black pearl stars. Trees breathing endless poetic rhythms and our signals to noise are disrupted, jammed by a system, red candelabras held in one hand and a smoking mirror revealing ourselves in great undulating colors, colors in tragedy and pain and conquest and music. It was the dark velvet blue and now black, black patches of a distant milky way, fading into a strange and unknown background, no longer in connection with the roots of my hands as they change the course of centuries old paintings. A universe unleashes its kryptonite poison, and we suck it up like fresh Columbian cocaine, midnight debauchery, with the blue and dark red lights of a nightclub, the rain pouring down from a silent firmament. We ejaculate our fears in a gas that is recycled by the polluted world of our creating. Civilizations shall crumble and fall below the Atlantic Ocean, and vanishing in sweet rainforest mist.

And I fell back down the freefall back into Jason's office and I came as soon as he made his final pull.

"Well, that was uh— a nice change of events. Thank you, Jay."

"You were zoning out. I had to bring you back."

"You certainly fucking did...." I lit up and opened a window. Smoking it out, I felt relieved that I was able to go into a trance in a way.

Jason walked around his office and rubbed his head with his hand constantly.

"What?"

"You have to tell me what fucking happened! You have to. Right now, Hugo."

I took another pull from my cigarette before flinging it out the window onto the street and stood there. "Why do you want to know?"

"Because it's killing you. And you're my responsibility."

"Jason—I... I don't know how."

"Right now, Hugo."

"He— it was just a freak— thing."

"Who's *he*?"

"This guy. Terrance. I went... to high school with. We all

went out for our senior prom, and we had some drinks and, I'm not going to lie, a lot of drugs..."

"Well, you know that never truly mattered to me. I just need to know."

I felt the weight of my stomach fill me with anxiety and a fear I never experienced before. Intense feelings of panic set in and my hands were perspiring.

"I don't think so, Jason."

"Hugo. If you don't tell me, I can't treat you anymore. This is a quid pro quo now. You know the fucking rules."

"What rules, Jason? What? Did I request for you to jerk me off and make me cum?"

"No. You didn't, but—"

"I didn't. So don't quote the fucking *rules* now."

"Hugo, I need to know. It's now or never."

"He—Jason I can't. I'm sorry I can't. Please! Please!"

"Hugo. You can't do this. I can't keep fucking—"

"Jason listens to me! I CAN'T! I swore. My friends and I made a pact! That means something where I come from! You make a promise in blood!"

"You made a promise to me, Hugo!"

"I know!"

"And I'm asking that you honor it! Now, I want the truth."

"Jesus Christ." I was hyperventilating; I was on my knees with my hands going up and down over my shaved head.

"What happened, Hugo? What happened on prom night?"

I looked at Jason, tears in my eyes. I closed them hoping for something to happen.

"From what I'm seeing, it's pretty bad, isn't it?"

I didn't respond. I was crouched on the floor, fighting back tears and pain.

"Release yourself, Hugo. This is a safe place. But I can't treat you if you don't open up."

I sat there. Quiet. Hand over my eyes. Wanting to disappear.

"Fine. That's it. This is our last appointment. I'm done." Jason walked toward the door.

I stood up and sighed. "The only way out is through... I'll, I'll tell you."

Jason, now at the door, turned around to face me.

"I'll tell you everything," I whispered.

My pain was insurmountable, and the light outside began

to fade. I felt the night repeat itself on an endless loop inside of my bones, my memory working overtime. And now there was nothing but the memory of that night facing me, in Jason's office with tears welling up inside of me. And I never felt more alone. Jason stood at the end of the office with his hands folded leaning on a filing cabinet. I could see it in his eyes, nothing but genuine concern and fear for what happened on that night, of all nights. Prom night, where everyone's life changed, all of us. One minute we were dancing, enjoying our youth, our freedom, and the next we were looking into an abyss. Little did we know that the abyss also looked into us.

"It's a safe space, Hugo." Jason uttered from the other end of his office.

"Nobody can ever fucking know this came from me. My friends mean too much to have everything destroyed."

"Anything you tell me is private, Hugo. You know the rules. I know our deal."

"Jason, if I find out it left this fucking room..."

"It won't. You have my fucking word, Hugo. We have all night. My last appointment called and cancelled."

He slipped! That's the fiction. Freak accident....

In remembering, I was trying desperately to forget.

CHAPTER 11
Dangerous Liaisons On Prom Night

Senior year of high school. 2002

Tonight is the night, the night of all nights where we can party and live the life we deserve. I felt the heat of the evening when he walked to the bathroom and was taking a shower, and where she called my house and left a message. Marvin Gaye's "Got to Give It Up" playing on the speakers in the tv room, the monster speakers that you can hear all through the house. It was Jocelyn on the phone, my date for the prom, she gave me head in my car last night after I wined and dined her at Blue Restaurant, the only Manhattan-like restaurant in all of Staten Island. Beautiful place with incredible food and drinks, never lets me down, constantly gets me laid. Bless its heart.

"Joce I can't wait for tonight..."

"Me neither, I enjoyed you so much last night."

"Oh, I know you did, my dick is happier than it's been in years."

"Yes baby, it was a pleasure."

"Believe me the pleasure was all mine, god that was so awesome."

We spoke for a little while longer, and after my one-night stand came downstairs and helped himself to coffee, we kissed goodbye and I got ready in a hurry. The shower was blazing with steam and hot water. For ten minutes I was doused in soap, and I kept thinking about the night ahead of me and all the wonderful things that my friends and I had planned. It was exciting and it makes me happy, we work so hard, we do so much and this night calls for debauchery. Of all kinds, big, small, or otherwise, it was a night to go down in history.

Little did we know....

He slipped. HE SLIPPED!

I was in a suit with no tie and the top buttons undone, my chain and chest showing, it's how I did it. Once I got downstairs, I did the line of cocaine Bobby gave me, to help pay for me coming to get him at the fucking movies after he saw *The Aviator* and was tripping balls on mushrooms. He always came prepared. I'll give him that.

It was fantastic how close I was with my boys and how close they were to me. I never had friends like the ones I had in high school, all the relentless ball-breaking we did, the countless times we skipped class and went to the movies to see *2001: A Space Odyssey,* re-released in theaters for the first time in decades on mushrooms, walking out of the theater in a strange and curious daze, taking a cab home, and sitting in my backyard staring at the stars. All the times we had each other's backs, I felt safe with them and they with me, perhaps I was the leader in a way. But we led each other, we bettered each other. Nothing could come between us that might jeopardize our close friendship, more than friendship. We were family.

I made myself a vodka cranberry with plenty of ice to compliment the cocaine I just snorted up my nose. It wasn't a lot, who the fuck am I? Scarface? I never really had much after this night in terms of the right friends, the best kind of people you can rely on when the chips are down and no matter how young or old you are, you need them, it's something life gives you, a gift of friendship, where you are loved and respected, they want your company, and are willing to die for you. What else did I need? Or even worse, want? Want is ego, need is soul. I would rather have soul, that to me was what true love meant. And love can be magic, but by now I know that magic isn't real either. Love is the potion; and we drink it down. Love is an answer. I'm just so fucking relieved I had the kind of people who I can call family.

I was sitting outside and glancing up at the setting sun, it was that beautiful time of day where the sun goes down, and it takes its precious time, where nature seems to sing its most beautiful songs, the end of a day, and the darkness gradually takes over, and it's the start of summer, where life can finally slow the fuck down. Finally. I needed tonight, I needed to just escape, and as I sat there in the backyard at the table with my feet up and a drink in my hand watching the summer sun descend into REM sleep, I began to understand just how desperate I was to let go of this part of my life.

I felt loved when I went to school, when I went to Anthony's nearly every day and Sunday dinner, and Easter Sunday, and Christmas Eve, or a birthday or even fucking Halloween, whatever it was, it was great, always a great time always a time where I felt more loved and relaxed than anywhere else on earth. When I was with Anthony and his family, I could be myself, I could bust their balls because they busted mine right back, and it was all good. I could laugh, I could eat anything, not be judged. I could smoke and do mushrooms, and nobody judged me because they did them with me all the time. We went to the Jersey shore every summer, to Lake George, New York every fourth of July weekend. Anthony's uncle has a cabin up there. Usually, it was about twenty of us all living in neighboring houses and coming together for the day. It was a nice and beautiful relief. I could just let go and be relaxed, content. I could mellow out by the lake, read my book. I remember when I was reading *American Psycho* and Anthony's cousin Benny sat down next to me and we spoke about it, taking mushrooms and smoking blunts all night long. Just us. Everyone else was sleeping or just sitting around. It was just Benny and myself, I think we were up until after five in the morning. I will never forget that night. One of the most interesting and passionate people I know.

Benny was older than us by three years but he made everyone around him mellow and relaxed and feel appreciated. It was a great moment of my life, to talk to someone I respected and admired. He had been through it all, and so did I for the most part. He told me about the first time he did DMT and Molly, and up until that point I had only done Molly, I think nearly one or twice a month for a year. However, I told him I had never heard of DMT. And he gave me quite an earful about his experiences. Saying how it was like being catapulted up into the stars, and beyond the horizon. I remember him saying that, that it was a catapult. And you're blasted from your body into the nether regions. After I heard that, I wanted to do it desperately. He mentioned his boy Frisco had it and that he usually buys once or twice a year, and that we could go together, and I would be able to try it.

Sure, enough I did. And it was everything he said it was. I couldn't think of the right word for it, and it was killing me, Benny then mentioned the word "shattering" to me and that's where it all began to make perfect sense. There isn't a more perfect word in the English language to explain it. Shattering. As if the Coliseum in Rome could come down. A truly unbelievable and terrifying experience. And I had only experienced it once to date. I was grateful, it doesn't happen once most times. It was so fast and vivid, that locomotive hydrologic feeling I had when I was soaring through the cosmos. Staggering, I felt upside-down, twisted around, and pulled as far as I can go, as if I were taffy being tugged by the beings that govern our existence. Maybe that's another good word for me to use, pulled. Stretched, yanked, dragged too. No matter what, I felt as if I could reach out and touch the beings as I lay my hand on theirs. It was thrilling, and something I don't believe I will ever have the pleasure of experiencing again. It was one of those once-in-a-lifetime things, it can never be repeated. Perhaps one day... one day when the chips are down, and everything is chaos I can call Benny and he can hook me up. Just one more fucking time before I die.

"Secret" by Madonna came on the speakers in my tv room, and I helped myself to another Vodka cranberry and I could feel the magical delights of pure Columbian cocaine working its way through my system. During my reverie of enjoying the cocaine and music and a couple of drinks, I had this alarming sense of disorientation deep inside. I'm not sure what triggered this feeling, but I knew it wasn't normal either. I stood there in the large space of my family's house and sat on the couch eventually letting this dark visitor leave as quickly as it came. I always worried about everything, what people thought of me, my bisexuality which I haven't mentioned to my family just Anthony and Tom, my real family, and of course Bobby but sometimes Bobby didn't use discretion, which concerns me too. I was stunned to discover just how comfortable they were with me being bi as I was with them being straight. It was a comfort and familiarity and it was in that specific moment where they became my family.

The phone rang and it was Anthony.

"You have anything I can do before tonight?"

"Oh, I do."

"Yeah? Beautiful. I need it. My date is making me fucking crazy."

"Oh, I'm sorry, you forgot to get your sister a corsage?"

"I was going to take your mom but she's not here."

"How sentimental."

After ten minutes of bullshitting over the phone and breaking so many balls, we needed insurance to cover the damage, I called Jocelyn again and told everyone to come over my house so we could pregame. May as well get this party started.

"I never had cocaine this potent."

"Easy does it Bobby, we need to be cautious."

"Your mom wasn't with me last night."

"I'm sure it wasn't anything to boast about."

"You guys..." Jocelyn uttered as she fixed herself and me another drink.

"We have plenty to smoke too."

"Incidentally, I think Terrance may be here with Deanna, I was hoping they would develop amnesia," Anthony remarked.

"Good, with any luck they'll forget my address," I quipped. We weren't crazy about Terrance and Deanna but there were times where they were good with us, so much drama not enough love.

"I can't take either one of them," said Jocelyn. She was fixing her hair near the mirror on the wall in the kitchen.

"I can't believe Terrance and I had a thing a year ago. The fuck was I thinking?" I sat down at the kitchen table and looked out the window and at my girl, who sat on my leg.

"We felt the same way. What a prick that guy is," Tom said as he took another sip of his drink and refilled his glass.

"He can be. He's not a bad guy though, it's-it's complicated."

"Not so complicated anymore. You have me." Jocelyn said as she kissed me softly on the mouth. Fly me to the moon, baby.

"I definitely do, thank god."

"Such a good woman."

"Eat your fucking hearts out; she's all mine."

"I *am* all yours, Hugo."

I felt such immediate and jolting love for this woman on my leg. She was beautiful tonight, and I couldn't wait to really dance with her later. Jocelyn was a beautiful goddess to me, somebody who had a light inside of them that reminded me of firecrackers which explode with kindness and beauty every day. I felt intrinsic love flow through me like a blast of pure light, it changed molecules. Her beautiful, rare gems that were her eyes, they shine in the dark, glowing like a sun in my heart, fire within my soul making me lose control.

"I think we are going to have one hell of a night," Anthony said as he filled everyone's glass with vodka cranberry from a pitcher.

"Absolutely." Doing cocaine made me want to smoke and, I excused myself and went out on the porch to have a quick cigarette. Anthony joined me. The sun was beginning to set. And before we knew it, *they* showed up.

"Christ. Fuck it all," Anthony uttered under his breath, taking a couple pulls from the cigarette before handing it back to me.

"It'll be fine. Let's just try to have a good night," I replied curtly. I wanted to have fun, to enjoy this night. I didn't have room for drama. However, with Terrance and Deanna, drama was sure to find its way to us. For the next ten minutes we sat and smoked and didn't say a word to each other, watching the setting sun depart from this world as it moved into another.

"How nice to see you guys," Deanna said as she approached Anthony and myself as I stubbed out the cigarette.

"Deanna. How are you?" I said as I stood up and gave her a light hug. *What the fuck was I thinking?*

"Well, it's such a pleasure to be able to meet up as we get our drink on."

"Yeah, why don't you pour us a glass, Hugo," remarked Terrance as he and Deanna walked in the house without even looking at us.

"It's right there on the table," Anthony quipped.

I shot him a quick look, and he laughed in spite of himself.

"What?" he replied. "It is."

I found myself laughing as well as we went back inside. Jocelyn always wondered why Anthony couldn't control what he said sometimes. I told her bluntly the fucking North Korean army couldn't control what came out of Anthony's mouth.

"Terrance, it's nice you made it. Deanna, can I get you guys a drink?"

"We helped ourselves to some vodka cranberry."

"Cherry."

We all toasted to a great fucking night ahead of us.

"'Cherry', huh?" Terrance interjected. "You haven't said that since we dated..."

"He probably said it when you guys broke up, too," Tom remarked.

"Tom," I said softly.

"That's right, he probably did," Terrance replied. "Oh well, here's to tonight."

"How are you, Terrance? It's been a while," Bobby said.

"Me, I'm great," he replied. "Are you still with that woman you were telling me about?"

"Who? Your sister? No," Tom replied with a smirk.

"What did you fucking say?"

"Fellas, fellas. We're not doing this... come on. Vibe high." I averted a minor disaster from taking shape. Terrance had a short fuse, shorter than anyone realized.

"Here's to a great night ahead of us," I said one more time. We all toasted and drank.

"And to many more to come," Deanna murmured in her sultry voice to nobody in particular. I was still captivated by her, and Terrance. As I glanced at Jocelyn and kissed her, those feelings faded away like mist. And I was enthralled by her again, enthralled by her voice, her eyes, her soul, everything. She is a Goddess.

"I ordered all of us a limo," Bobby said. "I figured we should show up the right way. And we can drink more on the way." Bobby always knew how to make an entrance and we toasted to him and his generosity.

We left twenty minutes later when the limo showed up in front of my house. We all did another shot and drank more on the way to the prom at the Waldorf. All together in the limo, cracking jokes and making memories. We also did some more cocaine in the limo too, each taking a snort. The driver didn't notice anything with the music blasting and the partition up all the way.

The fuse was lit now. It had a delayed reaction.

— — —

The sky was dark now with a shining white moon above. I felt its magnetic pull on all of us as we arrived at our destination, walking out of the limo and into the Waldorf. I looked up at it again and for a few seconds a silence overcame my body, a peace. I tried to hold it for as long as I could, when Jocelyn grabbed me by the arm, and we walked in.

"I think everyone is looking at me." Jocelyn observed as she smiled at me.

"Can you blame them?"

"I enjoy it." She had a Michelle Pfeiffer butterscotch voice that I found to be her most alluring trait. She is absolutely ravishing, especially tonight. I was completely entranced by her the way she entered a room, the sexy way she would cross her long athletic limbs, her romantic and thrilling laugh, an erotic laugh, her voice, modulated and soft like a mandolin.

I lifted her up in my arms and spun her around and shouted in the beautiful labyrinth hallway before we headed inside to sit down. We all embraced and toasted the night with shouting and dancing in the hallway. We were then led into the dining room, and with tables upon tables of everyone from school we took our seats. Lights were lit and music was blasting, a DJ of course.

"These tables are looking really nice," Deanna remarked. She sat next to Terrance, who glanced around and wasn't making much small talk with anyone. He had this air of superiority to him that turned everyone around him completely off. Despite it all, he had a charisma that was bigger than any of us. He was a great lover of mine back in the day, and everyone was aware of it too, they didn't seem to mind, as much as I had my own unburied resentment for our guest, I was still quite attracted to him. With all of my adventures with men and women, he was my favorite and still to this day, I was never truly over him either.

I saw my junior year English teacher, Mrs. Hoffman, Claudia. I always loved her, my boys especially, what a gorgeous woman. We actually smoked a joint after I graduated. In the back of the building of course, it was great. She has such a witty personality, striking and real. I waved at her and walked up from my table.

"Oh my god, here he is, Hugo Gold."

"Did you give me my final grade yet?"

"You better believe it."

We hugged and stayed that way for a few seconds.

"It's nice to know there are teachers in this world who take pride in what they do."

"Yes, it is, especially when I have to deal with people like you."

"There's that sharp tongue. Jesus."

"Congratulations, Hugo. You should be really proud."

"I am. I really am. You taught me a lot."

We let go of our embrace and stood there. She looked dynamite tonight.

"I hope so. I can see you're with your friends."

"Yeah, I'm a lucky man. I read uh *Great Expectations* like you told me. It was fantastic."

"Wasn't it devastating?"

"Yeah, yeah it was. Very much so. Pip."

"I always loved him. Just not Estella."

"Or Ms. Havisham."

"Oh no, not her! Nasty bitch. I have to get to my table. It was nice to see you, Hugo. Read *Dangerous Liaisons* next. It's excellent."

"I saw the movie, that is one fucked up story. I'll check out the book too."

"Fabulous read. Enjoy your night."

"You too Claudia—Mrs. Hoffman." I got so hard talking to her. I had to go to the bathroom and get myself under control. I went inside of the stall and had my back on the door. I looked down and saw my tumescence grow. Christ. Fuck it. I kept picturing all the hot men and women and made myself cum in the toilet. Got myself together. And walked out. I needed a cigarette desperately, but I dealt with it and sat back down next to Jocelyn and Anthony.

"You all good there, bro?" Anthony patted his hand on my shoulder as I took a sip of coca cola.

"Yeah, I'm uh I'm good. I was talking to Mrs. Hoffman."

"Yeah? I saw that. She looks fucking awesome. Wondering what happened to you after?"

"I had to go take care of something... I got a little hard from Mrs. Hoffman."

"Oh, and you had to go to bathroom to..."

"Yeah, you know... relax and take care of business."

"Little of this, little of that..."

"Exactly, brother. Exactly."

"Making buffalo mootzadel now, bro?" Tom overheard us and turned towards us. "Master cheesemaker."

"I wish you were there, bro, it was so hot."

"Hot."

"Really fucking hot. I didn't get anything on my suit."

"That's a relief. Fucking expensive dry cleaning."

"Where the hell were you?" Jocelyn asked as she put her hands on my shoulders.

"Just going to the bathroom."

"Are we going to dance or what?"

It was Madonna on the speakers now and everyone from their tables were walking up to the dance floor.

"What did you have to do?"

"Nothing baby. Politics with me and the boys."

"I see. Nothing important, huh?"

"I'm going to drop my load on you later, baby."

"So you say."

"Watch it."

We danced and forgot about everything for a while. She felt so good so close to me she was wearing her most delicious perfume, Dolce and Gabbana, absolutely erotic. She had a black sequined dress that went down her beautiful legs. And her hair was down, softening her fabulous face. I was drawn to her, drawn in a way that I never was before with any other woman I've been with. Men, well that's a different kettle of fish entirely. It was the seduction for me, it was her hand on my shoulder, her body against mine, my hands on her ass and rubbing it around her dress flowing nonchalantly around her back, there was nothing innocent about her. She had a fire in her belly with adamantine steel running down her back. She was the primal scream in all of us. Perhaps that is also what made me feel so relaxed when Jocelyn was around, Jocelyn had the ability to make you shine.

I saw Terrance with Deanna across the dance floor and all the old instincts came back to me.

I had just met Jocelyn the night Terrance and I hooked up at Anthony's eighteenth birthday in Jersey. It was a passionate night with Terrance. He had a daddy-is-home kind of feeling and I devoured it body and soul, I felt so weak in the knees when he was around so captivated. I never felt that vulnerable with a man before, it was usually me leading them to me, and here I was being controlled body and soul by my desire.

I remember I felt a little queasy in the bathroom from all the drinking Anthony and all of us were doing, and Terrance came in without knocking and saw me leaning over the toilet unable to vomit, and I sat down, we made some small talk, and he got down on his knees and blew me. It wasn't the average run through on Monday night, this was fully advanced next level fellatio. I never felt so exhilarated in my whole life like I did in that moment, and I came hard, so fucking hard, it was exhilarating. I moaned his name and was breathing heavily, I smiled and ended up on the floor with his arm around me. We lay there staring up the ceiling not moving not saying a fucking word. Just letting it all sink in. After an hour we felt the urge come back like a possessed tidal wave. He was sucking me again and throttling my dick into the next world. His body was on top of me as he shoved his himself against me over and over. My brain, my body, my mind, were opened completely now, like a violet in spring, the ends of their coarsened and darkened stems and the leaves with so many points and tiny veins in them. We tossed and twisted on the carpet.

Our tongues twisted around each other as he lifted me up and flipped me on my stomach and yanked my jeans off.

"Harder Terrance, come on baby. Come on. Fuck me. FUCK ME HARD!" He drove himself into my ass and I came so hard so forcefully I screamed in passionate ecstasy.

"Who's your fucking daddy, Hugo? HUH?"

"Oh God you. You are. You will always be."

I was pinned to the bathmat. We fucked on in the bathroom, his hard violent penis inside of me drove me insane, wild with festooned balloons exploding with light and purpose. He was going deeper and deeper inside of me, as if he was discovering the treasure he'd overlooked all these long years.

Harder and harder we fucked, and the harder my screams of passionate lustful heat expanded, there was a radio on the sink and when he flicked it on, it was "Love Machine" and for what seemed to be an endless string of passionate alliance with this gorgeous man, and the song we were listening to while he fucked me into next week, an orgasm was born inside of my body, and it rushed with locomotive treachery towards its roller coaster conclusion. It flooded the bathmat, we both came at the same time, moaning each other's name, holding each other's dream, remembering each other's thrilling release embedding it in our enlightened fucking brains.

"There you go, baby. There you go," Terrance whispered in my ear.

"Oh, fuck that was... that was amazing. That was amazing."

We stayed there laying in each other's arms lost in our separate worlds. Silent and full of curiosity.

"'Love Machine,' huh?" I whispered with a smirk on my face.

"It always got me off, always made me fuck harder. There's something about it."

"I know. It's a hot song."

"Hugo?" whispered Jocelyn as she stroked my face.

"Oh, sorry baby, I was just, I don't know remembering something..."

"Like what?" asked Jocelyn.

"Nothing important."

"Hey you alright? You seem..."

"What?"

"I don't know... just distracted."

"It's Terrance..."

"I figured. Listen, as long as he doesn't start anything."

"He was getting into it with Tom."

"Because Tom insulted him."

"Grass is always greener."

"Just dance with me, bitch."

Our night was everything I wanted it to be, some mild ball-breaking of course but that was par for the course. I never anticipated anything less. Terrance and Deanna seemed to be keeping to themselves occasionally talking to Tom or Bobby, certainly not Anthony. Anthony possessed a simmering contempt for both of them. I had them both, yet I had no ill will. I consider myself an anomaly.

That night with Terrance however was erotic, transformative, powerful, I never felt such exhilarating heat and passion, it felt different more meaningful. We kissed and held each other against the realities of our lives. We were both different people, but it didn't feel that way, I was connected on a deeper more compassionate level. Maybe he awakened something in me I wasn't sure, and perhaps I would never fucking know. He did lay waste my former self, sabotaging into dust, with that strong fucking cock of his. Turbulent it was, intense maybe even a little bizarre but that is where that Caribbean heat existed, that red hot heatwave that was Terrance.

"Can we smoke in here, you think?" I asked, still glued to the bathroom floor.

"Do you really think anyone would notice?" Terrance quipped back.

I nodded in agreement and smoked up.

"And we couldn't believe how fucking great it was to be in Florida away from this grimy city. Right, babe?" Jocelyn asked me, her hand on my face.

"Yeah. It was beautiful. Really nice. We stayed in Highland Beach."

We were talking to friends of Jocelyn and I saw Anthony, Bobby and Tony go outside to have a smoke.

"Excuse me for a minute, I need some air, baby. Be right back." I left the table and went to join my boys outside.

"Fellas, it's been that kind of a fucking night, huh?"

"And Jocelyn, a socialite."

"Those vagabond shoes..." I mocked. I lit up a cigarette and stood there with Anthony and Bobby, finally being able to breathe normally.

"Terrance doesn't seem to be saying too much," I remarked as I looked back inside and saw them by the dance floor holding each other and moving gracefully to the slow music.

"If he had anything to say, I have a boat to sell you."

"Come on, he's not that bad."

"Says the man who hooked up with him in a *bathroom*," Anthony uttered.

"In your house. I could still smell the cum on the floor, your mother's bathmat, I knew it looked familiar because it was the same one we used when we had to clean the sheets."

"She probably knew it tasted familiar," Bobby replied. "So sweet."

"You guys are really funny. I knew what happened that night. Completely. It was a nice vibration all through my soul, I needed it. I know Terrance isn't perfect."

"Far from it. People fucking hate him. I just hope nothing gets out of hand, what Tom said to him at your house..."

"Out of line, I think. But you know how he is."

"I do. I've known him for a long time. Let's just keep the vibe high and we can have ourselves the great night we want."

"Amen."

We stood out there for a little while longer, smoking, and breaking balls. I heard the music coming from inside the hotel, it was joyous to feel so enlightened and powerful at this time of the night. To have a beautiful lady by my side, my friends here, and two people from my past who could make anybody feel as if they were the only person on Earth.

Terrance had a presence to him that I rarely saw in other people, a powerful aura, detached yes and selfish, sometimes unspeakably cruel to everyone around him but he had a glowing smile, eyes that could level you, that could in their own sublime way, recalibrate your soul to never feel pain or hurt or agony. Perhaps he healed people occasionally too. I had a strong feeling that he might be mildly bipolar perhaps, he tended to have these waves of depression and joy and within hours of each other, it felt as if the bottom dropped out from under him each day and he was being sucked into a typhoon that would never stop wreaking havoc.

And I think it was only recently that Tom, Tony, and Bobby began to notice Terrance's mood shifts becoming so drastic and out of hand. I remember when he was having a fight with his boss Tatyana at a tutoring service company he worked for after school. She was a real miserable and hateful bitch, from what he told me. And one day he was eating lunch while his student was working on math problems Terrance wrote for him so he could practice writing and graphing inequalities, Tatyana came over for an observation which she did about three times a week and every week of his life. She was on her fancy cell phone with her fake nails and her even more nauseating perfume, well he was trying to explain how to write inequalities and since his student was struggling, Tatyana scolded him and told him to have his student figure out for himself. She also mentioned she saw him on the camera ignoring his student and just scarfing down lunch for a good twenty minutes.

"Are you kidding me?" Terrance remarked. "You were watching me on a camera? I've been with this company for four years..."

"It's just not something we tolerate here. The laziness and the eating lunch while you're working."

"I was hungry, Tatyana. I didn't have lunch today because I used my lunch time to make up work."

"What do you mean you didn't have lunch today?"

"You couldn't get that? You saw me on the camera; you can probably figure that one out for yourself."

"Terrance, it's just doesn't look good; your student should be a priority. Not eating food while you're working. We do not allow that. Frankly I'm annoyed, just really annoyed."

"So, you're annoyed?" Terrance quipped. He took his

student's work and checked it over.

"Good job, my dude. Do the ones on the back and you're done."

"Okay, Mr. Clark."

"I have work to do," Terrance said curtly.

"Excuse me, I am your boss and I'm not going to tolerate—"

"Yeah. Well, you'll have it on camera too. Anything else?"

"There is no talking to you," Tatyana got up and left, heading back to her office. Terrance felt the rage of inner demons crystallize in an atomic implosion.

"Listen AJ, do those problems and I'll be right back." Terrance walked to Tatyana's office and without knocking, let himself in.

"Who the hell do you think you are?!"

"Are you seriously breaking into my office?"

"Oh no, I'm simply walking in. Why do you have to speak to me this way?'

"I'm doing my job."

"Oh, being a miserable bitch? Is that it?"

"A miserable WHAT?!"

"YOU FUCKING HEARD ME!" Grabbing her keyboard to her computer and smashing it on her desk, the entire office suite immediately looked into Tatyana's window and there was dead silence.

"I'm out. I'll tend to my resignation tomorrow. Thank you." Walking out, he knocked on his student's desk and whispered, "Be good, little man." He never looked back.

I saw him at Denino's waiting for a table, he and I sat down twenty minutes later, and he told me everything that happened with his job.

Bipolar. He's bipolar.

He slipped guys, nobody shoved anyone!

He fell.

SLIPPED TOM!!! SLIPPED!

That was the last they ever saw of him. I know for a fact he was having difficulty at home and in school, began snorting cocaine in the bathroom so he was able to get to classes and do his work, feeling as if he was unstoppable. And he was. I remember he spent time at my house, in order to leave the abusive household he lived in, his neglectful father and toxic mother. It was a nightmare. He would come over my place, we would live like kings, fuck everywhere every day, and enjoy life.

He always said to me: "I love coming here Hugo, I forget about life for a while."

"That's what it's about. My parents don't give a fuck."

"They're never here."

"It's why it's so enjoyable. But I have to admit it gets lonely."

We made love four times that night, and he swallowed my cum.

"This means something Hugo. We fuck four times and I swallow your protein. It means something..."

"Like what?"

Terrance didn't say a word. He fell into a deep restful sleep. I was the one awake all night smoking on the balcony and staring into the deep velvet darkness.

Two hours of telling Jason everything that happened that night. I stared at him. I had no fucking idea how I was going to proceed with the rest of it. I wanted so desperately to forget all about it. Entirely. Except I knew the only way out was through.

"Do you want to pick this up tomorrow?" Jason asked me. For a second, I wanted to say yes and leave immediately. But it would still be there tomorrow, awaiting its second exorcism, its re-release. I had to do it now.

"No."

"Okay. So, you and Terrance were together. Why don't we talk about what happened after you left the prom that night."

"Jesus— I..." I became all chocked up and couldn't hold myself together, I didn't want him coming near me in this agitated state. I never enjoyed being touched by anyone when I was feeling vulnerable.

"It's okay, Hugo."

Prom 2002. The After-Party

Walking out of the prom, we were heavily dazed. A lot of dancing, a lot of sex, a lot of drugs, and we had an after-party to head to. The night was beautiful, clear and warm, with a breeze and the lights of our decadent and beautiful city lit up vividly along the streets, inside of offices, in convenience stores, everywhere and they seemed to move with me as we had walked to Blue Nightclub in the east village.

"I was thinking about our night back in high school," Terrance whispered in my ear as he walked alongside me and

Jocelyn.

"That flooded into my mind too... it was intense."

"It was, you were amazing."

I looked over at Jocelyn and she was talking to another friend of hers, she didn't hear what Terrance said.

"No, you were. It's great being bi."

"You get to explore so much, to be so much to men and women."

"I like it better with men," I exclaimed. I saw Jocelyn look at me briefly and smile. She knew I was bisexual anyway; it didn't matter to me too much. Who's better than me, right now?

"You look fucking amazing Terrance; you been going to the gym?"

"I want to blow you so hard."

Jocelyn heard that and she grinned at me ruefully.

"Well, who doesn't right?" she quipped.

"We had a thing back in—"

"Last year, yes, he told me, Terrance. It's all good. I know he's bi. It's his best trait."

"Indeed, it is, I find it alluring. He can have anyone or anything, including you."

"He does," Jocelyn replied curtly. "He always will."

"You love me?" I asked her with all the love in my broken wounded heart buried forever inside of me, deep within the sands of the world.

"I think the question is: are you in love with me?"

"What do you think?"

"I think you're trying to find a reason to be in love with me."

"Why would I look for it? I see it right in front of me."

"Then prove it to me." I placed my hands on the sides of her face and kissed long and passionately. I could hear our own shared breathing, our own connected admiration for our existence being exchanged through us, through the stars in the sky, the crescent moon, the invisible sun, everything around us, the molecules, all of our friends, the gods above, the neglected despondent demons beneath us. Everything and everyone.

"That was wild... you are wild." I said with a dazed look on my face.

"Too wild for you maybe..."

"Not too wild for you."

"We'll see."

Terrance glanced at Jocelyn and I with a smile on his face. No teeth, just a rueful grin, I always suspected that look was meant for me and me alone. Nobody else. Not even Deanna, who was quiet tonight, fucking relief. Her and Jocelyn were never on good terms with each other.

Anthony lit up a joint and we all passed it around, standing by a bus stop and getting stoned, on top of the cocaine, and the endless rounds of drinks we were enjoying, vodka cranberries and rum and cokes. Simply divine.

Jocelyn was on my lap, and I had Anthony next to me and Tom on the other side, Bobby was talking to Terrance and Deanna, I glanced at Terrance he had a nice tattoo on his arm, and it was the first time I noticed it tonight. Appeared as though he had been going to the gym too, chiseled chest as he rubbed his hand on it through his shirt. I felt the familiar pressure from both him and Deanna and Jocelyn. Christ, my hard-ons should be on the black market, wrapped in a big bow and sold to the highest bidder. Sexual healing never felt so exhilarating.

"I'm going to get some cigarettes, baby; I'll be right back. Anyone want anything?"

"I'll come with you," Deanna said, and Terrance followed us in as well.

We walked into a deli, and it was completely empty, the halogen light above us was potent and beaming down. Terrance and Deanna were grabbing beers and paying for them.

"More drinks for our wonderful night ahead."

"We can call a party bus. My uncle owns one."

"You've been quiet tonight, Deanna."

"I've missed you, Hugo; we both have."

"I know. It's—been a little much lately. But I'm happy with Jocelyn. I know she is with me; there aren't many women out there that can handle a guy who is bisexual. All my exes."

"Looks like you've found yourself the right woman."

"Yeah, I think I have."

"Come on," Terrance said as he patted my back. "Let's get this party bus here."

Terrance and I were standing away from the bus stop and smoking, making small talk.

"You think if I blew you right here, it would be a problem?"

"I can't say that I would stop you. Jocelyn may."

"Jocelyn. She is stunning."

"Don't."

"Don't what, Hugo?"

"Don't. Terrance. I know you," I said as I finished my cigarette and flicked it into a puddle near a sewer.

"Exactly. So why are you so surprised?"

"I find the more surprises I have with you the better it is."

"You mean when we fuck."

"When we do anything."

"You mean you weren't just after my dick?"

"Terrance, if I could suck it all night long, I would. I truly would. But I'm here with my lady tonight."

"I can see that. One step up from Deanna."

"She has nothing to do with it."

"What club are you thinking about?"

"I don't know... I'm open to anything. Look. I'll blow you in the club. We'll find somewhere to go, even if it's in a bathroom."

"Stalls always work. I would like that."

"I got you," I walked up to the crowd.

"Where should we go everyone? Limelight? SoundFactory?"

"Anywhere we can fuck around and lose ourselves," Bobby interjected. He was smoking a blunt with Tom and Anthony and they looked and sounded infinitely more dazed than I did.

"Exactly. Then SoundFactory it is. Maybe Terrance can get laid there."

"Or I can just call your mom and have her take care of it, Tom."

"Go for it."

"Do you have a fucking problem with me, Tom?"

"Guys come on..." I remarked, as Anthony passed around the blunt. We each took a nice hit.

"No, no it's fine. I do have a small bone to pick, yes."

"Oh God," I said.

"Well then, what is it? What?"

"For starters I don't fucking trust you. You're bad news."

"Bad news. For what? For you?"

"For everyone."

"Hmmm interesting. Well, I never had an issue with you but I see being a dick is something you take very seriously."

"Yes, I do. For years."

"Right, it's your first time in a suit and now you think you're Frances Albert."

"You see, that's where the issue is. Fucking snarky."

"No, just being real. Being honest."

"Right, you masturbating now too, right? Deanna must be relieved."

"Tom! Guys come on stop, keep the vibe high, this is supposed to be a good fucking night."

"You want to talk honesty, Terrance... how about during junior year you told everyone I was fucking gay and you made all these fucking disgusting comments about me all over the fucking internet and no offense, Hugo, but that was a slight against you too."

"No, it wasn't," I reprimanded Tom. "But it didn't make it right either."

"See."

"Tom, I did that because I felt like it."

"What did you fucking say?!"

"I NEVER LIKED YOU, TOM! FUCKING COWARD!"

"Terrance, stop!" Deanna shouted. It was the most she'd said all fucking night.

"Yeah, easy there guys, easy. First of all, that's a shitty thing to do, but we had a sit down and we resolved it, old wounds Tom. Alright bro. Terrance apologized."

"Fuck out of here Hugo, 'he apologized.' He did that shit intentionally. Is that a fucking apology?"

"Well, I—I just want to have a great night here. Alright. Deanna did you call about the party bus?"

"Yeah, it should be here in like ten minutes."

"See? Ten minutes guys alright, let's just bury the hatchet here alright."

"Three fucking years of hatchets, and one continuous blow job..." Terrance interjected. "They add up."

"I know they do and then they ejaculate, and you have to reload."

"It's usually all over his mother," Bobby remarked.

"And on the weekends, it's all over yours."

Terrance moved his hand on top of my crotch and rubbed it hard.

"You are making this really hard for me."

"That's the whole point, isn't it?"

"I told you I would... don't worry."

"It's not that."

Jocelyn looked over and Terrance took his hand slowly away from my cock and rubbed his mouth with it.

"What is it baby?" Deanna said as she kissed his neck.

"Nothing! Jesus!"

And just like that, Terrance shoved Deanna so hard she almost fell.

"Hey! Terrance bro! The fuck is wrong with you?!" I exclaimed.

"Not cool, you don't fucking shove a girl bro! No!" Anthony walked up quickly and took Terrance pining him to the wall of the deli.

"GET OFF ME TONY!"

"NO! Hey Deanna, you alright?"

"Yeah, I'm fine! THE FUCK IS WRONG WITH YOU TONIGHT?!" She screamed making us all jump.

"Bro, you push her like that?! Come on!!!" I shouted. "What are you on? Are you hopped on something!?"

"Funny coming from you. You're the one who has wanted me all fucking night and you show up with this new chick on your arm."

"Watch it."

"Princess of our dreams."

"What did you say? Fuck you, asshole!" bellowed Jocelyn. I took her in my arm and rubbed her back.

"There you go, have your man protect you like always. While I stand here. You want to take down my number, Tony?" Terrance wrenched himself free and took Deanna by the arm and started walking away.

"Yep, fuck it all up and walk away."

"Fuck you Tom, mama's boy."

"Ma—" Tom ran up to Terrance and shoved him to the ground. Deanna almost fell again as Terrance lay there with his hands on the pavement trying to push himself up.

"How do you fucking like it? Bitch!"

"Tom stop!! Guys what the fuck is wrong?"

"ENOUGH HUGO!" Terrance got up and started whaling on Tom. He punched him so hard in the face, his nose almost broke. And then hell broke loose. With Tom, myself, Anthony, Jocelyn, Deanna and passerby's all running up to the pit trying to take Terrance off of Tom who was pinned to the ground. They kept shoving each other, over and over. Finally, Anthony and I got Terrance off of Tom, he kept struggling but we held him hard enough for him not to move. The party bus took off and didn't come back. There was our fucking meal ticket.

"You want to fuck with me, bro! HUH!?" Tom ran up to him again and as we tried to block him from getting at Terrance, he cracked him straight in the face. Eye for an eye sort of speak. Terrance fell backward and in one last moment of horror, one that changed all of us for the rest of our fucking lives... he ran towards him and shoved Terrance so hard they ended up in the middle of the street. We all ran to them, but Terrance elbowed me in the throat and broke away from Deanna who sustained a black eye. Terrance socked Tom in the face and gut again and as we pulled Tom away to the other side of the street to call an ambulance... a car came speeding down towards us, I remember running up to Terrance and nearly cracking his face as the car hit him and sent him flying. It was like an explosion. The last thing I remember was Deanna screaming. So loud it muted the entire fucking world.

— — —

I wiped the tears away from my face. And I sat there not moving, staring at Jason. Who didn't move either. Or speak. The silence was heavy. And I felt as if I was losing my fucking patience. Jason had no other appointments. I got up, put my jacket on, made sure I had my phone, my wallet, lighter and cigarettes, and as I walked out, Jason's face registered desperation and disbelief.

I had just relived the most terrifying night of my life, every last detail. I didn't owe him shit. I shook my head and walked out. Closing the door lightly behind me, the horror returned, and the images of that night played in my head, I tried lighting a cigarette when I was outside, but my tears came fast, and as I got in my car and drove away, I found myself pulling over ten minutes later.

CHAPTER 12
A Pocket Full of Anesthesia

I didn't sleep at all last night. I couldn't. I was completely alone with my thoughts now, but I was used to being alone for most of my life. That lone wolf existence I have. Even when I was around my friends, I still felt isolated even though I knew without a moment's thought they loved and still do love me. And I them. But I usually just loved people from afar. Or just on my phone through texts and phone calls but I suppose that happens as you get older, and you transform yourself into someone you never thought you'd be. I didn't need a career, I had every luxury you could want, I didn't need a girlfriend or a boyfriend, they constantly gravitate towards me, they enjoy me.

I wish maybe if things were different with me that I could be happier, I'm sure many people understand this. When something happens, it can leave a trace of itself behind. Burning toast leaves crumbs along a plate, or when I... I accidentally push a kid into a car. I suppose we all have our demons, our ways of being that nobody can change, I had my friends Bobby, Anthony, and Tom. Friends that I loved and would do anything for, they were brothers to me, and even after what happened, we stuck together. We trusted each other, and they trusted me. Perhaps I was a leader, but on that night, the crown they placed on my head fell and I was no longer a leader, I was just like Terrance.

I was in my house, sitting outside. It felt warmer than usual, and I was slowly enjoying my pre-rolled joint. It was that time. Telling Jason everything that happened, and giving Frankie a completely different story felt as if I was being torn down the middle, and the facile version of me had disappeared. Evaporated. Something was slipping, and I felt the ground beneath my feet give out.

Frankie, I needed to be with him. I needed his company, and after what we discussed in the car and then again at my house, he was the one man in the world that could console me. Terrance was never consoling or warm, and seldom had a kind word for anyone, mean-spirited and bitter, resentful of anyone who would be able to make it in this world. I never knew or understood what presence of mind he had whenever we were together or in school, he had been reserved and had a snide remark for almost everything.

I do remember him almost driving me to murder one day, it was junior year and my boys and I were in Tom's backyard sharing a joint and discussing taking mushrooms for the first time. Terrance came over, because Bobby invited him and despite our strenuous objections, Bobby wanted him to be there. He had done a few lines of strong cocaine at a party for his girlfriend at the time, this chick Amy, we used to know. And her parents were swimming in money and took a three-month trip to Europe leaving Amy alone to call the shots. Of course he didn't let us know about anything, and he came over completely stoned out of his mind, his eyes were nearly bursting out of his skull, and he was loud and getting under everyone's skin. He was the first guy I was ever with, up until then I was just banging women I had no interest in men, but as junior year came around, I found I was aroused by them as much as women, perhaps more. Suffice it to say he was so fucking coked up, our secret to never reveal to anyone what happened between us last Saturday came pouring out of him like fucking word vomit, full disclosure—that fucking addict!

"Hugo, really?" Anthony asked me, but to my surprise and relief it didn't sound as if he were disgusted or put off by me. Bobby and Tom had indifferent faces on. They didn't seem to care either way.

"Yeah. I don't know—"

"You don't have to know anything, brother, you're our boy. We love you."

"Fucking right! It's something that's private and should be said on your terms and when you're ready!" Tom shouted the last part towards Terrance who stood there dumbfounded. "Is there anything else you would like to tell us Terrance or are you done being a miserable fuck tonight?"

"I mean, it wasn't anything to sound off about I just wanted everyone to know."

"Well, you just did sound off about it, you prick. But it seemed to have backfired," I remarked curtly. I felt the anger in me grow.

"I was talking about our night together."

"Really? I seem to recall you screaming my name a few times."

"I scream for nobody."

"So 'oh Hugo don't stop' is my imagination?"

"Fuck it, I don't care."

"Neither do we, asshole. Get the fuck out of here!" Bobby shouted and stood up from his chair.

"You fucking invited me."

"You don't seem to understand," Anthony interjected. "We don't care if our boy here was a serial killer, or a drug dealer, or that he was with you, perhaps that is one thing I'll never be able to fully understand because I find you to be a disgusting fucking bully. What we do care about is you leaving before this gets worse."

"Trust him," Tom replied. "It's not pretty."

"Neither are you."

"GET THE FUCK OUT! NOW!" I bellowed. And all four of my friends were slightly startled. "You are not welcome here. You don't matter. Not to us. And certainly not to anyone else. Do you have any fucking idea what people say behind your back at school, you sniveling mean-spirited little prick! They've always mentioned what a pussy you are, how you treat women, and just people in general. Bullies are not welcome here, you fuck! And your little plan here backfired."

"He's right, Terrance. Leave."

"Consider this the carrot, jerkoff, you don't want the fucking stick," Tom said. He stared Terrance down for a good two minutes and nobody said a word. "Or we can fucking throw you out. Either way the garbage men forgot to take you."

"I'm sure Hugo does."

"ALRIGHT." Tom got up from his seat, walked quickly over to Terrance and cracked him so hard in the face he fell backwards on his chair, his feet moving over his head was the best part.

"The stick. Not the kind you were hoping for tonight."

"You get it now?" I yelled. "LEAVE!"

Terrance slowly got up, blood gushing from his nose. He looked at us for a few seconds and quietly walked down to the street.

I yelled out: "It wasn't that special; in case you were wondering!"

"That was so gratifying, Tom. Because I was thinking maybe I'll just snap the fucker's neck."

"My fucking pleasure!"

"So now that you all know I'm fucking bi—" I started.

"We love you. Just shocked you didn't tell us sooner," Anthony said as he put his hand on my shoulder.

"Probably banging your mom too much," Bobby remarked.

"No, I think it was your sister *and* your girl at the same time," he quipped right back.

"You guys..."

"We love you, bro," Tom said.

We all hugged.

"I fucking love you all too."

"We are so blessed, fellas. Let's do these mushrooms now. It's still fucking early."

"Yes, let's do them. It'll be interesting. I've never done them."

A considerable amount of dramatic effect that night, but once we were hitting the peak of our trip, it faded into mist. We wouldn't see or speak to Terrance in over a year; prom night was the last night we would ever see him again. A memory that rewound itself like some insidious psychological torture. Christ, I needed a blow job.

While I was thinking about all this, my phone rang and it was Frankie.

"Well, I've been dreaming of your hot stiff cock all day..."

"We need to talk, Hugo."

My heart sank like a fucking anchor.

"Now."

"Oh okay... uhh is everything—"

"I'll come pick you up." And he hung up.

I still held my phone to my ear. And I couldn't fucking breathe.

Part IV

Meditations on an Afterlife

"Somewhere over the rainbow
Bluebirds fly
Birds fly over the rainbow
Why then, oh, why can't I?
—JUDY GARLAND
Somewhere Over The Rainbow

"The odds is gone, and there is nothing left remarkable
beneath the visiting moon.
Eternity was in our lips and in our eyes."
—WILLIAM SHAKESPEARE
The Tragedy of Antony and Cleopatra

"Every glamorous sunrise
Throws the planets out of line
And a star-sign out of whack
A fraudulent zodiac."
—THIRD EYE BLIND
God of Wine

CHAPTER 13
Metamorphosis & Kubrick

"Why don't you start telling me what actually fucking happened that night?"

"I didn't mean to lie... I didn't. It's a pact I made. These guys are my family; I don't have a family besides them."

"You fucking lied to me! You said he threw himself into the car, you didn't fucking say you PUSHED HIM!"

Frankie shoved me across the room and I landed on the floor. As I got myself up, he took me by the collar and pinned me against the wall.

"What happened?! HUH!? What happened? Do I need to ask your friends, your *family,* as you call them?!"

"You leave them the fuck out of this, Frankie!"

"I doubt you'll tell me what I need to know even if I did."

"Let go of me," I said as calmly as I could. I looked him straight in the eye. He let me go.

"Sit the fuck down. You better start fucking talking."

"I don't say a word unless you promise me it doesn't leave this room. Do you have any clue what would happen to me if I told you what happened, what we were all involved in?! I would never do that to you, Frankie! Never in a million years. And all I'm asking is that you extend me that same fucking courtesy, for Christ's sake! We go back, Frankie, alright, you know me. I- I should've told you what really happened, alright? And I'm sorry I didn't. I messed up, it was a terrible mistake on my part. I just need you to promise it won't leave this room." I was getting choked up and rubbing the tears away I stood there trembling, awaiting his response.

"They were complicit, Hugo. Frankie responded coldly, and he was barely looking at me.

My heart sank again and smashed on the floor. I almost

threw up.

His voice lowered, "I don't know what to tell you, I wish I could make it easier but you're not making it easier for me."

"How could you sabotage me like this, Frankie? How?"

He just stood there unmoving, his eyes cast down to the table as if the answer would just reveal itself there.

"I never told you... Maybe I should've..." he trailed off.

"Told me what?!"

"Terrance. He's... my brother."

"He's *what?!*"

Frankie stood there, not moving, not looking at me. I couldn't believe what I just heard. I felt sick, I felt as if the ground had dropped from beneath me and I was hanging in suspended animation over a huge cauldron of fire.

"This. Why the fuck did you never tell me, Frankie?"

"He was a mess. I couldn't help him, my family couldn't. Too fucking busy, I guess. He was just—he was helpless, Hugo!"

"Frank— I. I don't know what to say, he was bullying all of us, it got so out of control..." I trailed off allowing the tears to release this time.

"He was a bully from the time he learned how to walk. He even bullied me for being bi, but he didn't get very far."

"And yet so was he! He actually had the balls to bully you?"

"The broken nose I gave him put a stop for that. Permanently."

"I always wondered why it was a little crooked."

We both started laughing. I couldn't help it.

"Maybe if we had helped him, gotten him off drugs, those fucking pills he always took. Xanax. Fucking poison, mixing it with Vodka, and Scotch and god knows what other fucking drugs he was shoveling into his mouth. It was disturbing to see him slip away. I tried to convince him to go to rehab get himself back on track, he flat refused. He would leave for days at a time, going all over the place with that snake bitch he was dating..."

"Deanna?" I whispered. I just couldn't fucking believe it.

"Yeah. Soprano."

"She was there that night..."

"I know she was," Frankie responded curtly. "She didn't do anything to stop it either, did she?"

"No. I mean it all happened—"

"Did she even love him?"

"It's hard to be sure. But, no I don't think so. She's not

capable of it."

"Self-absorbed little cunt. I could fucking kill her myself."

I didn't say a word. My silence was my strength, but I certainly didn't disagree about Deanna. She was beautiful, but she was vacant and cruel, nothing to offer.

"I'm sure everyone agrees. Even me."

"Weren't you boning her for a while?"

"I was. We had a thing. That night I brought this girl Jocelyn I was seeing off and on for a good year and a half. But after what happened, we didn't talk. Felt a little awkward being there with Terrance and Deanna, they just made everyone—"

"Furious?"

"Yeah."

"To the point where you want to shove her into a car too?"

"He shoved her."

"Who?"

"Terrance shoved Deanna. He was having an issue and she asked if he was okay and for the time with her, she seemed genuinely concerned. And then he just shoved her off him and she almost fell."

Frankie looked up at me and for the first time I saw indescribable hatred in his eyes. He had beautiful magnetic eyes that drew you in to him, vivid blue shining beaming ocean blue, gorgeous. He was an Adonis; nobody could resist Frankie. But at that moment he looked at me, I saw how his eyes changed remarkably to a tourmaline black. It made me nervous.

"He shoved her. Why the fuck would he do that. He actually put his hands on her like that?"

I nodded. I remembered that moment. She almost fell.

"My time with him was exciting, however he was damaged goods. I wish I could make it sound less—"

"No," Frankie dismissed it. "No need, I was in a position to make things better for him, Hugo. He was addicted to more than Xanax. He was taking Lexapro, Zoloft. We thought maybe it was a bipolar disorder that went undiagnosed. If we had gotten him a doctor, somebody to talk to, maybe it would have been fine. He had such a hard time. He would hallucinate when he ran out of Xanax. We didn't have insurance so we couldn't afford three hundred bucks for a new prescription and he would have horrible withdrawals, convulsions, hallucinations, extreme mood swings, nightmares, night tremors, it was... I think by the time you started seeing Terrance he was flying off the rails already. He was smoking all the time; I didn't care that he smoked weed but when he began smoking meth... I had to draw the line. He did it twice and then even told me it was getting too scary for him, and he stopped cold turkey. And that's when my family and I noticed he began talking to himself, seeing things, hearing things, because the withdrawal from crystal meth is supposedly the worst kind of hell you can imagine. We're just relieved it didn't get worse than that, Hugo, that he didn't become seriously addicted. Oh fuck, this poor guy. He was nasty, I know; he had a mean streak. And the drugs certainly made it worse. I—" Frankie became choked up. And putting his head in his hands, began sobbing.

"And that was when I moved out, I couldn't bear it anymore. The mood swings became severe and I didn't want to be around him, nobody did. It was a nightmare, he became erratic and there was no money for his script refill, so we... I think we just gave up."

"He never mentioned he had a brother, Frankie. Why would he keep that from me?"

"Hugo he was out of his fucking mind. He wasn't thinking clearly. I could care less about that. We couldn't even afford to have him stay in a psychiatric unit at St. Vincent's. Things were fucking horrible for us! And what could we do for Terrance, my brother? His nightmares, the constant mood swings, I mean he was seeing things for fuck's sake! We couldn't take care of ourselves, much less him. It all unraveled... all of it. Completely unraveled. I met up with him one day for coffee in Manhattan. We sat down and he just couldn't sit still. He kept scratching and convulsing. I tried to help him through it, but he kept begging me for money and of course I wasn't giving him a fucking cent. It got so heated he got up and started screaming at me. I told him to calm the fuck down and he lunged at me! I had to push him off me and a few employees had to bring him outside. I was going to arrest him but I felt that may have made things worse, so I let him go and told him to never come back, not until he could get himself some help, proper help. And I think what my family and I did was actually worse than what happened on prom night, because that never would have happened if we hadn't given up and pretended as if nothing was happening. That's my great mistake... that is something I will live with for the rest of my life. And of course it became worse,

I'm thinking, since it was so bad if it was—if he actually meant to jump in front of that car, if it was a suicide attempt maybe. I don't know. But I wouldn't be surprised, Hugo."

Frankie was wiping away tears from his beautiful, haunted face. And I stood there feeling great pain inside of my heart too. We both sat down.

"I wouldn't be surprised," he murmured again.

"I'm so sorry, Frankie. I didn't know, I didn't know..."

Frankie had his head in his hand and was crying uncontrollably, not loud but I heard it and he couldn't stop.

"It's not you, Hugo," Frankie replied beneath a veil of tears. "Someone should have told you; he knew what he was doing, he knew I was getting into fucking law enforcement. It's why he never told me about you. Fucking manipulative sneaky prick. And now look... now look, Hugo. I'm sorry. It's my fault. It's all my fucking fault."

We hugged and cried. Not saying a word. We just let it out. All of it. And a minute later, a torrential downpour came down from a lonely firmament.

"I killed him."

"Frankie no, you didn't—"

"I killed him!! It's my fucking—" It was as if he had fallen off a cliff, falling into his own darkness. He screamed but it felt like a nuclear reactor, the kind that can break your heart. Mine was shattered.

He stayed the night. We fucked, smoked some weed, and watched Kubrick the whole next day. From *Dr. Strangelove* to *Full Metal Jacket*. We didn't speak a word. We just let his movies play out on HBO Max. And when we finished, after having some dinner, we ordered *Eyes Wide Shut* on Amazon Prime around one in the morning, and then he left.

I was there alone now, replaying everything he told me in my head over and over. I felt my stomach clench, tears welling up inside of me again. I missed Terrance. I wanted to feel his touch once more. There was something tender about him when we were lying next to each other in bed. We made passionate love and I had never wanted it to end. It had been so powerful, so moving, even a little weird sometimes. He had a whole other side to him, but who knew if it was real. I knew he had had problems, but I didn't suspect they were that horrible. I felt responsible for his death then and now and most likely for the rest of my life. Sure, Frankie admitted it was actually his fault, but I couldn't shake the idea of his family giving up. My heart felt heavy. I refused to cry again, though I felt the tears coming regardless. So, I cried a little bit to myself. Then wiping the tears away, I fell asleep on the couch and didn't wake up until nine the next evening.

CHAPTER 14
Chutes & Ladders

These memories of the setting sun become a blur, in summer they linger until late, obscuring the dark matter that lay beyond. Even inside of us. Four past midnight and we are still hungering for release, a deliverance. I only hope I can make the right decision this time. And something told me I would. I had to talk to Deanna.

"Hi. Deanna."

"Hugo."

"Are you driving?"

"What is this, the third degree? You've picked up when you're behind the wheel."

"I need to talk to you."

"About what?" She sounded irritable.

"Just about what happened on prom night, can you meet me somewhere?"

There was silence at the other end of the line.

"Okay, sure. How about Starbucks on Victory?"

"Alright see you there."

We sat in the corner near the window, facing the parking lot. I had ordered a regular black coffee; she ordered a tea. We didn't say much. Deanna had a look on her face that registered total irritation to me.

"So, what's the deal?"

"Do you remember what happened on prom night?" I asked her. My voice was tight, and I wasn't really drinking my coffee. Just sipping.

"Yes, how can I forget?"

"Did you know Frankie was Terrance's brother?" I asked in an off-hand way.

"He may have told me. I can't remember." Deanna kept looking out the window and playing with her hair.

"He told me the other day."

"Why would he tell you that? It's all water under the bridge."

"You didn't help him when you guys were going out. Did you?"

"I tried Hugo. He was sick. He was addicted to drugs, his bipolar disorder—"

"You never helped him. You just blew him hoping it would all go away."

"How fucking *dare* you? You were banging him too, Hugo. Why didn't *you*?"

"I should have, you're right. It's something I'll ask myself for the rest of my life. But what I'm wondering is... he loved you, and you didn't feel a thing for him. I'm wondering if that maybe sent him over the edge?"

"That certainly wasn't my fault, I did the best I could. I tried to love him—"

"Why is it that I don't believe you?"

"It's not my problem if you believe me or if you don't. He was a headcase, Hugo. When he was loving and normal it was great, but when he was having difficulty..."

"That's when you started seeing other people. Don't fucking lie to me."

"I'm not lying to you, Hugo. Have I ever lied to you?"

"I loved him. In my own way, Deanna. I did. He was bi, I'm bi... maybe it was just different with a man. On prom night you didn't look happy. Did something happen?"

"Hugo, that was twenty years ago it—"

"It matters!" I shouted and people looked over at us. I calmed myself down. "It's important for me to know what you were thinking, was he taking anything? He's taken quite a bit of drugs in his time, and I can't help but think that it was around the time he began seeing you."

"He was addicted, what can I do? I tried to get him to therapy. Maybe I should've thrown the bottles out."

"But you didn't."

"No, I didn't. I figured if that made him happy, then who am I to interfere?"

"So, you enjoyed it when he was unraveling and becoming addicted to Xanax and Lexapro and whatever the fuck else, he was shoving in his mouth?"

"Maybe."

"You're a real piece of shit, you know that?"

"Oh, *I'm* a piece of shit. Really? What about you? I seem to remember the two of you had a thing and he wasn't any better off."

"I listened to him. Maybe there was more I could have done, too, but I'm wondering if the real reason he died is because he killed himself."

"Terrance wouldn't kill himself."

"Are you sure? I mean, you seem so fucking concerned."

"I tried to be, Hugo. I tried to love him, maybe I didn't. It doesn't matter now."

"Yes, it does. The only problem is that it doesn't matter *to you.*" I stood up, took a last sip of my coffee, and flung it in the garbage can in disgust.

"You don't love anyone, Deanna. You don't even love yourself. You're not capable of it. Have a nice life."

"Hugo—" she called my name, but I was already out the door.

She followed me outside to the parking lot and I stopped near my car.

"The fuck do you want? I have to go."

"Come on." She rubbed her smooth hand on my chest and for a few seconds I wanted her next to me under the covers in my bed. But I knew she would never be capable of humanity.

"I can't do this. Not anymore."

"So, you're just going to leave me?"

"We didn't leave each other. I'm moving on."

"Hugo. Come on, please talk to me. I—"

"Does it matter? Truly. Does it fucking matter to you?"

Her silence was a response. I got in my car, backed out of the parking lot, and left her behind. While she stood there searching for an answer, I had already found mine.

I was back home and not around anyone. I had a cigarette outside on the porch near the pool, enjoying the silence. I was trying to understand everything that happened in the past few days. Frankie telling me Terrance was his brother, how it was a suicide not manslaughter, Deanna's complete indifference to it all, everything seemed to relate to Terrance and what happened on prom night. And once I had told Jason everything from that point on, I felt free. I was able to speak it into existence and leave it behind, the weight of it wasn't as burdening. Maybe it was all of us that night, maybe nobody was thinking clearly. I truly had no fucking idea he was so addicted to drugs, things that could kill him.

I remember getting high with him a few times with cocaine, or mushrooms, or MDMA, whatever we could get our hands on. Experimenting, enjoying life, not a care in the fucking world. When he was happy, it was as if the whole world could heal, and did. He had a radiant energy to him, and you felt as if the sun would only shine for you, but when this darkness would creep into him it was perpetual winter; dangerous, lonely, and unpredictable.

I knew he had a problem, problems in this case, plural. It was discouraging to see. It was as if he became a completely different person. Completely unfamiliar and dark. As if he were possessed. That's usually when he would force my hand to leave, nobody could be around him when he began acting that way, you would walk on eggshells for weeks. And then he would find his way out of hell and call me as if nothing had happened. I should've noticed right then and there, I should have intervened. Nobody else was. Not Frankie, not Deanna, and definitely not my boys Anthony, Tom, or Bobby. Forget about them.

"You know, sometimes, Hugo, I need more than you on my dick to get through the day. Life can be so hard for me. You're as mysterious as you are seductive, Hugo. You can never truly understand the depths of my heart and I can with yours. I suspect we are not as compatible as you might believe."

"What are you talking about?"

Terrance got up from, naked, staring out the window. "It's beyond my control Hugo; I can't do this anymore."

"Do what?" I sat up in bed and faced Terrance, who turned around in all his naked sensuality.

"I've become so bored, you see. It's not my problem anymore." He gathered his clothes and started getting dressed.

"You're ending it?"

"My love had great difficulty outlasting your virtue, Hugo, it's beyond my control," he stammered with his words, and I could see tears on his face.

"I don't believe this. What did I do? Something I said?

Did?"

"No."

"Did I not blow you often enough—"

"Hugo—"

"No, I want to know since you're so desperate to be rid of me."

"It's—"

"What?" I shoved him.

"Don't fucking shove me."

"No, why is it?" Huh?" I shoved him to the dresser and had him cornered. "You're fucking ending it with me?! WHY?"

"I CAN'T LOVE YOU! I can't! Not anymore. It's not who I am! You want to know who the fuck I am? I'm a fucking drug addict. I've done crystal meth more times than I care to think about. You see this on my arm?" He showed me his black and blue with a tiny hole in it.

"Terrance, what did you do? What happened?"

"It all just fucking failed me."

"Terrance... Jesus you're using drugs?"

"GET OFF OF ME!" That was when he shoved me hard that I nearly fell. "I don't need you! You fucking loser! GET OUT! Now! Just get the fuck out!" He took my shirt and dragged me out of the room.

"Terrance, get off me!" I wrenched myself from his tight grip. "Let's talk about this! You need help, how can you not tell me..."

"I don't owe you anything. I just need you to go! And never come back."

"You need help, baby."

"I'm not your baby. I'm nothing to you. You're nothing to me. Nothing. You're as desperate and pathetic as you always were. Look at you. You fell for a drug addict. Joke's on you, bitch."

I wanted to knock him out but the pain I felt was numbing.

"Get out. Don't ever come back."

"You're a fucking asshole!"

With the door slammed in my face, I stood there, broken, and unable to move. Rage ascended within me and its eyes were the color of dark stars. I walked out of his apartment building into the rain. I ran to catch a cab and told him to take me back to my house in Staten Island. For forty-five minutes I didn't say a fucking word, I just kept fighting back the tears and the pain.

I hadn't thought of that in years, and it was as real and excruciating as it was when it happened all those years ago. That's why he was behaving so strangely during the prom. It was all the drugs he had taken, his unshakeable guilt over ending it with me, the way he treated Deanna and Frankie and myself, he was more damaged than I knew. I was up all night, going over everything that happened. The hours changed but my broken heart remained the same.

The ambiance of my shattered self now in broken shards like the glass of a mirror on the wall. I didn't need a prophecy, or a crumbing civilization, there are worse things in this cold world than death and that is uncertainty. A release, a reassurance perhaps. As human beings, our unquenchable desire to change and improve is unbelievable.

Back in the day, I didn't worry about anything. I had my friendships, I had my life, and it was wonderful, and now things are different I still have a beautiful home and the friendships feel strange and unfamiliar. That night broke all of us, it all happened so quickly and without warning. The gravity was what broke us, the intensity, the violent outcome. It all fell apart. Or maybe Frankie was right, perhaps it was a suicide, maybe I didn't shove him as hard I thought. So many images flood through my brain when I remember that night, the sounds, the lights, the screaming, the sirens, everything. It all comes in waves from the dark. Unfathomable-sized waves.

My phone was vibrating now, it was Anthony. We agreed to meet at his apartment. Just us.

"So, I have some news. Your boy: Frankie."

"Yeah, what about him, Tony?"

"He's saying it was a suicide, apparently Terrance was heavy into crystal and had bad—"

"I know he told me. He told me everything."

"Are we okay, then?"

For the first time in my life, I heard a sense of panic in Anthony's voice.

"I think so, brother. I think so. We can rely on Frankie's discretion, if anything. But the four of us are fine. Did you tell the other guys?"

"Yes, they were fucking terrified just like us. I'm sure

Frankie will debrief us."

"He will. Trust me." Anthony removed a joint from his pocket and we sat on the balcony of his apartment, smoking and not saying a word in the still quiet midnight.

"I'm just so fucking relieved, Hugo. I never want to go through that again."

"None of us do, Tony. We were all there. We all witnessed it. But in a way, in a small way, I think he had it coming. He was a bully. But I had no idea until now he was so fucking troubled."

"Water under the bridge, Hugo. Don't sweat it. It was bound to happen no matter what we did. He didn't listen to anyone."

"Deanna doesn't seem to care. She's such a cunt."

"I agree. Nobody likes her. She's not a nice person."

"Agreed. Maybe she'll find peace one day."

"Hopefully," nodded Anthony.

I left half an hour later and on the drive home, Mozart came on my speakers. I felt the night wrap me up.

CHAPTER 15
Deliverance & Retribution

For the first time in my life, I felt more in control. Coming clean with Jason and with Frankie helped me to see beyond the veil of what happened. And what happened changed all of us, Bobby, Anthony, Tom, and myself. I would include Deanna, but she was still the cold uninterested selfish bitch she always was, it doesn't take much to be the same person you've been since high school, she just has a lighter temperament since getting laid more than once a year. Perhaps the PMS has subsided, and her broom was given the proper oil change.

In high school she was beautiful, respected, admired even by the older students in our school, she had a certain bitch virtuosity that I was able to tolerate, I even praised her for her coarseness and cold demeanor. Perhaps I was the same in a way, disconnected and disenchanted by this new chapter in my life, my parents never projected humanity or compassion or understanding; they were too impressed by themselves and their money to care and it rubbed off on me. I was in trouble constantly. It was almost laughable but my teachers, some of them at least, exhibited great humor and interest in me, perhaps they were impressed, and a bit taken aback by my ability to do whatever I wanted because I never cared for the consequences. You can't live your life on the margins all the fucking time.

I slept with Deanna in high school and continued on and off with her for years afterwards. She was beautiful too, a charmed and effortless beauty that glowed from within. I desired her in silence. I never was the one to make the first move and one day she was over Bobby's house for a pool party, Anthony, Tom, myself, Terrance—everyone was there. And Deanna and I had our own little party upstairs in the attic where the spare yet spacious bedroom was. For hours on end just enjoying great passionate sex, we locked the door too. And two blow jobs, three muff dives and sometime later, we walked down after a really hot enjoyable shower and joined the masses in Bobby's backyard. It was a wild and wonderful night. However, the next day changed everything.

June 2001. Staten Island, NY.

"What do you mean it wasn't enjoyable, Deanna?"

"Come on Hugo, I tried to be enthusiastic but more often than not, my mind goes vacation."

"You can do that all on your own," I replied flatly, and I stood there, not feeling anything but a fusion of empowerment as a curious energizing sense of self emerged from the depths of me. I smoked another cigarette by the window regarding the stars with a mild detachment.

"That's the nastiest thing you ever said to me."

"I find that hard to believe. As if your lying to me is any better?"

"I just—didn't know how to tell you."

I laughed in spite of it. "Have you been practicing in front of a mirror? Because you're doing a phenomenal job. Truly. The inflection, the flatness of your big announcement right before you launch full steam ahead into your big speech about your lack of sexual charisma."

"What the fuck do you know about depression?"

"Well for one thing I didn't live in a freezer before meeting you, and secondly, you have no fucking clue what I deal with, nor could you understand it if you did."

"Right, I don't understand depression? Why because I'm banging you *and* Terrance?"

"So, the happy-go-lucky cheerleading slut *does* feel things?"

"What?!" her voice changed, but I only heard underwater tones. "I'm the—" She stormed out of the room walking to the bathroom and slamming the door so loudly the house shook. Maybe it would fall on her, who knows. It couldn't be more excruciating than sleeping with a hyena with chronic PMS.

"I think your broom needs another oil change too. And let me know when you want to sleep with me again. I'll try harder next time. You know it amazes me that someone as sexually evolved as you can be so judgmental. I mean I didn't think humping two men at the same time would be something to proud of. But whatever floats your boat. The tramp in you must be so proud, having this kind of ego boost by experiencing both a man and some wimpy ass faggot who can't maintain an erection."

Deanna came back out her tears turned her face red; I looked up at her, finished my cigarette, flicked it out the window, and headed for the door.

"I need you to go," she said evenly.

"I'll be more than happy too. I don't respect what you told me, it's cruel."

"So are you."

"Let me ask you something, Deanna, do I know Terrance better than you? Because I'm telling you now the guy's no fucking good!"

"You sucked his dick, too. You made your fucking bed."

"But unlike you, I sleep in it." And with those last words, that final crucifixion of her wounded self, I walked downstairs and headed out the door.

I can't fix stupid. I walked back to the backyard.

"Fucking annoying cunt," I said through gritted teeth. I had a second cigarette and sat in silence. Quickly inhaling and exhaling, I could punch a hole into someone's fucking heart, I was so fucking livid!

For a good ten minutes I sat and smoked. Until Tom sat down next to me.

"She is such a nasty and infuriating bitch. I'm sure plenty of men wouldn't mind oiling her broom before the night is through. Making sure the miserable witch gets back to her fucking castle before the fucking sun comes up, sniveling little wench!"

I was venting to Tom and Anthony heard our conversation as he sat down across from me.

"Are you talking about Deanna?"

"No, I'm talking about Rene Russo," I quipped flippantly. "Of course I'm talking about Deanna!"

"What happened?" Tom asked.

"I don't know. She's a frigid, moody cunt who doesn't know how to love anyone. Does that work for you?"

"I'm not surprised. She's always been this way."

"She's upstairs. Not sure if she decided to melt herself with a shower but who knows right?!" I shouted so she could hear me.

"Hugo... Hugo, relax. Relax. Come on."

"I didn't fucking start this!"

"I know. I know. Just take a breath, just breathe. She's the same way with me too. Pretty much with everyone, incidentally, does anyone know where Terrance went?"

"Oh yeah I've been *so* worried," I replied dryly. "Christ. No wonder my anxiety is so out-of-fucking-control. His well-being is so important to me."

"He probably did," Anthony remarked. "Who fucking cares though?"

"Definitely not me," I replied. "His once and future princess is still in the bathroom though."

We all laughed, smoke some weed, and didn't say a word to each other for a good three or four hours. We had Radiohead on the speakers from the stereo set Bobby's father set up. It was glorious. The four of us were blessedly, happily stoned; it was wonderful. I think that is what makes a friendship like ours have such strength and resilience. The four of us can all sit and enjoy the night with constellations in the sky and Radiohead on the speakers. The world is wounded enough, sometimes we need to leave and let it fucking heal.

We all sat back in our lounge chairs, glancing up the sky seeing them dance together in unison. The sky was a sparkling black tourmaline, festooned with galaxies we will never know, beings we will never meet until our time is up. That is God to me. I suppose we are pretty insignificant when we consider the size of the universe, but mushrooms make me feel differently.

We are not insignificant; it's our idealism of what the universe should be that is insignificant. Human beings want everything to fit into a neat little box, convenient and contained. But something like this, something like the universe, the planets, the stars, the new horizons only serve to horrify me to some degree. We return to where we came from, with perspective, intellect, wounds, dreams, memories, but do we ever really leave earth behind? I should hope not. And as my mind became flooded with these thoughts, I relaxed myself again, another deep breath, the answers are hardly important. It's the question that drives us.

I continued to look up at the sky. Each star seemed to tell a story. Illustrations of a lonely universe. I found them fascinating. I could write them a poem. I can do something. For they give us liberation, they turn the tide, change the course of the wind, they gather around us, a Milky Way in our trembling hands. For what is beyond it? Beyond the boundaries of perceived space-time. I had no fucking idea what made Deanna say what she said. Perhaps I wasn't the right man, maybe not.

She is beautiful. She is unpredictable. But there is so much more to her, Terrance was in love with her, and his drug habit was pushed to the edge with her constant and persistent obsessiveness. I loved them both, contracted to them both as Edmund in *King Lear* remarked at the end. Two women loved him, yet he played them both. Manipulated the two of them to no end. I had to admire his gumption.

I enjoyed reading Shakespeare. I still do. The power his words exuded when I was enjoying some marijuana and having some beer, reading *Macbeth,* and *Othello, The Merchant of Venice,* the list goes on. I slowly became interested in poetry too and I wanted to write the perfect one someday. Fuck, I had so much ammunition, so many stories, so many doomed relationships, after a while I began to imagine myself in these plays becoming these flawed characters, only to realize real life is the most flawed of all.

She was sinister, Deanna. Her eyes emphasized a black ocean with no recognizable depth, just a bottomless pit. I felt myself sink into her almost every night, I was beguiled by her, she was different from women I've been with but perhaps that was where everything fell apart. And I wanted to feel her on top of me each night, I just kept coming back for more. She was funny, she was nice to be around, charismatic, and beautiful, an effortless beauty that never faltered. And after being with Terrance, I think that was when everything changed.

I loved the guy, but he was unpredictable as well, you never knew when the bomb would go off, and he was constantly on medications all for different reasons, his depression, anxiety, headaches, back pain every little minor infraction required surgery, a doctor's appointment, or some kind of pharmaceutical intervention. I would go over his house, we would fuck, smoke, watch tv, order food, and do the entire process over again the next day. I never had a strong emotional camaraderie with Terrance, perhaps that was my fault maybe it was just who he was. Who the fuck knows. But just when I thought I'd seen it all, I had stumbled upon something that I'll never forget.

I was getting dressed in his room and I dropped my watch under his bed. I leaned over to pick it up and saw a handgun inside the bed frame with the handle sticking out. At first, I couldn't move. I had never actually seen a gun up close before, except for in movies of course, but that's on a screen. I took the gun by the handle and slowly removed it from under the bedframe. I held it in my hand and found myself shaking. What was Terrance thinking to do? Suicide? Did something happen that he wasn't telling me? I—

"You found it?" I nearly jumped out of my fucking skin when I heard his voice, turning around to see him leaning on the doorframe.

"Jesus Terrance—you scared the fuck out of me."

"It's just protection, okay."

I stood there with the gun in my hand not saying a word.

"It's not loaded. I just—I owe some people money and they've been harassing me."

"Owe who money?"

"Hugo, it's not your concern. It's nothing to worry about, okay?"

"I am worried here. I find a gun under your bed; I don't know what to think."

"You don't need to think anything, Hugo." He walked up to me and held his hand out and I lightly placed the gun in his hand, which didn't move.

"Are you alright, Terrance?"

"Right now, I'm not," he responded coldly. "But I just popped a Xanax, so I will be later on."

"Oh alright. I uh... would I be able to get some too? My anxiety is spiked right now."

"Because of the gun?"

"No, it's the fucking UFO on your front lawn. Of course, because of the gun!"

"Yeah, you can have one. It's the two milligrams. I've been taking them two times a day. They're strong. So, I can break one in half for you."

"Be careful with this shit, Terrance. Please."

"You know me, Hugo. Who can fuck you better than I can, right?"

"Not many people, as I recall."

He got out the container with Xanax, picked one out, broke

it in half, and handed it to me. "This is still really big."

"You never had any problems with something being big, did you?"

"Not since we started sleeping together."

"Exactly." Terrance placed the container back in the cabinet and we went downstairs.

"I'm sorry, baby."

"For what?"

"The gun. I shouldn't be prying that way."

"Oh, don't sweat it. It's fine. You can trust me."

"I know I can. I just hope you're not in something you can't get out of."

"Nothing of the kind, okay. It's just some harassment. To be honest, it's my father's gun. So, I didn't buy it. I couldn't even if I wanted too. I'm not twenty-one yet."

"I never knew your father kept a gun."

"Now you do."

I walked up to him, and we kissed, and I felt his own handgun in his pants jutting out.

"Yeah, that's my other gun."

"This one is definitely loaded. I can tell. Didn't you shoot last night?"

"Yeah, but I may need to do it again..."

"I guess an extra inning won't hurt either one of us."

We fucked so hard and so long we were nearly out of breath by the time we finished. There was something wild and fantastic about it, and we'd fucked countless times, but this night felt the most powerful, the rawest the most mind-blowing. Maybe it was the conversation about the gun under his bed, and for some reason, as scary as it was, it also turned me on.

"God it really was loaded huh? Holy fucking mother of Christ, Terrance." I was catching my breath as we lay down on each other. I had one more cigarette left, and we shared it in silence. After a good forty-five minutes of restoration and sleep, I got up and got dressed again.

"You can stay, Hugo."

"I know. But I have to get home and get some things done. I'll be around tomorrow. That was amazing, by the way, I never knew you could arch your whole body back like that. It's like you're some kind of love machine..."

"I am the love machine."

"And you work for nobody but me," I sang along as I moved my hips backward and forward with my hands in the middle.

"Do you really have to go, baby?" Terrance said as he placed his foot between my legs and moved my cock around.

"It needs to catch up on some sleep, Terrance. Been working overtime."

He placed his foot back on the bed I finished getting dressed and Terrance glanced out the window.

"Alright, let me know if you change your mind. I'll be here all day. Alone."

"If it's any conciliation, I'll be alone too, alright."

"Then what's the big fucking deal about going home?"

"Nothing. I just—I just have to get some things done. Believe me, it's nothing glamorous."

"It can't wait?"

"Why are you breaking my balls? We just had a nice afternoon."

"I'm not running anything, Hugo. It's just..." He put his fist through the wall next to his bed and cast a dark look in his eye.

"Jesus, Terrance! What the fuck? Come on... I'm sorry alright."

"I'm sorry." He got up out of bed, embraced me, and kissed me heavily on the mouth. "I've been feeling lonely, baby."

"I know, I get it, it's okay. Alright. It's okay."

"Sometimes I don't know what to do. The fucking medication isn't helping."

"Did you consider maybe going to a—"

"A therapist. No. No fucking way."

"It's discreet, baby. It's nobody's fucking business. Not even mine."

"I know that," Terrance responded curtly. "I'm just not sure that will be enough for me."

We let go and he stood there, tears in his eyes, rubbing his face.

"Listen to me, and I'm only saying this because I love you so fucking much baby, maybe ease up with the pills, okay? I don't want anything happening to you."

"Ease up?"

"Yeah, you seem to be taking them a lot. When did you have that Xanax script filled?"

"What are you insinuating, Hugo?"

"I'm just curious."

"You're just curious but there's some meaning in that, isn't there?"

We looked at each other and didn't move our eyes away.

"No, but I want to know when you had that script filled."

"Why?"

"When, Terrance?"

"Fuck you. Get out, just get the fuck out."

"No."

"Get out."

"Not until you fucking tell me when you had that filled!"

"GET OUT! NOW!" He began shoving me out of his room and into the hallway. I went into the bathroom and glanced at the open medicine cabinet and saw the bottle staring me in the face. Terrance moved in and nearly knocked the bottle out of my hand; pills went all over the bathroom floor.

"Terrance, what the hell is wrong with you?!" I shouted.

"Give me the fucking bottle!"

"Where is—" I found the bottle next to my foot.

"Give it to me!" Terrance managed to get it from my hand and shoved me on the floor. "It's not your fucking business."

"It *is* my fucking business!" I stood and pinned him to the door. I yanked the bottle from his hand and saw the date. A few days ago. The bottle was nearly half empty already.

"Terrance, this is for three fucking months, and it's nearly fucking gone! What are you doing!?"

"I'M DYING, HUGO! I'M FUCKING DYING! AND I NEED TO DO SOMETHING ABOUT IT!!"

"What do you mean you're dying!"

"I need these drugs. I need them. I can't hide it from you, but I need them to function. I have bipolar disorder on top of everything. And to me that feels like dying. Every day. There is no relief with anything, it's a constant reminder that I will never find peace. I will never find any relief. I'm a fucking..."

"Baby, I love you; I love you so much Terrance, we can get through this. We can do this."

"No! Nobody can do anything! NOBODY CAN DO ANYTHING, HUGO! NOTHING!" Terrance was shrieking at the top of his lungs at me, with tears of rage and fear pouring from his face.

"Ask Deanna about the fucking gun!!! She'll tell you!"

"What do you mean 'ask Deanna'? Did she fucking give you

it?! You lied to me!?"

"She didn't... it's my father's. But she—she did give me something. Hugo, get out! You're going to stand there and accuse me! Get THE FUCK OUT NOW! JUST LEAVE!" He nearly shoved me down the stairs.

I was able to get my footing and run out of the house. I could hear his torment from outside. And even still as I was lying up in bed with a spliff. I didn't fall asleep until after three in the fucking morning.

The next morning, I bolted to Deanna's house, and she was sitting outside reading a book and as I stormed in, she flung the book on the ground.

"What is it now?"

"What the fuck did you do to Terrance?!"

"Excuse you, Hugo!?"

"He said you gave him something. He was fucking having a nervous breakdown. He's bipolar, you sick cunt!"

If she was a man, I would be beating him so badly.

"I didn't!"

"Don't fucking lie to me, Deanna, do not fucking lie to me! WHAT DID YOU GIVE HIM!"

"I... I gave him something to help him cope."

"Drugs?"

"I—I wanted to help, alright. It's—nothing. He'll be fine."

"Fine?! When I ran out of his house last night, I could hear him screaming. You heartless bitch! Is *that* your definition of fine!!! It was like he was fucking possessed!"

"I don't know what to say anymore. He's been that way for years."

"Oh, I forgot you only bang him when he's in a good mood. Answer my fucking question."

"Who says I have to do that?"

"You're fucking crazy, you know that."

"It was just some cocaine... my cousin always said crystal meth helped with her..."

"You—you g-gave him crystal meth?"

"Housewives used it in the fifties to clean their house, are we any better off now?"

"How can you fucking do that?"

"Terrance needed me to help him. And now he owes money. But I can't fix that. He'll recover. I told him to go easy with it, but I guess he decided differently. He left me for dead; he dumped me and now he's trying to mend the frayed bond. Well, it's too late, I suppose there is no telling what he's capable of fucking doing, is there? Nothing at all. You know, sometimes madness is like butterfly wings: all it needs is a fucking push!"

I lunged for Deanna and flung the chairs over near her pool. I was fuming and I wanted desperately to grab her and hold her head under water. She was sublimely dangerous and I was seeing for the first time just how pathological it really was.

"No! Don't you lay your fucking hands on me, Hugo."

"He can die, Deanna! Don't you fucking care at all?"

"It's not my problem."

"WHO ARE YOU!?"

"I'M NO ONE!" She spat hard in my face.

I grabbed her by her arms squeezing her tight. I pushed her so hard into her pool, the water exploded. And as guilty as I felt, I did feel slightly relieved to see her in there alone, in shock.

"Don't you ever fucking come near me or Terrance again, you fucking evil cunt. Or I'll fucking kill you myself." I spoke so quietly, she recoiled, standing there in her pool, her hair and makeup in disarray. Her real self now revealed to the world. I walked out of her yard without looking back. Slamming the wrought iron gate behind me.

Present Day Brooklyn. 2022.

Those memories, those haunted kingdoms I visited seemed darker now than they were when I closed them down for good, foreclosure. I thought I'd never have to revisit them again, would never have to see the dark castles for which there is no light. Some wounds go too deep; we can never fully heal. My own arrogance had cost me dearly. And now my friend and lover is gone. He's dead. There was nothing I or anybody could do. But when I thought back on that incident with Deanna and that afternoon with Terrance, I figured I understood why the shoe fell the way it did. I hadn't really seen Deanna after we met up again a few months ago. But maybe I should. I needed her to know what happened with Terrance, that it was her fault. That it wasn't manslaughter, but suicide. She was the executioner; she dropped the blade from above. Her hands were soaked with blood now and forever.

Out, out damned spot! Out I say!

I sat by the pool, stretched out on the lounge chair. I was smoking a joint tonight, cigarettes after a while make me really fucking dizzy and I can't think straight. Marijuana was different, it had a clearer perspective to share. The more I remembered everything that happened that night, with Terrance, Deanna, Anthony, Tom, Bobby, me... we managed to really fuck it all up. Royally. He was a wonderful lover, when he wasn't using and before I found out, he was wonderful.

I remember being so furious with my mother for not showing up for a track meet when I was in middle school and she never said anything about it. She saw the look on my face when she answered the door, Anthony's parents had dropped me off. I stormed inside and went upstairs to my room slamming the door behind me. My father was in Europe visiting, I don't remember giving it too much credence but when my own mother, my own family let me down, it was excruciating. I was always meant to be alone, completely untethered from the world around me. And for no good reason either. It was the way things were.

Now I sat there sobbing and I wiped the tears around my face off. I wanted to be completely exonerated of all of this. I wanted to put it all behind me, to move on. The ghost of once was will always be here. Frankie called my phone. And at about a half hour later we were making love on the couch in the living room.

— — —

I woke up and it was still dark; I didn't bother to consult my phone for the time. It all happened so long ago, but I still felt connected to it on every imaginable level. Frankie was still sleeping and I had the silent house to myself, it was a relief. Just to have some silence meant everything, some fucking stillness, something to hold onto besides Frankie's arm on my chest. It'd been so long since we'd fucked, it was a relief, a rejuvenation, stronger and more powerful than I remember it being the last time, which seems to be centuries ago now. He stirred in his sleep, and I saw his face in my field of vision, so erotic and beautiful. He gave me fever when he held me tight, I felt it caressed my soul. The elemental effects of true love, I never felt this way about anyone, it changed me somehow, to know I could feel these feelings again in my life, the only other time was Terrance, before that night. Not even for Jocelyn had it ever been that strong. I sat outside on the porch and had my coffee it wasn't even six-thirty am, yet I was up and refreshed.

The wind was light and wonderful, I heard an owl in the trees, the rustling of leaves in the trees, and on the grass. I felt a permanent grace. The quiet stillness of morning light, the rising sun, the first rolled joint of the morning, just a few lights pulls and I was back on Earth once again, the vagabond loner, sipping his black coffee trying to reconstruct my past to suit my isolated present. I suppose things happen for a reason, perhaps that's why we are here in the first place, because there is a fucking reason for everything. I did miss being with Terrance, and I never really thought about him or our relationship until it was too late, until after he died. Despite his mood swings, his erratic behavior, the addictions he had, it was more than one, cocaine, heroin, crystal meth. I had no fucking idea.

It broke my heart. It just broke my fucking heart. He was worth so much more than anything he ever faced. Not even Frankie, his own brother could help him. He was a man who slipped through everyone's grasp, a man who didn't have what I had, perhaps it was his anger his jealousy his unending fury... and certainly the fucking drugs. He was experimenting, he was self-medicating, he was trying to find a way out of the fucking darkness, without realizing he was the fucking darkness!

As I sat there smoking a cigarette, mulling it all over, a car drove by, and I heard the lyrics "*Somebody is gonna hurt someone... Somebody is gonna come undone,*" "Heartbreak Tonight" by The Eagles played, not loud but just enough to put everything that happened into perspective.

It was me that came undone, and every time my mind wandered back to that night of all nights, the more I began to understand why Terrance wanted to end his life, why it was so imperative that he construct every minute detail so meticulously. He knew nobody would care, not even the fucker who hit him with his black BMW.

That fucking sound he made when the car hit him and he went rolling up towards the windshield and seeing it crack that way, and Terrance's body flying off into the street for the last time. It remained in my head until this very day, and it made me feel his pain as it started to rain. The car taking off, Anthony, Bobby, me, and Tom all frantic and helpless trying to come up with the perfect alibi.

He was pushed.

No, he just threw himself into the car.

No! NO! He was pushed.

That's what we'll say... he was pushed.

Tripped. He tripped it started fucking raining and he slipped.

He slipped. That's the story. That's the fiction.

Terrance saw the car coming and it was coming around the street at a furious speed. He antagonized Deanna on purpose by shoving her, he knew that would incense me and my boys to the point of fucking murder, mission accomplished. He did want to have some blood on their hands too I just didn't know if I was part of that equation too. I was his lover, but things went down with us too, especially that violent argument we had about finding out he was doing all those drugs. And—

"Baby what you doing up so fucking early?" Frankie put his hand on my shoulder, and I jumped slightly in my chair.

"Jesus! You scared me."

"I could say the same..."

"I'm sorry, I just couldn't sleep so... I wanted to sit outside in silence."

"You're upset by what happened, aren't you?"

"No, I'm upset because *American Horror Story* is only on once a week." I glanced at him but he didn't look back. "Of course that's why I'm upset! I just I can't stop thinking about it."

"You alright?"

"I don't know, Frankie. I just don't fucking know anymore."

Frankie patted my shoulder and walked into the other room, getting dressed and ready for work. I was alone again. Cut off and in total delirium. Ruminating about the argument I had with Terrance a week or so before he died was weighing heavy on me. I wanted it to stop but it refused. It played over and over like a diabolical tune you can never sing. I felt the perpetual hit of panic consume my body like rushing water from a fountain. A nightmare is fed before it is born. I finished another cigarette, stubbing it out on the bottom of the chair, and went back inside for more coffee.

Frankie was standing in the kitchen with a coffee mug in his hand eyeing me steadily. He had something on his mind. I was always able to tell when his anxiety and suspicion revealed themselves in a thaw. It was the presence of a shadow, festooned with strength and anger. One that could easily kill you if you lied or withheld information. A dark paradise, Frankie had a rage, a wrath, and it's only been once in my life where I met this other side of him.

We all have demons; he let his dance. But in that moment of profound rage, I saw a light in his eyes, his deep mysterious eyes and found a calm as well. Usually anger was nothing without peace, a yin and yang situation, but usually that tranquility took its time long after the anger had dissipated to silence. I poured another coffee and stood next to him, glancing down at the floor; all I craved was release.

"Hugo, it's alright. My brother was fucked up. I loved him very much, but I couldn't save him from himself. What happened... it happened."

"It's not alright, he died because of me. Because of all of us. He didn't just—"

"Yes, he did. I'm amazed he didn't die earlier because it was so fucking severe, but things happen even when we are careful. Even when we safeguard our every move. We are never at our best in high school. It was a freak thing. I miss him and I loved him."

"Sometimes I think we all died on that night. That somehow what happened changed all of us, eroded our life, and things were never the same after that. I lost touch with Tom and Bobby, Anthony I spoke to off and on, nothing crazy. Living with this, though, it's horrible. I seem to be just barely surviving."

"But you are, my love, you are," Frankie said and we hugged it out in the kitchen.

"I'm sorry, Frankie," I sobbed into his arms. "I'm so sorry! I lost it that night, I fucking lost my nerve that night."

His arms were wrapped around me and in his strong embrace, I felt the release I needed.

"Don't apologize, baby. Don't apologize. It's alright. Everything is alright."

Later that night we were in bed together with the shades turned down after he came on top of me, ejaculating his sperm onto my bare chest. We kissed and lay there staring wonderingly at the ceiling fan, which spun on low. The second release that I needed.

"Not smoking tonight, baby?" Frankie whispered in my ear

that made me more ravenous for him delicious body than anything else. An addiction I could never fully satiate.

"No. I just want to lay here. I'm out anyway. Too many cigarettes." I felt a little lighter and the heavy burden of tragedy slowly but surely eased up.

"I see. You alright?"

I shrugged my shoulders and didn't say a word.

"Hugo?" Frankie tried again.

I lay there with my hand on his chest. The mystery abounds in a tightening vise around my neck. Deanna had given him drugs, Deanna was the one who was responsible, I can't fully believe it was something he wanted to do. To kill himself.

"Fucking cunt," I whispered out loud.

"What?" Frankie turned to me.

"Nothing I—sorry. Deanna."

"What about her?"

"She gave him drugs, Frankie. She just gave them up toots sweet, no questions asked."

"I seemed to remember her pilfering him Xanax and—"

"Jesus, it's not just the pills!" I snapped and sat up in bed. "It was worse, it was heroin it was..."

"She—she gave my brother heroin?"

"That's what she told me."

"Heroin? I should smack the shit out this bitch... where did she get it?"

"Nothing would make me happier."

"Where did she get it, Hugo?"

"I don't know. She never mentioned it. I should have asked."

"Fucking outrageous," he kicked the sheets off and got dressed in a hurry. "Where does she live?"

"Frankie, we have to be careful."

"Where the fuck does she live, Hugo?"

"Frankie, I think we—"

"I ASKED: WHERE THE FUCK DOES SHE LIVE, HUGO!?" he screamed. And his magnetic eyes were fire, pure black electricity from deep within.

I told him her address and when he finished getting dressed, he roared out, slamming the door behind him. My apartment shook violently. I sat there, head in my hands. Waiting for the next drifting nightmare to find its way to me.

Rain came down, it didn't wash away my guilt. I sat there

in my kitchen, and an odd disorientation overcame me. It was a harsh reality of everything in my life, the wheel coming full circle and never finding my way out of the rabbit hole. That cunt. That evil conniving sniveling cunt. She could fucking die now and I would be perfectly fine. She should die. She killed him. She fucking killed him and she killed me dead too.

I called her cell and got her voicemail. After listening to that fake sweet voice of hers, that disenchanted little princess twat, I nearly slammed my phone against the fucking wall. Frankie did me a favor, he awakened an anger in me. I felt awake now. Charged up.

You fucking whore! YOU FUCKING CUNT! What did you do to my friend! What DID YOU DO! HE NEEDED HELP! AND YOU GIVE HIM HEROIN! HOW COULD YOU?! WHAT THE FUCK IS WRONG WITH YOU?!

I sobbed uncontrollably. And after a few minutes, I picked my phone up again.

What the fuck is wrong with you, Deanna? I'm guessing a lot. You're even more fucked up than Terrance. You did to him what you did to me, to Frankie, to every man who comes into your life, you destroy them, you lie to them because there is no real you. You're just a figment. A ghost. You're fucking nothing! YOU'RE NOTHING! You selfish little cunt. You know why you're so alone Deanna, you want to know why... because nobody fucking loves you. Not me, not anyone. Especially not your father. He told me. How does that feel. Take the knife you stuck in Terrance and plunge it into your own fucking bones! I hope you fucking get cancer and die you evil bitch. I really do. AND I'M NOT THE ONLY ONE WHO FEELS THAT WAY!!

I heard my phone crack into a thousand pieces and at that moment... I felt better than I had in months, maybe years. She was always a horrible disgusting human being, but Frankie's anger worried me most of all. I knew he loved Terrance very much, and now it felt as if everything was unraveling.

I lay on the floor of my kitchen, riven with pain and guilt for what happened. As if I kept reliving the night over and over again, bound upon a wheel of fire and torment, no freedom, no emancipation from my actions, we were all so drunk that night, so high on drugs, so laced, out of touch with reality a bit too, but there is something I wish I had done. I wish I had stopped him. I wish I had maybe intervened better, taken a stand, spoken to Terrance, maybe I should've stayed with him instead of walking out, maybe if I was a better friend and lover, it never would have happened, and Terrance would have received the help he needed but didn't. It didn't work out that way.

I loved him, he saw something in me that maybe was hidden from everyone else in my life. And that night, I think all he needed was love, all he wanted was someone to care about him, and he reached out to me as a friend, and I wasn't there, I shrugged it off because I was angry and hurt, and now look. There is no going back, there are no second chances, there is no time machine, there is no way to make up for the choices I've made. I have to accept that which I have and move on... which, if I'm honest, I haven't. I think you can accept plenty of things and take a longer time to move on with your new knowledge. I was stuck here; I was in a fucking void I couldn't find my way out of. Jesus.

There on the floor, I glanced over at my sabotaged phone. Which was fucked. I felt the pangs of guilt and rage wash over me in a terrifying wave. I would never find my way out of here.

I continued to sit there until I passed out. Sleep. That was what I needed. And craved. I needed rest. Metamorphosis too, maybe. What dreams may come? Please no fucking nightmares.

It was three hours later, and I heard knocking on my kitchen door. I jumped awake and wiped the crust from my eyes. It was Frankie, it felt as if it had been forever.

"Open the fucking door, Hugo," he barked.

Yeah, it was him alright. I nearly bolted to the door, opened it, and he came storming in.

"Hugo, I need to know something right fucking now because that twat is a fucking deranged lunatic!!" Frankie shouted.

"I always thought she was just lonely..." I mumbled under my breath. My sarcasm and bitter jaded existence never ceased to amaze me. I lit up a cigarette and stood there, my heart pounding but not as heavily anymore.

"Hugo, right now... I could rip your throat right out of your fucking body. I'm a detective I can make it happen."

"Alright, aright. You're right man, I'm sorry. I make these horrible statements I can't help it. You know me."

"Yeah, that's for fucking sure! I think if Ghandi had to spend any prolonged period of time with you, he would've wound up kicking the shit out of you."

"Probably." I wasn't going to deny it. Frankie knew me best.

"She told me everything. She told me everything that happened that night. Weird part is she even told me she gave him all those drugs, just confessed to everything. She mentioned you a few times. I knew you guys were hot and heavy back in the day..."

"It was nothing—"

"Yeah, and I couldn't give less of a fuck right now or for the foreseeable future, fifty years down the line."

"You're going to be even sexier..."

"I can't believe she fucking did that, and I'm pretty sexy now."

"Goddam right you are, Frankie. I am not kidding; you are a fucking Adonis." I took a few pulls of my cigarette and handed it to Frankie, who did the same. I stubbed it out and we stood there in the kitchen.

"I just wish things had been better for all of us, for Terrance, even Deanna I suppose."

"We all feel that way. I know I do."

"My brother." Frankie wiped the tears off his face and stood there sobbing, and falling through a rabbit hole, this immovable tragedy inside of his blood. I was there with him in the quiet peaceful kitchen. The sabotage, the fucking sabotage, fucking Deanna! We didn't kill him, she fucking pushed him, and what's worse is that he planned it that way!

"Terrance he... suffered. He couldn't help it, the depression got worse every day... he had nightmares. I told you all this, right?"

"Yeah, you did. I'm so sorry, Frankie."

"Everyone around him walked away, I don't know if it was actually bipolar disorder, but I could sense the pain in his eyes and the slight infraction or perceived inconvenience would set him off too—the fucking drugs certainly didn't help him either. That—"

"I could murder that bitch, Frankie. I could..." I wanted to have another cigarette, but I stopped myself.

"I want to know something, what was she like, when you were together?"

I sat down at the kitchen table and looked at Frankie. I had a pair of boxer shorts on and a t-shirt and seeing Frankie in his uniform, I wanted him on top of me more than anything else in the fucking world.

"I was never happy with her, maybe there were times when I was, but not too much. She was difficult, selfish, mean, not really capable of love the way you and I are. Or other people who aren't heavily medicated."

"Deanna was medicated too?"

"You seem shocked."

"Believe me, I'm not." Frankie took a cup out of the cabinet and nearly slammed it shut. He took the coffee pot in his hand. "Is this fresh?"

"Yes... sort of."

"Good enough." He filled his mug and nearly gulped half of it down. "Listen Hugo, I think she was more fucked up than we realize. And she told me something that happened between you two a while back?"

I felt the floor disappear beneath my feet. Like I was being pulled down into a fucking abyss. "Yeah, I shoved her. I found out she was giving Terrance drugs. And I—I lost it."

Frankie took another sip of his coffee and placed it on the counter and glanced at me with his beautiful dark blue eyes.

"You put your hands on her and threw her into the pool?"

"I was angry Frankie; I know it was wrong, alright? I was angry. And scared about what happened..."

"You can't fucking do that, Hugo."

"I know."

"I could arrest you right now and that's not code for 'let's go upstairs and I'll read you your rights'."

"It could be..." I said with a rueful smile on my smug face.

Frankie wasn't having it.

"Alright I'm sorry... I'm sorry." I put my hands up in surrender. "My mouth is going to get me in trouble one day. Maybe I should be shoved into a moving car, I could use a good ass kicking."

"Yeah, I'll fucking say. This isn't fucking funny, HUGO!"

"I'm sorry..."

Frankie had this newfound rage I'd never seen before.

"You put your hands on Deanna and flung her into the fucking pool! Deanna. Of all people!!! Are you out of your fucking mind!?" He flung the half-filled coffee cup against the wall of the kitchen. I actually didn't mind flipping out that way. Just as long as he doesn't burn the house down, I'm good. It was a relief to see my parents wall with a nice stain on it. I'm leaving it that way too.

"You don't go fucking near her, Hugo. Ever again. You just sit here, cool down, go do some fucking cocaine or something while I clean up your shit!"

"What do you mean, *clean up*?"

"What do I mean? You don't care what people fucking think? We have to shut her up somehow, so I'm going to talk to Deanna. There's a chance this may work out to our advantage but who fucking knows. So, keep your hands off her and keep your fucking mouth shut!"

"Okay."

"There's something else I need you to do for me."

I knew what Frankie was capable of and I felt relief for the first time in months.

CHAPTER 16
Blood on Their Hands

I was in Jason's office again, and waiting for him to get out of the bathroom and sit down to talk to me before I snapped completely felt like a prolonged fucking eternity. I heard him washing his hands before he came out of the bathroom and sitting on his regular chair.

"Sorry about that. A lot of coffee today."

"I know the feeling..." I mumbled under my breath. I hadn't slept for the past two days, not since what went down with Frankie in my kitchen.

"I thought this was all resolved."

"Tale as old as time... you really think it all just *goes away,* Jason?"

"I never said that."

"Maybe it'll never go away. I need help, Jason. I need something... I need something to help me cope..."

"What do you need?"

"Something. Xanax?"

"You have to understand, since I'm just a therapist, I can't write prescriptions."

"You did one time. Please, Jason. I've been having these panic attacks in my sleep; I haven't slept at all in days. I feel like a fucking zombie. For fucks' sake, I feel like I'm seeing things!"

"I can probably do this... I have a few pills in my medicine cabinet. Or I can give you the bottle, but we need to have a session. I'm not just slipping you some benzos and hoping it all goes away. You're my responsibility, you're under my care."

"I know I am. I'm willing to do that."

"When did the panic attacks start?" Jason flicked his pen and began taking notes.

"A few days ago, I would go to bed and wake up panicking

it felt like a fucking heart attack or something, but I knew it wasn't and I couldn't breathe, and I would lay back on my pillow clutching my chest. And after a few minutes it would stop. Abruptly."

"So, they last a few minutes... is there anything that might be triggering them? Besides the obvious..."

"I don't think so, I just want them to stop."

"I understand. Has this always happened to you?" Jason inquired and as I saw his pen moving rapidly along his notebook, I felt assured that it was going to work out. I needed them desperately. There was nothing else for me to do.

"No, I was able to manage my stress, manage my anxiety every day. I never had an issue with anything like this. Maybe some mild depression but Jesus Christ the state of the fucking world today."

"I know, it's bad out there, I agree. Is there anything else you want to tell me?"

"I don't think so... unless you know something I don't."

Jason kept writing notes in his book, and I sat back in my chair. He was a godsend to me. It's a shame I hadn't come seen him more frequently. We had a deal, and Jason understood that.

"How is everything else in your life?"

"Not too bad. I just I want these fucking panic attacks to go away. That would be nice."

"I'm sure. Well, from what I gather you certainly need something to help you cope with your anxiety and you mentioned you were experiencing some mild depression. So, I'm going to mistakenly put some pills in your hand that you're going to put in the pocket of your coat and you're going to keep your mouth shut because I have no idea what you have in the pocket of your jacket. Do you understand me? You say one fucking word, Hugo..." He left the rest unspoken.

"I swear on my life, Jason."

He got up and went into the bathroom again and came out with the bottle of benzodiazepines and slipped them into my hand. I did what he wanted me to do, dropped them in my inside coat pocket and not saying a word.

"You don't have any pills because I didn't give you those pills, I never gave you those pills because the pills no longer exist. I flushed them down the toilet."

"Good plan."

"It wouldn't be a plan if you say one fucking word to anyone. It would be a crime."

I sat there and didn't say a word. For once keeping my mouth shut.

"Because if it was a crime, I am fucked. FUCKED. You keep those pills at home in the medicine cabinet; do you understand me?"

"Yes."

"I hope so.

"I find out you have them on you..." Again, he left it open to interpretation.

"You won't."

"I better not. In fact, give me the bottle. The label has my name."

I handed him the bottle that didn't exist without argument, and he rapidly peeled the label off and crumpled it into a ball before flinging it in the garbage can.

"I have no idea how those pills ended up in your pocket and you don't either."

"No clue. I found them on the floor of my bedroom. If anyone is going to go down for this, it's going to be me. Not you. I give you my word Jason."

"You're the happy fucking wanderer, alright?"

"I can manage that."

Twenty minutes later my session was up and leaving Jason's office, I saw Frankie waiting outside his office.

"All good?"

"Yes. Between us."

"Of course!"

"Hopefully this helps us, Hugo. I'm at my fucking wit's end."

"I'm the one not sleeping, Frankie."

"Yeah, well get used to it. I've been walking into fucking walls all week."

I got some lunch at Yellowtail Sushi and headed home right after. I took a pill and a nice hot shower. Changed into some clean clothes then I sat on my couch and watched *A Clockwork Orange* and *The Sopranos* season five, keeping it on even when I was falling in and out of consciousness. It was a long and luxuriant rest. My body craved it and my mind desired it even more. I knew Frankie was experiencing anxiety as well, but I had no idea it was this debilitating. For as long as I had known him, Frankie had never suffered from anxiety or depression the way I had. However, given the circumstances, I was not about to step on anyone's toes and accuse them of anything, least of all my best friend and passionate lover.

I saw my copy of the book *The Amsterdam Experiment,* and I recalled how a friend I used to know wrote it and gave me a copy of it to read. He even had a brief inscription inside of the book flap.

Things are fucking chaos. Let this book I wrote offer you a reason why.
Your friend,
Jesse

And as I held the book against my chest and felt myself deconstructing from the inside out, I was overcome with significant emotional power. As if everything I had ever done had been reduced to nothing. That my life is gone. My family is gone and never truly loved me. They loved the idea of me but they never loved me. I grew up comfortably, but I never felt comfortable here. I didn't know it then, but I fucking knew it now. It's not a welcoming place to be, it's huge, it's beautiful and yet cold and detached, as if a museum of art opened up in my living room and you were never permitted to touch anything. Just standing in the middle and watching from a distance, always at arm's length were my parents, they held me, but I never felt their heart with mine, I never felt a warmth and tangible love there, it was as if I was a bomb and they were looking around me trying to determine which wires to cut. Perhaps I was not the son they had in mind. Maybe since the love I had for them was the wild wind, storms approached and never ceased to devour us.

My friends however, they were my safeguard and when Jesse gave me this book, I was in awe of him. He was the man who could lift anyone's mood off the ground and turn it into silk with his friendship, his warmth, his ray of light in your body, awakening all of those mysterious doorways that were locked, things that have led to disaster and tragedy, a leaf clinging to the tree.

Holding *The Amsterdam Experiment* in my hands, I opened the book up and flipped through the pages and felt myself sobbing and attempting to hold it all back, the cover design alone was stunning, absolutely stunning. The candles and the globe in the corner, and the mirror, and the decorated marble fireplace. It was almost exactly the way I visualized the house in the story to be. A decadent kind of beauty, sexual freedom and power in every crevice and marble fixture. This heady steam, it made me crazy, fucking insane, to know my boy wrote this fucking thing with all he was dealing with. The anxiety and depression; it was unbelievable to me. It's no easy task writing and completing a book. It takes time, effort, diligence, and consistency. But sometimes consistency can be fickle, but if there is a fire in your belly man, you write that fucking book.

And he did. Jesse wrote this fucking book, and I kept reading passages within its pages, and I felt so in love with it. So wonderfully in love with it. The dialogue in the scenes, the moments where my imagination began to take shape and help me see it in my head, the way the walls felt in my hands, the sounds of Isabelle's voice and Hugo's voice. Hugo was my favorite character. He was so wonderfully evil and captivating. He had such a dangerous and unstable energy to him, but you're drawn to him too. An engaging and menacing presence in the story and it was exhilarating. He had me on edge in some scenes, especially when he's speaking to Carlo late at night when the mansion is plunged into darkness and he's sitting by the fire sipping cognac having a cigar and holding a cane in his hand. Eerie.

I remember how Jesse's eyes would light up every time he spoke about it, every time you mentioned books or literature, or poetry and he would come alive. How many people in the world are like that? Few. A shattering few. Jesse was lonely but he also mentioned, "So are all great people who want to write for a living, we live a solitary life," he told me. I couldn't fucking write a book if I tried but he did it, he fucking did it and I was so proud of him. My friends really didn't read but I enjoyed a great story like this one, stories that had my heart racing and blood pumping. I never read books that made me as hard as the one my boy wrote, every scene had a truth to it, and yes, they're wealthy powerful untouchable but I felt a humanity to them as well. Perhaps we're all damaged goods, they just made it look fucking beautiful, darkness is elegant decadent, exquisite. Darkness can be comforting at times; a magician's magic trick is the moon at night.

I remember him writing that in a poem he had published. The guy could fucking take a fucking leaf off a tree and just by a wave of his hand it turned to silk. Perhaps it was the price of all great minds, to be lonely. I was still trying to find my niche, luckily, I had a tribe to help me do it. Anthony, Bobby, Tom they were different, they were and are my boys and guys I trust and respect. And they enjoyed Jesse's company, I remember one time in high school it was our junior year and Jesse was caught cheating on a math test and the funny part was it was mine and I didn't cover my answers I wanted my boy to pass, and we were both in the principal's office. I never understood it, yes okay it was a Catholic school but part of it was being a good Samaritan. This is what I get for being nice.

"So, you decided it was a wise idea to have your friend here cheat off you, Hugo?" the assistant principal said. This woman was a piece of shit. It was rumored she slept with the gym teacher.

"What's the big deal?" I quipped back. "It's math. When the hell are we going to need algebra here or anywhere? I'm going to law school—"

"At this rate, Hugo, I would imagine a trade school would be a better fit for you," she said in response.

Jesse had a look of disgust for this piece of shit. I wanted to bash her fucking skull in. Men in my family made more money as an electrician and plumber than this woman made in ten fucking years. This arrogant cunt.

"What would be wrong with that?"

"If that's something you're passionate about rather than law school, then by all means..."

"They make a lot of money," Jesse chimed in as he sat up in his chair.

I loved this guy; he wasn't afraid of anything. She had her voicemail playing and the tv turned on low, she even had the radio turned on low. It was bizarre. She hovered over us like a dead animal and still decided to reprimand us when she was talking on the phone, listening to the radio, and watching tv. Fascinating. My boy Anthony did Applied Behavior Analysis over the summer one year at A Friendly Face on 1887 Richmond Avenue in Staten Island, New York and made good money, and he told me Tatyana was his BCBA (board certified behavior analyst) and when she was observing for the fifth time in the week, she had her phone on FaceTime, scrolling through her iPad, and talking to another employee at the same time. Old dog, new tricks. What really drove him over the edge was how she was observing him on the cameras claiming he was giving his student a break for forty minutes, that was outrageous. And then had this skanky little wench Kristen tell him he was in there for ten minutes, meanwhile she was some crack whore BCBA STUDENT! A STUDENT! A WHITE TRASH CUNT in other words. He then told me on her way home Tatyana was crossing the street and was killed dead by a drunk driver. The wicked witch was dead. I remember spending over $200 on Saki and sushi, that night Anthony and I were like kings, feasting and celebrating. We even told the waitress his cunt of a boss was killed by a drunk driver. It was a wonderful night.

He would entertain me constantly on the stupid things Tatyana said to the kids and I would fucking die laughing.

"Hello, do you have a hug for Ms. Tatyana?" Who the fuck is she Roman Polanski?

"How was school today?" Who are these kids, fucking Walt Whitman?

"So can you tell me three things you did today?" I can't. She needed ABA. It was unbelievable. Was she always this ignorant of what autism really is? Oh man we were cracking up so badly it was invigorating.

"Last time I checked it was easier to be a Monday morning quarterback. I want you boys to write me a three-paragraph essay about what it takes to show respect. Handed into me by tomorrow."

"Respect?" I said flatly.

"Correct, Hugo. Although if I were you, I would look it up first."

"You don't need to insult us, Ms. Tatyana," Jesse replied. My rage was growing exponentially, a fired time-bomb.

"Oh, see that's where you are wrong, Jesse, because I feel you both would be better served working at some McDonald's counter then having to complete your degrees here in the summer."

We just looked at her with contempt. For once I wanted to control what I said.

"Out. Go back to class," she curtly commanded.

We got up and went outside. Even the secretary looked at her cross-eyed, as she slammed her door behind her.

"She won't last much longer, boys. Just hang in there." The secretary winked at us as we walked out. We glanced back at her.

"Thank you, Ms. Maria," said Jesse.

"Yeah. Thank you is right," I added.

"I can't believe she made that ignorant crack about electricians. They make a shitload of fucking money. She's so awful."

"Yes, she is," Jesse agreed.

We walked slowly back to class.

"You alright man?" I asked Jesse as I put my arm around him.

"Fuck her. She's ignorant, you can't fix ignorance, Hugo."

"No, you can't. You're absolutely right." I flicked a joint out of my pocket. "But we can try."

"Holy fuckin' Jesus... Hugo," Jesse whispered as we admired the intricacy, and with just looking at it, it meant release and freedom.

"Out back behind the bleachers. Nobody will find us."

"Let's light this puppy. GODDAMN!"

"Jesse! Jesus," I laughed, despite Jesse yelling in the hallway.

"Sorry."

I remembered I had a lighter in my jacket pocket. A blue Bic lighter. Always the best. I had started smoking cigarettes when I was a junior in high school, and I always came prepared. Ralph Lauren Cologne and plenty of breath mints.

Luckily neither one of us were caught that day. It was beginning to rain anyway and the pungent odor could have come from anywhere. We nearly finished it as the rain began to really come down.

"There's this story I've been working on. And I can't wait to finish it. I'll share it with you, Hugo."

Three years later he published *The Amsterdam Experiment* after finding his girlfriend hooking up with another guy at a party. A month after that, he had overdosed on Xanax. But I can still remember that day. I'll always remember that day. He was fucking great, a kind and beautiful soul, and it shows in his writing too. Every word has meaning, every scene radiates.

That was my friend Jesse. And I missed him. And I sat, holding this book, reading the chapters, the erotic sex scenes, Hugo, Isabelle. I wished I could just tell him how much I loved his book and how much I loved him for writing it. And how much he made a difference in my life and everyone around him. I couldn't stop turning fucking pages and I kept reading like crazy, it was such a captivating story. I guess in a strange way, I wanted the book to be just mine and to have that memory of Jesse for myself. Not for anyone else. He left something behind for me, perhaps for everyone. And that's immortality to me. That's how you sometimes live forever. A book is a wonderful thing, and it's worth it. It's all worth it in the end.

I took a pen and wrote his name in the book. And a little passage.

Brother.
The world wants to write a book. Half of them don't even fucking finish and the other half doesn't even have the fucking balls to even start it. You're doing fucking amazing. Keep writing. I don't think Heaven has bleachers.
Keep shining on man,
Hugo.

And though I knew he would never be able to read it, I still wanted to write it inside of his book. Maybe I believed that he could read it in a way, from above. Anything is possible right? I closed the book and lay down on my bed. A few minutes later. I fell into a deep sleep, not waking up 'til the next morning.

Part V
The Sound & The Fury

"Life's but a walking shadow,
A poor player that struts and frets his hour upon the stage
And then is heard no more.
It's a tale told by an idiot,
Full of sound and fury, significantly nothing."
—WILLIAM SHAKESPEARE
The Tragedy of Macbeth

"You can easily judge the character of a man
By how he treats those who can do nothing for him."
—JOHANN WOLFGANG VON GOETHE

"The saddest thing about betrayal
Is that it never comes from your enemies."
—ANONYMOUS

CHAPTER 17
Cruel Intentions

If heaven were above me, I was barely touching its hard edges of marble and stone. I was lying on a floor of fire which shifted into an eerie velvet blue and surrounded me. It wasn't hell, perhaps just fucking purgatory. Brimstone is for liberal cunts. Not me. I'm not a fucking charlatan either. Far from it. The man who orders the execution never drops the blade, and I wiped my hands clean long ago.

Terrance was dead. There was nothing we could fucking do about it; ruminating won't bring him back. What? I have to spend the rest of my life being maudlin and full of self-pity? It's a beautiful fucking day. It's a normal thing, death. The trees don't give a fuck when they die, why should humans be specters at the feast? Witnessing our own undoing is a lifelong process, and perhaps I enjoyed the bottom falling out at any time because what the cunt did was beyond reproach. That irresponsible sniveling cunt. I wanted out. I wanted to lose my mind—I just—

"What is it, Hugo?" Jason asked me.

"I don't know. I WANT TO FUCKING STRANGLE THAT FUCKING TWAT!" And I took my cup of coffee off the table and flung it across the room.

We stood there and I felt better. I imagined flinging Deanna in front of a speeding subway train. Jason looked at the chaos on the floor. The coffee soaking and staining his carpet.

"Did that feel good?" he asked me in a flat tone.

"It did, actually," I said and I sat back down. I smoked a joint and opened the window behind me. "Maybe I should do that more often."

Jason started picking up the shattered coffee mug. Placing the pieces one by one gingerly on his desk.

"Alright. I'll do it." I kneeled down on the floor but as I reached over to grab a piece, Jason flung my hand away.

"I need you to go. Now. And when you calm the fuck down, come back."

"Excuse me?"

"Excuse you. What the fuck, man? What is the point anymore?" He placed all the pieces on his desk and it looked like a fractured miniature statue at the MoMa.

"She killed him, she seduced him, she fucking loved him as much as a heartless spoiled envious old bitch can love and she fucking... lied to him. She killed him—"

"That's not the point right now. I'm talking about *you*. I need you to go."

I stood up and faced him. I felt crestfallen. Was he really kicking me out?

"Excuse me, you have no fucking idea what it's been like for me."

"YES, I DO, HUGO!"

"Whoa. Chill the fuck out..."

"NO. *Nothing* I have done has helped you. You don't want to be helped. You want to be reminded of your own immortality."

"My own—I really fucking hope you're not thinking that I don't care?"

"Do you?"

"Yes, I do. I've been depressed. It's why I'm fucking here. And you're calling my bluff. That is ridiculous! That is fucking absurd! Maybe I *should* leave."

"Well, it's your call, but don't expect to just get over this."

"I'm trying to make things better for me! He didn't deserve this!!! He was my love; he was fucking wounded, and I didn't help him either!"

"I know you didn't."

"Then what is it? What?"

"You're trying to cover it up and I don't know if I can be involved."

"I'm not trying to incriminate you here."

"I already feel as if I am. It's a tragedy what happened, Hugo. I feel terrible. I do. I may not be the warmest guy, but I think I understand your pain and loneliness, what Deanna did was unspeakable. I personally would feel better if we turned her in."

I sat down on the couch. "So, would I. But retaliation would beget retaliation, and I would be fucked. So would my friends. That would fucking ruin everything for me. Frankie knows but I have his trust. And I need yours too, Jason. "

"What am I supposed to do?"

"I just need your trust. No more, no less."

We stood there in Jason's office and his silence, his chosen reticence, was becoming increasingly deafening. He took a few deep breaths, made his way back to his desk, staring indifferently at the stack of pieces from the flung coffee cup and finally looked straight at me. In the depths I could see us making love forever and weekend getaways in France, or Spain, or Italy, anywhere in the world, where we could lose ourselves, where we could be as one with everything. Where nothing would manage to break my spirit, where perhaps the wound would heal itself, would close up inside of me.

We could make a break for it. We could leave. Nobody would have to know, nobody would ever know. Not Frankie, not my friends, not my family, nobody, especially not our very own Lady Macbeth over there, that crumbling psychopath. All the rage would eventually evaporate like a spring rain. We could take on different identities, we could become different people, a different life, different dreams. Or maybe there would be no dreams, no acting, no life on the fringes, no sadness, or looking over our shoulders, everything would eventually become nothing. And we could live; we could move to Italy and live. Why not? Is there anything left for us here?

As I thought about all of this, I began to believe it could be a possible exit strategy for the both of us. I looked at Jason, who was writing something on his MacBook, and I took a deep breath again.

"We could leave here, Jason; we could just lam it." The words came out of me in a rush and I saw the inevitability of them taking shape.

"Hugo, how the fuck could you ask me to do that? I can't leave here. I have a life. I have patients."

"Well, you just tell them Christmas came early this year."

"Hugo, it doesn't work like that. I have patients who are suicidal."

"And it's not going to do them any good if you're here or not anyway."

"What does that mean?"

"Jason, I'm just... it's not going to change anything. You did mention to me how you wanted out."

"I think you're angry and I understand why, Hugo. Deanna."

"Deanna is a cunt, a sneaky manipulative bitch."

"I know she is."

"Trust me, she'll get what's coming to her."

"How do you mean?"

"You'll see."

"Is it something I should worry about?"

"See, this is the visceral reaction I was hoping for..."

"I can't do it, Hugo. I can't. I get it with our relationship but... I would be implicated."

"Why don't you trust me?"

"I do trust you." He walked up to me and laid a passionate kiss on my mouth. I felt all of the dark negative energy releasing itself from my bones. He had a seductive energy to him and after all the women and especially men I had been with, he was the most potent of all. Not even the world's leading love machine Detective Frankie, could even come close. Or maybe he could.

"Fucking Deanna, she caused all this that..."

"I think she needs more therapy than you do."

"She needs fucking electroshock therapy... fucking Faye Dunaway."

"So, what are you going to do now?"

"Can I blow you?"

"Do you really need to ask?"

I went down on Jason. And I put in some extra effort to really make him explode. And he did ten minutes later.

"Christ Hugo, well done. Well fucking done. It's been a while... Fuck, where did you learn that tongue trick?"

"Choate. Consider it a tip."

"Fucking retainer."

"You taste so good, so sweet."

"For you. Only for you. Goddamn." He zipped himself and sat there still in his heavenly state of euphoria.

"So... what about leaving? Just leaving it all behind?" I tried again.

"Let me think about it. I just don't want to make anything worse for you."

"I know you don't. It's okay. It'll all be okay. I'm sorry about the coffee cup."

Jason waved it off. "Be careful, Hugo."

I walked out of Jason's office without looking back. I did two small bumps of pure white cocaine and drove off into the misty afternoon. I never considered myself to be a great fan of coke, but I know those long nights spent at the clubs in Manhattan in high school after drinking all that vodka and cranberry, it definitely helped to straighten me the fuck out for the journey home. I turned on some Biggie on my phone and as it blasted through the speakers, the light mist that overcame the afternoon quickly switched to heavy rain. The wind blew its rage, and the rain came down in buckets. A storm we needed perhaps but I think calmly in the rain, it reminded me of Shakespeare, how a thunderstorm or hurricane can wash away all of our evil deeds. We all do bad things, don't we?

I—

My phone blared, cutting off the beginning of "Hypnotize," flashing the name I was dreading all fucking month.

"What the fuck do you want?" I pulled over and the heavy rain continued to invade the earth.

"To talk."

"No shit."

"Hugo, please. It's serious."

"Serious as in giving a guy drugs..."

"Hugo—"

"No, I want to know. You've piqued my curiosity."

"I've peaked more than that with you, Hugo."

"You do that with all the guys..."

"Not as many as you think."

"Yeah, right okay..."

I lit a cigarette. Cocaine always made me want a cigarette. And I was on my way up now.

"Why are you like this?"

I exhaled the smoke out the window. She made me want to drive my car off the Verrazano sometimes.

"God doesn't make mistakes."

"Are you smoking?"

"Oh Jesus, Deanna...Oh yeah. Talk down to me, oh god, I love it. I'm gonna... I'm gonna."

"Hugo..."

"Who's your daddy, huh? Who's your daddy." I waited a minute, took another drag off my cigarette, and smiled to myself.

"You're a real asshole you know that..."

"Oh no sweetheart, you take home the gold remember."

"Right, you're just the runner up."

"It was a fellatio competition."

"And yet you loved every minute of it."

"Well, when you work hard..."

"You weren't as hard as I liked."

"Zucchinis. You should be used to them by now."

"Frankie's now..."

"Good, I don't give a fuck. Enjoy it. He's demanding though."

"Oh, I know he is."

"Yeah, I figured you did."

We remained on the phone without saying a word to each other. I continued to smoke, and the cocaine rush was hitting me now. Nice and pure. Perhaps the only innocent feeling I had left.

"Can't we talk?"

"So, it's now it's my fault?"

"No."

"Do you have any idea what you fucking did!?" I grabbed my phone and shouted into the speaker.

"I didn't do anything!!"

"YES, YOU DID, YOU CUNT!" I screamed into my phone. I hung up and slammed it down on the passenger seat. I rubbed my forehead, took another drag off my lingering cigarette, and flung it into the rain.

Deanna's fucking stubborn refusal to see the reality of her actions is what makes this entire thing fucking unbearable. It was worse than what she did! It was worse! It's like this cold-hearted selfish cunt is IMPERVIOUS to feeling anything! NO GUILT NO EMOTION. She's a sociopath!!! If I made a deal with the devil, if I sold my soul to him in exchange for making her get hit by a car and die I would. Perhaps I should. It's not hard. Evil conniving bitch. How could she?! Terrance had a chance; he just needed to get himself help. I needed help to help him cope, I was weak!

"No, you're not. But she is." Frankie was next to me in bed. It was still daylight we had the shades down and the air conditioner on high.

"Then what the fuck are we waiting for?"

"Hugo, you need to calm down. I can't just arrest her. I need proof, incontrovertible evidence that she did this! A trail of some kind..."

"That's the whole fucking problem. I don't have a trail. I just have a feeling. Maybe it wasn't really what happened on prom night. This has been happening for a while, Frankie. Longer than I thought."

"It doesn't mean you're to blame. I'm his brother, or was, and I couldn't help him. He slipped through everyone's grasp."

"Just because you couldn't help him, Frankie, it doesn't negate the fact that someone could. Not for nothing, but you were there from the beginning, I just found him hot at first and that's where it all began, my sexual reawakening. Maybe nobody loved him the way I did."

Frankie sat up and put his arms around his legs and looked at me. His eyes were magnetic and possessed a curious anger that I found to be rather eerie.

"You're fucking stupid if you think I didn't love my brother. Younger brother and granted yeah, he needed more help than I could give, but what about me!? What about me?"

"What about you?"

"He died. He killed himself. And..."

"And if it wasn't for Deanna and—"

"And what?"

"Nothing."

"No. What, Hugo?"

"I need a shower."

"I wasn't his fucking lynchpin, Hugo!!!"

"No. You were an ambitious cop."

"Yeah, fuck you."

"I thought you just did." Slamming the door hard, I turned on the music on my phone and got the shower running. I closed the shower curtain and let myself burn to death under the stifling hot water. My respite was short lived because two minutes later he stormed in and nearly ripped the fucking shower curtain.

"Round two now?"

Frankie cracked me hard in the face and my head hit the wall. I was dazed and disorientated for a good minute and a half. Everything was fuzzy and blurred and I nearly slipped in the shower. He stood there, a cold detached look on his face.

Still, he kneeled down and put his hand on my head, but I smacked it away and stood up. Then he did the same.

"What the fuck are you doing?" I asked; my world had just come crashing down.

"I loved Terrance. I fucking loved him," Frankie whispered in his deadpan voice. He stood there unmoved by what he did, which only enraged me more.

"Is that it?"

"Yeah."

"Then get the fuck out of my house and never come back."

I didn't hear him leave the bathroom but I heard the front door slam violently behind him. And all that was left was what had just happened. My face stung. And I stood in the shower, unable to move. Just letting the hot water suck me up in a hazy cloud of steam.

An hour later, I woke up from a bizarre dream and felt my face which was swollen black and blue. Looking in the mirror I saw the damage Frankie did, and just how deeply it was embedded in my memory, how quickly it made itself at home in my bones. I was still attempting to figure out why he did what he did, but I remembered quite clearly what people have told me about Frankie. You never knew when he was going to snap and lose his shit completely. He went from calm and charismatic to a violent fucking psychopath at the turn of a dime. I'd seen him fly off the handle over the simplest shit but then he was a detective, a corrupted one, but a detective, nevertheless. And I understood the pathology behind it. He was dealing with lowlifes constantly, drug addicts, pedophiles, serial killers, and the like. There was no break. There was no sense of ultimate release for him, and he could have anyone he fucking wanted.

The mark on my face was nearly swelling to look like a fucking plum. He really decked my hard. He had never hit me before. And what bothered me was how much of a fucking moron I was for not retaliating. I know hitting a cop is a felony, but my rage was triggered, being bullied in high school and then one day, I didn't sleep very well the night before and I had a huge fight with my mother for not being able to pick me up from school because she had a meeting in the city. Well, I took the bus in and there was this bully, this one motherfucking prick named Matt. We were never friends, not by a longshot, but I dealt with him a few times. He had sold me weed, mushrooms, cigarettes, anything. For a while it seemed fine, but he would bully me. Then when I came into school that morning, he made some ignorant crack about my haircut and the shirt I was wearing. And after everything, I snapped. I went ape shit on this fucking guy. Bloody nose, broken jaw. I was suspended for a week. My fucking golden ticket out of that shit-hole school. My parents left for Europe. I had the world by the balls.

I was grateful for the opportunity; he gave me a chance to redeem myself. And it felt great. And then to my surprise, everyone who was friends with Matt couldn't believe he was beaten so badly and so violently. They stopped hanging out with him. The irony of it all. Fucking jerkoff. All bluster; there was nothing behind the mask. Just another vapid doorway to nowhere. All he did was intimidate and lie to get what he wanted, textbook delusional narcissist.

Well, luckily for him, he got what he fucking deserved that day. Spoiled little shit that he was. And as the cherry on top of the cake, his on-and-off girlfriend, Tiffany, and I went to dinner and a movie, *Cruel Intentions* to be exact. Suffice it to say, she was so turned on by Ryan Phillippe that she got on her knees and blew me, I was turned on by Gellar and Phillippe too. She swallowed that protein shake like a pro, wiping her lips with the tip of my t-shirt, which I never washed. Fucking beautiful white gold for me to treasure forever.

As a sidenote for *Cruel Intentions,* it's more of a question, a reasonable question... why couldn't we see Phillippe's cock? Why not. Just one fucking time man, Jesus. We can see pussy in *Eyes Wide Shut* but god forbid they show a nice dick? I mean it's different now, we have OnlyFans. But now and then it does bother me. I just have to use my imagination, which is fine too, because it can be as big as I fucking want it to be or medium-sized, too. I don't want to give him too much credit; he's not Shemar Moore or anything but he is gorgeous. I saw *Eyes Wide Shut* in theaters too, absolutely unforgettable experience, shattering. Kubrick's final masterpiece. Impeccable film. Great fucking night too.

Things end so quickly. And I could still hear the sound of Terrance's body hitting the car, being flung in the air, the sickening sound of it landing in the street. Over and over the sound and the fury of that night played in my head in an endless loop. It wouldn't stop. Sometimes it went away, sometimes it was nothing but that sound and I'd wake up in a cold sweat, drenched in my own crumbling guilt. I wish I had just spoken up, told the cops that it was an accident, and that it was all me, but I had to listen to my friends I had to listen to Anthony, Tom, and Bobby and go along with it, and now it's eroding me and I'm sure them.

From what I had been hearing from Frankie, Anthony was crumbling away in depression, Tom had been having anxiety attacks and losing sleep at night, Tom had been on a downward spiral for years, dabbling in cocaine to deal with the weight of that harrowing night. I suppose we had grown apart over the years and had never been able to put the pieces back together. I wanted to cry. To just lay down in my bed under the covers and cry it all out, maybe find some fucking clarity but it was not forthcoming. Perhaps I was bound upon a wheel of fire, perhaps that was my hell.

I took two Xanax pills, took a long hot shower, got into my warm bed, I saw a few messages on my phone and put my phone on silent. I didn't speak for the rest of the night and slept away the wilting hours. I wanted to miss it all; I wanted life to pass me right by.

CHAPTER 18
The Life & Times of Danny Ether

I stared at the wall in my room hoping a fucking UFO would come and whisk me away to another fucking galaxy, but all that happened was a blurred representation of alternate reality. Out of joint with the rest of the world and the world behind it. Downward spirals. Nothing interested me anymore. I saw a text from Anthony, and I wondered whether or not I should respond and I did. I told him to come to my place and we could smoke all day and not go out, not be with anyone, just us. It was better that way, less aggravation. Because the last fucking thing I wanted to do was talk to people, especially Frankie, Deanna, or even Jason.

I saw the nice mark Frankie left on my face and I laughed to myself. It was the first fucking time he decked me and of course it was right in the face. I almost had to admire him. Falling in the shower was a deft touch, however.

Round two now? I can't control my fucking mouth sometimes. Maybe I *was* fucking asking for it. I went downstairs and it was a bright beautiful morning. I sat outside with my coffee, smoking like a maniac, and enjoying the quiet, the wonderful peaceful quiet. The birds were chirping. I felt a relief.

But I recognized the dark patterns inside of me that were making themselves known to me. My coffee tasted especially good this morning too, Maria took care of me in more ways than my parents ever could. She always looked out for me, and she was a blessing every day she was here, working her fingers to the bone for very little in return.

Anthony came a few hours later and brought breakfast with him, plenty of pre-rolls. some mushrooms, and his own cracked heart. His soul was wounded; his face was drawn, and he hadn't touched a thing. I was smoking steadily and looking out towards the pool. I looked over at Anthony who was laying on the lounge chair and he appeared to look older since the last time I saw him; time was a cruel, tricky motherfucker.

"I've been losing sleep, Hugo."

"I've noticed you look drained, brother."

"Yeah, it's just I can't live with this anymore. I just can't do it."

"It's eroding all of us man, it's not doing us any good."

"You said Frankie was going to take care of it."

"He knows it was a suicide, but there is the issue of Terrance being shoved, and the fight..."

"What?"

"There was more to that night; I've been piecing it together. Terrance kept antagonizing all of us and Deanna. He wanted to piss her off so she would shove him and since he's such a fucking psychopath anyway, flying off the handle isn't uncommon. But it was that last split second, it's a split second but I think I recognized the car that hit him. I just have no fucking idea who was driving."

"What kind of car?"

"It looked like a BMW, black with grey or maybe a tan interior. Had that logo piece on the edge of the hood. I seem to remember Frankie owning a car like that..."

"No fucking way. You—"

"I don't know. But it scares the shit out of me because the last thing I want to do is accuse him."

"What's up with your face?"

"Take a wild fucking guess..."

"Fuck. What happened?"

"He flipped out, that's what fucking happened, and this... sudden realization. First, he admits to being Terrance's brother, now this, I can't keep up. I just can't... was he working with Deanna? Did they both fucking plan this? She gives him fucking drugs and Frankie—"

"It makes sense."

"Oh, Jesus this is SO FUCKED UP! How is everyone else handling it?"

"Not very well. Tom called me last night in hysterics, been having nightmares like the rest of us. How are you?"

"At the end of my rope, man. Wish none of this happened, Terrance was fucked up. He was troubled. We fell apart as a couple, and Deanna, after everything that went down between the three of us bro, and Frankie too."

"You guys really had a turbulent time with it all huh?"

"Too much sex and drugs. We were all fucked. All four of us."

"I hear you. That wasn't the first time for Deanna, I can tell you that." Anthony smoked some of my pre-roll and lay back in the lounge chair. "She is dangerous, Hugo. Just stay away from her."

"What do you mean it 'wasn't the first time'?"

"You know what? Maybe I *will* have one of these. I'm going to need it."

He took a pre-roll from the bag and lit it. He exhaled slowly and I was waiting on pins and needles for what he was going to tell me about Deanna.

"I have to say it feels nice to smoke out here, been fucking miserable for so long, man."

"Anthony, what about Deanna?"

"She's really troubled."

"Oh yeah? Fucking girl interrupted over there," I said in such a flat tone Anthony paused a minute to digest my words. He shot me a look and went about smoking his pre-roll.

"Do you remember Danny Ether? He was Benjamin Ether's cousin?"

"Oh yeah for sure. He got us into Limelight in high school."

"Yes, he gave us those MDMA capsules."

"Such a sick night."

"Well, he also knew Deanna through us." Anthony flicked his pre-roll into the ashtray on the table. "And she gave him drugs too. He was already addicted to heroin, but he used every now and then. It wasn't a daily fix with him. He was smart, but so wounded. And they had a thing I think for a little while and it got worse between them. Danny could be a bit of a whirlwind sometimes and Deanna was already..."

"A backstabbing slut...?"

"Yes."

"I've been blind through this whole thing, Tony; I can't help but think I was the reason why it all went down that night the way it did. "

"I think it was all of us, not just you, trust me. It happened and it was unfortunate, I remember Danny telling me so much about Deanna. She was abused by her father, and then her father died when she was in high school."

"Abused how?"

Anthony took another leisurely pull from the pre-rolled joint and exhaled quickly. Handing it to me, I did the same and wanted to lose myself in the smoky clouds before me. The sound Terrance made when he made bodily contact with the car resounded in my mind over and over, an unending succession of terror and pain that played in the far corners of my memory like some demonic set of drums.

"I think emotionally. He was a full-blown fucking alcoholic, and her mother was not much help either. Constantly shopping and completely self-absorbed. She was fucking the landscaper."

"I should have cut their grass that summer..."

"She would have loved you long time."

"Tell me about it."

We sat there in the sunshine. I needed release, I needed to leave this place and possibly begin a new life.

"Your phone is ringing, Hugo," Anthony mumbled.

To my dismay, it was Frankie. I picked up after a minute and some heavy breathing.

"Yeah?

"Hugo. We need to talk."

"What do you want, Frankie?"

"Look, I know I lost it the other day; I apologize. But we really do need to talk."

"About what?"

"I can't say over the phone. Can you meet somewhere?"

"Let's head to Panini and get something to eat. I'll take an Uber." We hung up.

"I have to go, brother. Stay here. I'll be back later."

"All good?"

"I hope so," I replied. "I really fucking hope so."

"We'd like two glasses of chianti please. And some bruschetta to share," Frankie told the waitress at Panini. It was crowded tonight; I think Frankie was counting on that.

"Sure."

"I've been wanting to tell you for a long time that I think I know who hit Terrance on that night. Someone tipped me off, and they're willing to help us."

"Who?"

"I don't want to burn my sources, Hugo. This person wishes

to remain anonymous."

"I see. Well, what kind of car was it?"

"2019 black BMW, with a dark tan interior. It had a slight dent just under the right headlight. And a bigger one on the hood."

As Frankie described the car to me, I was dumbfounded with the sound Terrance made when he was hit by the car, that kind of thundering explosion of pain and shock that ran like a locomotive sickness through all of us. The sound seemed to grow exponentially the last few years, and with it the lightning crack of silence I heard. Silence that was deafening. The more I attempted to shut the memory out of my tormented brain, the stronger it became. I was a sitting duck.

The waitress brought us our drinks and food. Frankie winked at her. She smiled and left to attend to another table at the other end of the restaurant.

"What was that wink about, you sexy love machine?"

"I'll show you what a love machine really is..."

"And you won't work for anybody but me..."

"Yeah, sure."

"I want to put this all behind me. I want this to end. I've been through enough, and I'm sure you have too, Hugo."

"I have."

I sipped my wine and picked at the bruschetta. Frankie did the same. It was a strange night, and I had a headache now, too. It was as though as I was slipping down a rabbit hole and there was nothing below my dangling feet. It was a dark plunge through an abysmal nightmare. My stomach was in a knot and all I wanted was a cigarette maybe some coke and a night in bed with Frankie for the hundredth time in my life.

"You alright?"

"Yeah." I sipped my wine again and whatever blue demon I had awoken inside my soul was now resting. I took a few deep breaths and closed my eyes. I didn't say anything for a few minutes as Frankie told me everything he knew about the car.

"Would your friends know anything? Any details?"

"Everything is a blur, I'm not sure they would. We were so drunk that night and flying on drugs. It was a powder keg from what I remember. I wish I had seen it coming sooner, but nobody suspected anything until it was too late. Horrible."

"None of us wanted anything like that to happen, Hugo, but it did. I'm not implying that you were the culprit. My brother was fucked up. He was on drugs, abusing alcohol, in and out of rehab, until it all became too much for any of us to handle."

"Yeah. You told me that. Twice."

When we finish, he paid for our meal and drinks. And then we fucked in Frankie's car.

"This smoke feels so nice," I whispered as Frankie was putting his pants back on.

Walking porn. I mentioned that before, right?

"Always after we fuck right?"

I didn't respond. I just looked out the window, hoping for a giant asteroid to collide with earth. I saw the giant white moon in the velvet black sky, no noticeable signs of stars, although I'd been walking into walls all fucking week.

"Look baby, it'll be okay. I know it will be okay. We just have to... find some way to move on from this. I know it's a tragedy, and I also know how much you loved my brother too."

"I know."

"He was not exactly the nicest person in the world. I understand that. Just fine. He was a bully. I told you how he batted me for being bi...yet. So was he."

"And me." I took a drag off my cigarette before handing it to Frankie who slowly took a heavy drag and exhaled a dizzying cloud of pain into the open night air.

"His pain stretched deeper than anyone could've imagined. Poor fucking guy."

We didn't speak for the duration of our time together, and the drive home we only plated music. "Formant" by Office Gossip. This beat stretched into my bones and repaired the wiring. Completely numb.

When I got home, I thought of Danny Ether again. A nihilistic chill overcame me as I stepped into the vacant hallway. It was something out of Citizen fucking Kane, a haunting sense of wide-open castle-like hallways and bedrooms, a massive underground pool with little to no lights, an abandoned tennis court in the yard. And when I stood there, remembering how while in high school I did the exact same fucking thing because my family was in Italy while I stayed here and got high with my friends watching Scorsese and Kubrick all week because it was fucking snowing nonstop. I suppose it's meant to be ironic, a broken and lost motherfucker like me coming home every day to this, and yet so unhappy... that's a cliché. But does that make it any less true?

It was the first time I had experimented with harder drugs, MDMA, mushrooms, anything. But one night we had tried crystal meth. Just once. And it was as if we were on the moon looking down through a telescope and seeing the planet.

You're out of the woods
You're out of the dark
You're out of the night
Step into the sun
Step into the light
March up to that gate
And bit it open. Open.

That song played on the tv when we were watching *The Wizard of Oz* on acid and the snow looked as though it had invaded our fucking house, and the potent sun the way the fucking sun shone through the fucking window, man. Acid. We were doing fucking acid bro, it was fucking... I can't even explain what that shit was like. It is absolutely fucking devastating. I think the word. Devastating. And then I had a bit of a meltdown because I was fucking flipping out because we had put on *2001: A Space Odyssey* and the scene where Dave is deprogramming HAL and the chilling decomposition of his voice got to me, it got under my skin for some reason, and then my entire house was black, just plunged into darkness as the film then descends into space and Jupiter... fucking stargate sequence. I was crying, I was... crying. Thank god for my friends, things went a little south suffice it to say.

"Hugo... Hugo. It's alright man, it's alright. Take a deep breath. It's... it's all good. It's just a movie, you know. It's just a movie. Fucking Kubrick, it's a fucking movie." It felt as if the voice, were a disembodied entity floating around me and from the back of me, a kind of alarming disorientation coursed through my frozen blood, and I could not see straight, all these multidimensional octagonal shapes kept moving in and out of themselves.

"I know. I—I – I don't know what's... what's happening. I just—"

"Bro..." Anthony this time. Or the aliens. I was never sure.

"Nothing. It's all good."

"Danny?" I was shaking, convulsing, laying on the nice marble floor of my kitchen, and sobbing like crazy. And the kitchen was now under water, everything was shimmering and spinning, and revolving, and morphing in and out, out and in.

As if I was inside a jellyfish floating in the fucking Atlantic Ocean and that jellyfish is struck by lightning and a space time continuum takes over. That was acid. That is the best and most concise way for me to explain it. It definitely had its charms. After the movie, we went outside and sat on the chairs around the pool that were now submerged in snow. And for a good hour, we were bundled up and just staring at the falling snow.

"See it's snowing bro... fucking planet is covered in fucking snow. Covered."

"This white crystal..."

"We did that already."

"I know."

"Yo, that was fun."

"Scary."

"Yeah, it was."

"Fucking rocked, no?"

"Yeah."

"Who in high school can fucking say they did crystal and acid on different nights in one week."

"Fucking nobody."

"Not a chance."

"Not even fucking close."

"It's how we love each other, right? I mean we love each other..."

"We do. We don't show it but we fucking do."

"I love you both very much. Couldn't be happier."

"Agreed. And Tom."

"Bobby and Ether."

"Yeah of course. "

"You said Danny and Ether."

"I know."

"No, it's all good... I feel like different people."

"See."

"I understand it now. How there are so many versions of you and me out there, of everyone."

"Being the gods who made us bro."

"Amen. Fucking amen."

We all sounded as if we were locked inside a vast and beautiful elevator that went up into the clouds and showed you rooms with multiple colors and different music in each room. Several different dimensions existed on this one plain of consciousness.

It was me, Danny, and Anthony. Tom and Bobby were staring off into space while the screen was black, while "Blue Danube Waltz" played delightfully over the speakers. The music had taken them away, flying them towards Jupiter and back again, in a graceful *Fear and Loathing* meets *The Big Lebowski* kind of way. Metaphysical in a way. The need to escape, to surrender to nature's turbulence. Life is turbulent. It all feels as if it's a tornado, devouring all in its path. The way life is meant to be lived.

In the Ether... that was the name of the book Danny gave me to read. His cousin wrote it, and to me it was more than just a book of poetry. It was a mind fuck, a surreal almost incendiary mind fuck about addiction, anger, pain, the darkness. I devoured it in one sitting. I started it in the morning after a horrible night with this girl I met at a party. She was a frosty cunt and she made me feel inferior for some reason, couldn't even try to fuck her because I would freeze to death. But I digress,

Men are just easier, bro.

And it just struck a real tough and bad chord in me. And I don't mean "bad" as in it pissed me off. It just woke me the fuck up. I wish I could remember some of the lines to it, but I can't. I know I wrote them down somewhere. It was a visceral reading experience for me, it was poetry you could feel in your heart, your bones, you became afflicted by the renegade nature of it, it was so powerful. I don't remember reading poetry as moving before or since *In the Ether.* I know I had a copy of it; I had moved with my family from Brooklyn to Staten Island and I lost it. I wasn't sure if I had left it at the old house in the bookcase in my room, or it just got lost in the shuffle. I'm sure I will find it.

I wish I had a second copy, because I could really use it. Danny was the best, just a fine man, loads of integrity, sincere and personable, he was wounded but those wounds didn't bleed on everyone else, he would give you the coat off his back. I remember, this girl Jessica in high school her boyfriend dumped her for no good fucking reason, and he was taking her to the prom. She was furious and hurt and decided not to come with us. When Danny got wind of what happened, he got himself a tux got dressed went to her house and told her "We are going to the prom, put your dress on." She smiled beaming from ear to ear and at the end of the night she blew him in the limo to the club. Like magic.

I do remember one called *Candlelight Euphoria* and the last two lines of the poem go:

"We are her gospel
We are her euphoria"
-Benjamin Ether

And nearly falling down on the floor and reading the book over and over again, different poems at different moments. What he did was like Mozart. Ben finished his requiem, however. And I marveled at his talent. This fucking gift he had. I could never come close, I liked to write poetry, but I never put my time into it. Benjamin and Danny *were* poetry.

They were a part of me. They gave everyone around them wisdom, insight, confidence. People like that are rare gems indeed. They had gifts and they fucking gave everyone around them something you never find anywhere else. There is pain and cruelty everywhere, men and women alike, it's an inevitable part of life, the brutality of it. The massacre. The horror. They provided a key in the imprisoned life my friends and I lived. We had everything we could ever need or want, and when we met Danny and his cousin Ben, it all changed somehow. We woke the fuck up.

Before Danny passed away, he told me to be careful around Deanna, to not trust her and to just tread carefully. I told him that I would, that I wasn't her biggest fan either, but things happened, and we wound up having that brief fling. I never knew someone so hateful and so broken in my fucking life, she was horrible. A bottomless black hole.

"Deanna, is bad news Hugo. Stay away from her."

"I know man, I'm not a fucking idiot."

"Sometimes I wonder, Hugo..."

"So do I." I didn't quip back too frequently with Danny, he was different from me, and when he spoke, I listened. But I wasn't then. I was just placating him. Hindsight is always twenty-twenty.

I think we all looked up to him, he wasn't like us he was different, he was a loner, but we respected him enough to have him by our side. Even when things were out of control during classes, or in the auditorium for some fucking movie showing or the lunchroom or the school yard, something was always done about it.

Let the water wash over you
Wash it all over you
Swim to the ocean floor
So that we can begin again
Wash away all our sin
Crash to the other shore

"Swim" by Madonna had this unbelievable way of making me feel better again. Every time I was home, I would listen to it in my headphones, smoking a joint outside. It was such a poetic song, and it filled my heart with such love and light, it made me feel as if the weight of my life was once and for all removed. I loved and greatly admire music and artists, anything that involves creation, building from within your soul is a wonderful and cherished gift, a precious commodity indeed. I remembered Danny introducing me to new music constantly, everything from Tupac to Red Hot Chili Peppers, to Biggie and Radiohead, Wu-Tang, everything under the fucking sun. And I was wonderfully, gloriously stoned. Danny had everything you could ever need and we needed it; there was little to no warmth in our lives before we met Danny Ether.

One day when I was a junior, I was struggling. My grades were slipping, my parents were off in China, I had broken up with my girlfriend, I wasn't sleeping, I felt as if things were tumbling down on me. Ether approached me in the lunchroom, sat down at my table, and asked how I was feeling.

"Not too good, man. I feel like I'm fucking losing it or something." I gave this nervous laugh and he looked at me with concern in his eyes.

"Listen to me, why don't we just leave after lunch, sneak out, rent a movie, get obliterated and I mean fucking *obliterated* with some Modelo beers and a nice big fat joint? You down with that, bro?"

Twenty minutes later, we had ditched that fucking prison.

"I find what helps me when I'm feeling this way man, is a good fucking horror movie something that will scare the shit out of me, for some reason I forget why I was feeling down in the first place. I also have some cocaine at home; we can do that, too."

"Let's do that first, watch the fucking movie, get stoned later on."

"Good idea."

We took a cab to Blockbuster; we rented *Angel Heart* and

we went to Danny's house. His parents were away too, I forgot where, but we had the pad to ourselves. We did a couple of lines of pure white cocaine, and I was already feeling my anxiety begin to organically dissipate. We turned on the movie, finished our dinner, and my cocaine high was at its highest peak. I felt as if I were floating almost on the couch, and that movie... Jesus Christ. That movie was fucking scary! I never felt so drawn in by something, it seemed to possess this unnerving air of reality, as if I were being sucked in. I think it was DeNiro as Cypher that pushed it over the edge for me.

"What do you think so far?"

"Jesus Danny..."

"Fucking movie is no joke, right?"

We both laughed so hard, most likely a knee-jerk reaction to the movie itself that triggered our unstoppable laughter.

"I fucking can't believe how fucked up this movie is, man."

"Louis Cypher." I uttered to myself. We watched the rest of the movie in silence, not moving a muscle and since my cocaine jolt was so potent, I could also hear all the noises in the apartment, all the tiny unnoticeable clicks and movements of the home, I was so fucking scared, I never told Danny that either.

"FUCK NO!! He was—"

"Yep! He was Johnny Favorite!"

"NO FUCKING WAY, MAN!"

Let me just say that the ending to that movie, where Cypher's true identity is revealed, was terrifying. Him sitting there quietly, calmly, holding the staff in his hand, I felt so freaked out. When the movie ended, we sat there. I was processing the horror that seemed to fill my brain and Danny was right, I did forget about my anxiety. It was gone.

"How do you feel, Hugo?"

"I feel... pretty fucking great, brother. First time in a long time, things have just been hard and strange for me, but I'm actually taking a dump in my pants because that was one scary fucking movie."

Danny couldn't stop laughing.

"I'm fucking serious, I may take another one when I get home, I'm turning on every fucking light in my house, and setting the fucking alarm... fucking DeNiro! I can't!"

"See, what did I tell you? It works wonders with anxiety, right?"

"Dude, I can't believe it. It's like horror movies are good for you in a sense."

"I know. It's what I watch when I'm going through things or just not myself, I understand everything you spoke about at school bro. I get that way; it can be lonely it's a horrible feeling. But for some reason, some cocaine or some horror just wipe it all away."

"Sometimes all we need is a fucking jolt to our system..."

"For sure. How's the cocaine treating you?"

"Really well, actually, I get it wholesale. It's top tier, right?"

"Yeah, brother really nice energy inside of me, Danny. I'm glad we did this."

We both split a cigarette outside in the yard, I always needed to smoke when I did a large quantity of cocaine. We spoke about school and other things, my on-and-off girlfriend, our families, life in general, and before we both knew it, it was close to eleven at night.

"Fucking great night, Danny, thank you for this, bro."

"Anytime, you know that." His voice had a genuine love inside of it, a light that was seldom seen in anyone else. His eyes were magnetic too, almost hooded eyes. They possessed a real sense of having lived through a great deal of hardship, of tragedy. He was the kind of guy who would give you the coat off his back whenever you needed it.

We said our goodbyes for the night, and I headed home, fucking stoned and relieved of my anxiety. It had evaporated like a fine mist.

The next day, I stayed home from school. Fuck that place. Fuck it all man. I needed rest, silence, and contemplation. Quiet days at home with nobody around me. All I wanted to do was to sit outside and not think. Just flow, just live. Just fucking live. That was Danny's point. And I was following his advice entirely. I was fed up with making fucking allowances for people all the fucking time, people know exactly what the fuck they're doing. Let's call a spade a fucking spade. Pieces of shit, those fucking selfish miserable cunts.

I do thank God for my friends the ones who have been there for me since the beginning. Anthony, Bobby, Tom, and Danny. He had been dragged through the ringer more times than he cared to think about. However, I was the closest friend he had out of the four of us, and I think he knew that too. And we also were friends with his cousin, Benny, another fucking awesome human being, his poetry hit my bones like shattered glass. I bled from within. His words... his words are fucking daggers. These fucking ice pics. And he was a warm guy, had his view, very cool view of humanity he loved animals and movies and music and New York, he had moved to Cali and I hadn't spoken to him since.

One day I will find his book of poetry, *In the Ether,* and his words will heal me from within. Cauterizing the demons with fire, silencing them forever.

In the middle of the night, around 3am, I had awoken from this vivid and disturbing dream and noticed a message on the answering machine. At first it was static and then I listened a little more clearly.

"Yeah... Hugo. Call me back, it's Danny. I'm just having a hard time right now." And he had hung up. I had no clue he even called, and then the answering machine said it was around midnight when he'd called. Not that long after I'd left his house. He had never called me so late before. I felt as if something had to be wrong. I called him back but there was no answer. I tried a couple more times. My anxiety was awake and I began to panic.

I was still feeling mildly stoned from the night before and all the cocaine we snorted. As I was driving to his house listening to Perry Como's "Sunrise, Sunset" my heart was palpitating uncontrollably, and my palms were sweaty as I walked the one mile to his house. And after fifteen minutes I arrived at his house and walked up the stairway to his front door. I rang the doorbell repeatedly abut there was no answer.

"Danny! Danny! It's me: Hugo... answer the door!" I shouted in the bleak darkness of the quiet neighborhood. I was trying frantically to get him to come to the door and not wake the entire world with my shouting. It was the last thing we needed right now. I rang the doorbell over and over and knocked so hard I felt as if my hand would come off my fucking arm.

"Fuck! FUCK FUCK FUCK... what the fuck is— Oh!" I recalled how Danny kept a key under the mat along the sliding door on the side of his house near the pool. I walked around there and pulled the rug up and there it was. I ran back to the front door, unlocked it and let myself in. There was no alarm set.

I called out: "Danny! Where are you, man? I got your

message. Are you alright?"

I walked into the kitchen but it was empty; the lights were on but it was an eerie silence which surrounded me. The whole house was still. Not a fucking mouse stirring.

"Danny! I'm coming upstairs, man... better be important. I told you not to bang those broads from Staten—" I got to the top of the stairs, hearing "Somewhere over the Rainbow" playing on the tv in his room. I walked into his room hoping to see him there.

"Danny..." I turned the tv off and walked toward the bathroom from which I heard the shower running. The door to the bathroom was left slightly ajar with steam floating from the sides of the doorway and the threshold.

I stood there feeling the steam hit me like a tidal wave of warm heat and pushed the door completely open. The shower curtain was pulled closed around the tub.

"Danny?"

I drew back the curtain and he was laying in the tub, a needle in his arm, shower water running. He looked pale and his eyes had a blackness under them; his arm was dripping with blood where the needle had been plunged. At first, I could not breathe or move or think. He wasn't sick or passed out... he...

"Oh my GOD! OH FUCK!" I screamed and fell to the floor of the bathroom, backing quickly against the door. I kept hollering into my hand and screaming for Danny to be alive, to be alright. I crept back to the tub and turned the water off, trying not to touch him.

"No NO!!! Danny! What did you do! WHAT THE FUCK DID YOU DO? OH MY GOD!" I was sobbing and screaming at the same time. And then I ran out of the bathroom and called 911.

"I need help, my friend is dead in the tub. He lives at 349 Forest Avenue! Please!!" I was crying so much I couldn't breathe.

The ambulance showed up ten minutes later.

CHAPTER 19
Crime & Punishment

speed of light
rambunctious chaos
and theories of relativity
immersion of light
your smile is my favorite
i try to write simply
humble
be humble...
silence
forty minutes till midnight
your glory days are coming
youth is a taste of eternity
dream as if you've never dreamed again
feel deeply
be passionate about something
anything
art is music in motion
poetry. Everlasting love.
constellations
artists need support
wings mended in time
artists need tragedy
for it to bend time
they remember wounds
old souls
fire places
rain storms
each glass of wine
literature
books

film
they feel art
others will just enjoy it...
they see themselves there
inside the words
the inevitable space time
of where they are
and where they came from
the mortality of words
they linger on my tongue
i can never quite figure them out
but they have a soul
a blended music
a tempo i swoon for
music
it is god
it is butterflies
raindrops
a pin drops
and you are free
the moment before it rains
when you see leaves dance
when you feel nature
when you remember words
sweet words
quixotic
mysterious
beautiful
candles
glow
and be your art
yourself
you are art
imperfect
a dazzling love spell
one which will never break
a whirring fan
a summer night in June
half hour till midnight
time
bend it
squeeze it

love every split second
every sound
every roar of your heart
a vociferous cry
to heaven
to your art
to everything you create
a splendid darkness
lit by your eyes
as they dance in lightning beats
of red and violet shades of words

"The night was pain. Pain I never felt before. The dream that we dream of, right? He can't dream anymore, but maybe he can. Hopefully he can find peace. I remember wanting to be dead then too, that it was me and not him! I couldn't believe the fucking pain, it was unreal. It still breaks my fucking heart. He was such a happy guy, he was a happy fucking guy, he was so loving he didn't deserve that! Why would he fucking do this? Jesus Christ. I could've stopped— I could've... done something. If I just heard the fucking phone sooner! He didn't deserve it, Jason."

"I'm so sorry, Hugo."

"I wrote that poem for him. I folded the paper up and put it in his pocket. Give him solace. Some release."

I sobbed into my hands as I covered my face.

Jason waited for me like he always did. It's funny though... most of the time I always thought it was cumming into a sock that made me feel better or cumming inside of a man or a woman, but it wasn't. It was crying it out that was the real release from the fringes of life, the margins I found myself living in each day since Terrance killed himself on that horrible night in high school. All the pain, all the tragedy, how much can I fucking take? And Deanna that fucking... bitch. That evil bitch.

"Do you want me to—"

I stuck my hand out and he immediately became silent again. He knew me. He knew how short a fuse I had lately. I wiped my face and looked at him.

"That night we were all so done. So wasted man. It just completely fell apart all of it, it just went haywire so quick, and now we're living with it."

"You said Terrance's death was a suicide. Why the guilt?"

"I could have saved him. I could have done something... and I didn't."

"Why do you keep blaming yourself?"

"I—I don't know. Danny... he had such a light inside of him. He could make life better for anyone and now he can't do that anymore. He died. BECAUSE OF THAT FUCKING HEROIN SHIT! THAT'S WHY!!! I have a feeling it was—"

"Who?"

"Who the fuck do you think?" I said this so flatly even I was taken aback. "The same one who fucking planned that night. The same conniving sick demented bitch who gave Terrance drugs!!"

"Deanna."

"Sharp as a fucking cueball. Yes, Deanna!" I took a second to take a few deep breaths before I responded again, before the acid landed right on his face. "I'm sorry."

"Don't be. It's fine."

"I'm so livid right now and hurt and in pain. I want to take Deanna's face right the fuck off. She is the bane of my existence, that evil, sniveling bitch. What the fuck is wrong with her? I want to know. If I knew, I could maybe..."

"What?"

"Save someone else's life so they don't end up like Terrance or Danny."

"Do you believe she may have given Danny drugs, too?"

"If she did, Jason, I'm telling you right now, my face will be the last one she sees. Not the doctor's."

Jason considered my words and I could tell he agreed with me.

"It won't be cinematic," I added. "I should look up his cousin Benny. I had a book of poetry that he gave me and I can't fucking find it in my apartment. I'm assuming it got lost in a box or something..."

"I hope it turns up for you. That's nice he gave you a book."

"Yeah, it is. I always appreciated it and treated it like gold. Mint condition even to this day. I don't fuck around..."

"Not like that anyway..."

"Well, you know better than anybody, don't you, fucking sex addict?"

"I'm the addict?!"

"Maybe I should be more adventurous?"

"More adventurous? You? I'm amazed Onlyfans wasn't shut down because of you. More adventurous."

"You know what I mean. Been living on the edges."

"I understand, change is good."

"I'm going to go now, J."

"Okay no problem, Hugo, I understand."

I got up, put my leather jacket on, patted him on the back, kissed him hard, and walked toward the door.

"Don't stiffen up on me now," I muttered.

"It never lasted very long anyway..."

"Tell me about it."

"Prick," he whispered as I stepped over the threshold.

I was hungry. I ordered ahead for some sushi and ate it in the car. I was originally going to just go the fuck home and maybe do some reading. And she popped in my head again, like an aneurysm. That walking terminal cancer herself. There was no cure to this walking disease, Deanna was the cancer in the cell, she was the dangerous unstable lover of Frankie, me, Terrance, everyone. Promiscuous and cruel. I wanted to destroy her. I wanted to ruin her, manipulative fucking cunt. And I found her to be a seductive woman. She had the ruthless conniving sexuality I couldn't resist, perhaps her darkness and pain matched my own. I was as much to blame for what happened to Terrance as she was, as Frankie was, everyone that whole night. We were all there, all of us, and it just went south really quick.

Things went down that night, it got out of hand, we were all drinking heavily, all smoking heavily, all of us dazed and fucking confused, stoned, drunk. It was a fucking disaster. Nothing could have made me believe that it was to happen for a reason. I certainly fucking hope not. Words were exchanged, harsh mean words, quips that usually began as jokes or mild ball-breaking. Sprinkle in some marijuana, Jack D, Vodka Crans, arguments that become heated, a slow fucking burn, another drink, another bump... ticking time bomb. Tick, tick....

HE SLIPPED!

TERRANCE SHOVED DEANNA!

Boom.

I went to the cemetery where they buried Danny, standing over his grave in Staten Island, New York, Shaolin's poetry. Nobody fucking knew him the way I did, and I only wanted more time with him. I wish I could have been there earlier, if I had fucking known... I remembered walking upstairs trying to find him, maybe passed out on his bed, or snorting cocaine and listening to Wu Tang. He made all of our lives better, more meaningful. A genuine loving soul, there was no malice in his blood, no cruelty in his bones, he was absolutely incapable of behaving that way.

I knew cruelty, of course. I had seen it for years and I inevitably became cruel myself. He would kick the shit out of me if he would have found out what happened with Terrance, or how all of us had gone along with our lie until we found out too of course that it was a calculated suicide. Deanna's heartlessness and lack of morals is what caused Terrance's death, I was sure of it, but my friends and I getting into an altercation was something else, something far worse... we lost it that night. Especially me. I remember Anthony's rage that night, when he saw Terrance shove Deanna to the street. I remember my blood becoming cold and my fuse being lit, exploding within seconds. Atomic rage.

"He didn't know how much we all loved him."

I nearly jumped out of my skin hearing this. I turned and saw Frankie get out of his car. He walked up and stood next to me.

"Probably not," I replied.

"I need you to get more pills from Jason. We need to keep it going."

"This is what you bring up, Frankie? When I'm visiting my friend's grave?" I was dumbfounded, what the fuck happened to this guy? He was cold, detached, withdrawn. It wasn't like him. Frankie was filled with life, lust, a great body, but now it was different. He was so angry, so removed.

"He was my brother. And I never understood why he was so hateful either, why it all happened the way it did, why Deanna kept giving him drugs but that's all in the past now, Hugo. I need you to do this for me. Because something tells me you owe me a little more information."

"I told you what happened."

"We believe it was a suicide, but that car... we have to get rid of it."

"Why?"

"Evidence. I can't be implicated. Nobody can."

"No, I don't... I just... it can be risky. For both of us."

"I'm a detective, baby; I won't let anything happen to you."

His hand touched my face and we kissed hard on the mouth. It was an electrifying energy surging through my bones, a reawakening to who I was before all of this spun so hopelessly out of control, to who I was before the guilt and pain set so vividly inside of me. Despite the distance that was between us now, I was still truly attracted to him, I desired him, and it was the first and only time in my life where I have ever been controlled by desire. Single combat.

Perhaps that is what Deanna and I had in common.

"One hand washes the other. You help me dispense of the car, get me Xanax to keep a cool head and everyone is happy."

"Frankie, I love you, but I am trying to stay clean here, if Jason finds out...."

"He won't find out. I'll make sure he doesn't."

"He knows me, he's my fucking therapist—"

"You mean the one you're fucking? Or is it the other way around?"

I was struck by the callousness of his words and their stinging truth.

"It's mutual, okay?"

"Hmmm... I mean, I love you, Hugo, but it can be construed as unprofessionalism on Jason's part and I would hate for anyone to find out."

"What the fuck are you doing, Frankie?"

"Protecting you."

"You're sabotaging me!" I shouted in the quiet desolation of the cemetery. "Don't fucking do this! You know what happened with Terrance!! It's horrible but if you are going to go after anyone it should be that cunt, Deanna. That evil bitch."

"It's Deanna I'm thinking of. Get rid of the car with me and have Jason dispense three months' worth of benzodiazepines."

I stood there confused and truthfully, a little scared. He just wasn't the same Frankie I had known and loved and fucked. His whole demeanor has changed to somebody entirely different, as if he were poisoned within his soul, a toxicity I have never known, a dark side. And it was unexpected, submerged somehow within him this dark nature. His eyes at once so magnetic and erotic now seemed empty, devoid of compassion and life, a dying sense of self. It was beginning to rain, and I stood there for what seemed an eternity. No end in sight kind of eternity.

"It will all be okay, Hugo. I need you to trust me. You trust me right?"

"Yeah I—I do you just seem different lately... that's all I'm saying."

"Once you get me Xanax, I'll be that same hot fuck you loved."

"You're still a hot fuck I'm sure..." My heart was beginning to pound and not out of exploding sexual thrill that I normally felt whenever Frankie grabbed my throat, but it was fear, an unprecedented fear, with definable features. And now that was the end of it.

"Then let me suck you off later alright. You need a nice blow job Hugo, I can tell, you were never wrapped this fucking tight."

"At least one of us is." My words were daggers and they sliced into his soul. I even shocked myself.

"Yeah, you're probably right but you still have those errands to run for me. I'll sweeten the pot. I'll get rid of the car. I know a guy. In the meantime, help me out here."

"Xanax is dangerous Frankie..."

"So, is this relationship with Jason, but you seem to know that already, don't you?"

"What, like you never did anything like that? You were banging your high school teachers, and yeah that was hot bro... real hot. You're fucking good."

"I know. It was worth it each fuck."

"Oh, I know it was... you're a sexy guy, my baby, yet this is how you treat me? Blackmail?"

"I'm not blackmailing anyone, least of all you, Hugo. The truth is when I was in bed with you, it was the only time in my life where I ever felt real joy and..."

"You know my feelings for you Frankie, I just can't imagine how you can..."

"Jason loves you then?"

"He has nothing to do with it. I'll get you the fucking Xanax..."

"See, I knew you were going to fold."

"As long as you don't destroy Jason."

"What?"

"That's my condition."

"Okay. I won't. You have my word."

"Do I?"

"You do." Frankie's eyes told me the truth that I wanted to

see not just hear.

"You say one fucking word and I'll blow this whole thing wide open. Could be pretty damaging to a detective. Shouldn't you be the one setting the example?"

"I always loved your mouth, but I can break it right now and not have a second thought."

"Assault now? Don't fuck over Jason!!"

Frankie approached me again and kissed me so passionately as I tried to pull away but his power to bind me to him to feel his intense sexuality on my wounded body was splendid and gloriously hot. He put his hand between my legs...

"Just—fucking promise me... Oh—"

"I promise, you weak slut... I fucking promise."

"You fucking better... Jesus—my G—just do this for me..."

I felt his stiff cock on my legs and then between them, God he was so lustful, so fucking gorgeous, even with this dark cynicism to him, I never could resist him, no woman or man ever could.

"You're going to make me fucking cum right here in a cemetery..." I was breathing so deeply so passionately, he was rubbing and tugging me against my car, I didn't want it to stop.

"I certainly hope so, Hugo...Oh god now I-I'm almost there myself..."

"Oh god baby... Oh god..."

"I still have it, don't I?"

"Oh, you really—really do baby."

"Who's your fucking daddy, bitch?!"

"IT'S ALWAYS BEEN YOU!" I came so heavily in his hand and all over my pants it was as if I were paralyzed, my joy juice was all over his hand. He smelled it and licked it clean like he always did.

"That's right, baby... that's right."

We stood there, not a soul or car in sight. Thank Fuck. I had never enjoyed a hand job in a cemetery before.

"I have to go. I'll be by later tonight. We'll talk. I love you, Hugo." Kissing me on the lips: it was sugar in my veins. I watched him go. I wanted a fucking cigarette so fucking badly. He drove away and I was left with the massive cum stain on my jeans.

"Nicely done, Frankie, you made me cum in a cemetery. Nicely done." I got in my car and found a pack of cigarettes in my jacket pocket.

Thank God. I lit up and waited there. Basking in the resonating silence, taking everything that just happened and burying it deep within. As far down as it could go, ocean depths. After ten minutes of sitting there, quietly smoking my brains out, I drove him in complete silence, wet and filled with a horrible sinking dread.

Driving home a mist had settled over the streets and the houses, enshrouding it in a strange cloud of damp rain. I had the radio on, and I was listening to the soundtrack to *The Social Network,* I never enjoyed that movie, but I found the music to be powerful, Reznor had skills I never found to exist in anyone else. A class act. All that aside however, the change in Frankie startled me. I had never seen him act that way, desperate and scared at the same time, willing to make me his accomplice now. I still wanted him in my bed, but his jealousy and bitterness...

"I love you so much," he had whispered into my ear one early morning last winter. It was pitch black in my room and we were doing shrooms and laying under the covers shivering because the heater wasn't working and he breathed that into my ear. Love can be consuming. It had a voracious appetite. Frankie could swallow me body and soul and suck up the marrow. I was his prey, his favorite fuck, his victim, his lover, I wore many hats in this relationship and despite the twisted nature of love, I could never leave him. Not really. Perhaps there was something infinitely wrong with me then.

I had to tell Jason, if Frankie even thinks about it, God help me. God help him. God help us all. One thing you never do with Frankie is cross him. I've seen him arrest people and when they resist him or give him probable cause, he will make it look like an accident. It can be a bruise on your face, a black eye, a few broken ribs... a broken arm. It didn't matter. He had the upper hand. And everyone knew to never get in his way. Even other detectives knew not to piss him off.

I sent him a text at a red light and took a deep breath.

Frankie, if I've angered you or done anything to make you question my loyalty, I would want you to tell me. But I haven't. You know I haven't. You know how much I love you, as a person as a friend and lover... I couldn't live with myself if I knew I betrayed you. I just wanted to let you know that.

Five minutes later he wrote back.

I know that. It's exactly why I can trust you. You have a lot more to lose than I do.

My soul felt cold again. It was inevitable with Frankie; he can be hot and cold in minutes. A mean streak in him a mile long. He was never especially warm or over-friendly with anyone, he was dazzling in bed, the best fucks I ever had were from Frankie, but loving and compassionate, not particularly, not once.

Hugo if you fuck me on this, if you say a fucking word to Jason...

I said I won't, and I won't.

You see what happens when we help each other out?

I'm not helping out with anything. Just for once we happen to want the same thing.

To live happily ever after... why are you texting me? Why can't you just call?

I have to go Frankie. I have things to do.

I pulled into the driveway to my house and sat in the car for another five minutes turning on the air conditioner and listening to the soundtrack on my phone. My phone blared again.

You're not afraid of me, are you? That's my Hugo... always looking out for me.

You know I do.

I plunged my phone inside of my pocket went into my house and collapsed on the couch. I felt numb, anesthetized somehow. Finally. It was nice not to have to feel anything for a while. Removed from it all, I smoked an entire bowl of herb until I was fucking numb from top to bottom, I refused to feel a fucking thing. I needed to sink below the depths of an ocean; I wanted to attach a fucking cinder block to my ankle and live among the strange and horrifying sea life where the sun never reached.

At this point does it fucking matter? Frankie was a fucking maniac, Deanna was distributing heroin like girl scout cookies, that demented fucking freak, Terrance's voice in my head at night, the sound of the car hitting him in the rain, all of us losing our fucking minds, the dominating thunder and heavy rain outside my window, my friends and I hanging by a fucking thread, Jason's career on the fucking line, being haunted by Danny's horrible suicide.

That cinder block sounded wonderful right then. I needed something right now, I needed to feel better, to be happy again, to go back to the way things were before this all happened, where I was just living with it, sleeping dogs and all... and I had to go and fuck it all up for myself. I had to just find a way out now. I'll get the Xanax for Frankie, he can fucking choke on them I don't give a fuck anymore, that's my life, that was how I was raised, to not care about a fucking thing, to fully invest in my life and myself. Well look how fucking well that's going for me! I fucked up, I fucked it all up. I was in hot water, my friends, Jason, everyone involved. And I had to unintentionally throw them all under the bus, and whether they would ever believe that is simply out of my control. There is no going back, this is the forward motion from now on. Killing myself on the other hand, the weight of the world on my fucking shoulders right now and I had to keep walking...

The phone rang in my pocket. I didn't bother to look to see who was calling me. Instead of answering, I flung it across the room, and it landed on the couch. I refused to talk to anyone about anything. I lay there sprawled out on the couch staring blankly up at the ceiling, not making one fucking sound.

I woke up and it was pitch black outside the living room windows. I had passed out while hoping a UFO would crash through the fucking ceiling and beam me up. No such luck, however. I sat up and rubbed my face and yawned. I felt around for my phone, before I saw the light come on in the darkened room. I went over and saw five missed calls from Anthony and a bunch of texts from Bobby. I didn't bother reading them or calling anyone. I didn't have the energy. Enough shit has gone down in the past month or so, Frankie turning into a fucking Nazi, learning the truth about Deanna, everything. "Please UFO, any kind, shape, anything. Just beam me up. COME ON BABY! CRASH INTO ME! BEAM ME UP!!!!!!" I shouted in the giant empty dark house. I went upstairs and fell asleep in my bed within moments.

— — —

I woke up again at four in the morning. I smoked a great deal of weed for a nice twenty minutes. I wanted the numb feeling to last, an entire pocket full of anesthesia, to cloud my memory, relax the nervous system, and up the dosage accordingly. Otherwise, I would go into my garage, sit in the car... what Frankie put me through, what both him and that horrible woman are putting me through. I knew it. I fucking knew they were together on this. I had to tread lightly, no sudden movements, no retaliation, no threats, nothing. Silence. Quiet. I loved Frankie I knew I could eventually get through to him. He was angry, not vindictive. He just was not that kind of person. Except I knew with every fiber of my being who was and is.

"It should've been me, Jason."

"Don't say that!"

"It should've been me."

"Don't say that, man."

Once again, I sat in his office, dark circles had formed under my eyes. I had to have this session. It was eleven in the morning. He would know what to tell me. I was reluctant to inform him about Frankie; the last thing I wanted to fucking do was antagonize or provoke him. Mum was the word of the fucking day.

"Confront Deanna. That's all you can do, Hugo."

"I understand that. What I can do too is snap her neck."

"Yes, and it's completely understandable. There is a way to do it however."

"I don't fucking care. She's a horrible person, a sociopath and how can you deal with a sociopath? There is no reasoning with this dreadful human being, there is no logic or emotion with her. So cold so detached...."

"What I'm going to ask may sound a little delicate..." Jason replied.

I glanced at Jason and sat back in my chair.

"Was she molested when she was a young girl...?"

"What the fuck?"

"I know it sounds a little extreme, but oftentimes this behavior stems from something traumatic that happened in childhood, possibly from a family member?"

"I don't fucking know; however, I don't think I would be surprised."

"I see."

"I don't feel a fucking thing for this self-righteous piece of shit. She's a corrupted soul."

"I know she is. Believe me. I don't know her personally but from everything she's done, there is little to no love in her life. Certainly, abuse is a factor here."

"Frankie showed up at the cemetery yesterday, he was..."

"What?"

"He wasn't himself, Jason. Something is fucking wrong, beyond the obvious of course. He just... I don't know if he was on something or there is something happening that I'm not aware of but I think I'm going to need some Xanax. I'm running out of fucking patience and I am constantly fucking alone here!"

"I'll write you a prescription."

I wiped the tears from my eyes and took a few deep breaths. It was hard-hitting to think I was faking all of this, this emotional overflow but despite everything with Frankie, I was still very attracted to him.

Jason wrote the script for me.

I rushed to the drug store, had it filled, and brought it to Frankie at his apartment.

"Got them."

We fucked, lit up and lay in bed.

"I'm proud of you, Hugo. These pills come in handy. I just can't take all the misery you know..."

"Yeah. Frankie... are you being careful? This shit is addictive."

"I'm being careful, baby, I'm sorry about the other day I should never have confronted you that way."

"What's going on with you lately?"

"I—I just have some things on my mind. Unraveling maybe..."

"Unraveling?"

"Yeah, Hugo please I don't want to talk about it."

"I just want to make sure you're not hooked on them. I was on them remember. It was hell getting off them."

Frankie took two Xanax pills at once and gulped them down with beer. "Yeah, you were practically useless to me. I never saw you so unhappy..."

"Exactly."

"Don't worry about me Hugo, I don't need it." He got back in bed with me again and we slipped under the covers. "I'm fine. It's after all the shit that's happened. It's been taking a toll on me." The wicked side of his personality was revealing itself now, and it was as if the dark side of the moon had just plunged down to earth crushing everything in its path.

"Alright. It's fine. Goodnight."

We didn't speak a word for the rest of the night and the next morning I woke up alone. He had gone to work and not woke me to say goodbye.

I called her phone and she answered.

"Yes." That voice of hers, that clipped, out-of-joint sound of her voice. It just made me feel the nauseating hatred I had for her all these long years come back to life.

"We need to talk."

"I don't want trouble, nor do I want you here, either."

"That's too fucking bad I'm pulling up to your house in five fucking minutes..."

"What makes you think I won't call the cops?"

"Because you would have done that already. Besides, Frankie is busy. We just fucked last night. So just have yourself a nice cup of coffee and I'll will be there shortly."

Two minutes later I pulled up alongside her house, stubbed out my cigarette on her front steps, and rang the doorbell. She answered on the third ring, and I walked right past her.

"Oh yeah just come in."

"You have some fucking balls, you know that?"

"Well how about we go out by the pool, and you can prove to me how big yours are."

"Not necessary. Besides you've seen them."

"Oh, I have."

"I want to know something. My friend Danny, right... did you give *him* heroin too?

"Danny Ether? Are you kidding me? His cousin Ben would have me killed."

"And right now that doesn't sound too bad, but I want to fucking know the truth, Deanna."

She stood there, implacable and detached, which was her from the beginning. Deanna was heartless, cruel, not a normal functioning person; she never let anyone get the best of her.

"No, I never did."

I smiled to myself for a second.

"No? So, he bought heroin on the streets, not from the vicious twat next door?"

"That's right."

I walked around her living room, absolutely indulgent home décor for an innocent Staten Island chick with a fast money side hustle. It's true, crime does pay.

"Blood money buys a lot of fancy shit, doesn't it baby?" I picked up a vase, a huge decorative vase with black and white lines going around it, it was heavy, and it felt smooth in my hands. I flung it hard across the room and it smashed into thousands of pieces on her hardwood floor.

"YOU ARE FUCKING LYING TO ME!!!"

She stood there. Unmoved and looking right through me but I saw her jump and that was enough evidence for me today.

"So, I want to know: did you give him drugs?" I waited for an answer. "If you lie to me again, I swear to fucking God, it won't be cinematic. I want to know! Right now, Deanna!"

"No, I didn't."

"You're fucking lying to me!"

"I'm not lying."

"You *are* fucking lying to me!" I was smacking my hand against the blank wall of her living room over and over. My rage was boiling over, consuming me from the inside out. It was as if I were possessed, and perhaps maybe I was but I had to know.

"Did you?"

"No!"

"Deanna, I swear to God..."

"No."

"Tell me, did you?"

"I JUST SAID NO!"

"You—I'm giving you one more fucking chance..."

"I'm telling you the truth, Hugo."

"No, you're not!"

"Yes, I am!"

I grabbed her and pinned her against the wall. "You killed him! You evil sick bitch!"

"HUGO!" I turned around and saw Frankie standing by the dining room. "Take your fucking hands off her."

I let her go and she walked briskly away from me towards Frankie.

"What the fuck are you doing here?"

"Hugo, I think it is best if you just keep your fucking mouth shut."

"What is going on? You're working with her, huh?"

Frankie whispered into Deanna's ear and she walked upstairs, slamming the door behind her. It was just Frankie and I downstairs in Deanna's house.

"You seem surprised somehow, Hugo. That maybe Deanna

and I hated each other, you're right we do. But after what was happening with Terrance, I found it to be incredibly challenging to just pick up the pieces and go on with my life. He was so fucked up I didn't have a life. I never went out with friends, I never enjoyed myself; I never felt relief or joy or love, what about me? I deserved all those fucking good things that you take advantage of every day of your miserable life. It was infuriating to see how you moved on with your life when I didn't have one of my own!"

"Move on? You call what I've been going through for years *moving on*? Are you fucking crazy?"

"Yeah, I'm fucking crazy. Crazy enough to fucking shoot you and not give it a second thought."

"Shoot me. Do it. I have nothing to lose, you were fucking right about that, so just shoot me. Come on. Do it. Do it. Actually, why don't you suck my cock and then shoot me. And then we can go from there."

"Everything is a game to you, perhaps that is the problem right there. Let me save you the suspense. Deanna was right."

"What?"

"She wasn't the one giving Terrance drugs. I was. And that included Danny as well. He began asking questions about Terrance's state of mind, he was concerned, he was also concerned for you as well, I just thought— well why not just make it fun? Push the blade in a little further. Make things worse, have them die slowly more and more each day. And by the time Terrance was hit by the car, which I disposed of myself, thanks for helping me with that. It was my car. I'm a detective. I can make anything happen. I guess you just forgot, you've been losing it lately."

"Deanna went along with this, then. He was your brother!"

"Oh please, for fuck's sake Hugo, he didn't mean anything to me. No more than dog shit. The guy was a prick, a worthless degenerate. I couldn't let him bring me down the way he was. I had a career to think about, to care for. So, the drugs helped, and during prom night, I planned it all and he wanted to die, he was begging for an excuse. It was liberating to finally give him one."

I could not for the life of me believe what I was hearing. It was Frankie all along, all of it was Frankie. I—he slept with me, he was... he was in love with me, but he's been lying to me. Over and over. Deanna was his accomplice.

"FUCK YOU!!!" I ran to him, bashing his head against the wall before he recovered and body-slammed me on the floor. His hands wrapped around my neck.

"Choke me, you can't fucking run forever," I whispered.

"Yes, I can, and I will. Just have to take care of this first." His grip around my throat tightened like a boa around a rabbit, and I found a piece of ceramic from the vase I had smashed. I had it in my hand, but Frankie's grip was so strong I found myself losing consciousness. I had it in my hand and my grip tightened too.

"Not before I do this."

I took the piece and plunged it into Frankie's neck. Blood spurted out everywhere around me and Frankie's lifeless body fell to the floor. I scrambled back away quickly and watched him die. Then I called 911. It was my turn now. It was my turn to tell them everything that happened.

Everything.

CHAPTER 20
No Rest for the Wicked

It was as if the chaos had permanently ended, and now all that was left was the debris from the storm, picking up all the pieces and moving on. That to me was depression, the storm was anxiety, and now the storm cleared and there were blue skies for days. I was on Lexapro from Jason, and I was now seeing him twice a week, I decided that was best.

I told the cops everything that happened to me and it was ultimate salvation. Verbatim what Frankie confessed to me a month ago, Terrance, Deanna, Danny, it was surreal to think Frankie was the one pulling all the fucking strings this whole fucking time. I didn't think in a million years it would be him but the more I dug, the more questions I asked, the more people I spoke to about what really was happening with Terrance, the more sense it made to me, the more our relationship was strained because of it. The more I felt the pain of being in love with Frankie, someone as desirable and strong and wild as Frankie, he was beautiful and I was still in love with him, and it broke my heart to think I had to defend myself the way I did.

But he was suffering too, perhaps more than all of us combined. I remembered all the wonderful times we had, in bed together, laughing hysterically, smoking weed until we were numb, eating mushrooms, going out to dinner, nightclubs, just being with each other, he was an exciting guy, and my feelings were complicated, except I knew my life was worth saving, too. I knew he would have killed me.

They arrested Deanna after she confessed about being Frankie's accomplice. I would have more to say about her, but there is nothing for me to say that would make the slightest difference. She was a selfish cunt, who needed too much. She was addicted. Frankie was banging her too. I suppose I can't blame her, I think all of us had a little piece of that over the years.

The cops walked her downstairs and I stopped them for a second.

"Yes?" she said indifferently. Her tone alone was enough for anyone to want to crack her hard in the face but she wasn't worth it, she'd never been worth it.

"Don't worry. I can't be bothered. It's just nice to see you like this."

She had tears in her eyes, and I grinned at her. The cops walked her out and she didn't look back. They drove away and later she was convicted on an aiding and abetting charge, sentenced to ten years in prison. I almost came in my pants when I heard that glorious fucking news. Jesus Christ. Conniving sick cunt. No rest for the wicked.

The charges against my friends and I still stuck. But Frankie had actually indicated all of us, according to the lieutenant. To keep us quiet about what was really happening with Terrance and his role in his own brother's suicide. That fucking sick prick... perhaps he did us all a big fucking favor. We all went to my house, dropped acid, ordered food, and escaped the rack of this tough world.

The next morning, Anthony was on the couch on his phone, and I came back downstairs, my memory was fuzzy and out of joint, I preferred that than being in prison of course.

"Good morning."

"Hugo... that was something last night."

"Yeah, it was. I'm just so fucking happy we are all alright. That we can live our lives now."

"Something like that, Terrance was..."

"Anthony, he was troubled. We all are brother..."

"I know."

I thought for a moment, rubbed my face, and fought back the tears. "I'm sorry I didn't mean to snap, I just miss him so fucking much. He didn't deserve it, bro."

"I know he didn't."

Now I was sobbing, and I refused to stop the tears from coming.

"He was in so much pain, so much he wasn't dealing with. He had nobody to turn to, certainly not Frankie."

"He had me Tony, why didn't he just talk to me?"

"I don't know, brother. I don't know believe me I wish he did. I should have reached out; it's the right thing to do."

"Yeah. It's on me too. Who knows why things happen."

"They happen. There's nothing anyone can do."

I wiped my face and looked around, I didn't hear Bobby or Tom, it was just Anthony and I there.

"Where are the other two pricks?"

"They left a while you were still sleeping."

"You want some coffee, bro?"

"Sure. Coffee sounds nice right now."

We walked into the kitchen I poured some coffee into the maker and filled it with water and got it brewing.

"It's so quiet."

"I know. It feels nice, right?"

"Yeah, it does. I like mornings like this."

We sat there in the kitchen, the only sound we heard was the coffeemaker brewing our coffee. I always enjoyed that too for some reason.

"You alright, Hugo?"

I didn't answer Tony for a few minutes and after I thought about it, I looked him in the eye. "Personally, I don't know, bro. But I know that in time I will be. But Frankie he kept his own brother sick... it just, oh God. Maybe we will never really know why."

"Maybe not, but maybe we will someday."

"I don't think I want to Tony."

"That's okay, we don't need to know everything."

We sat there and after a few minutes of shared silence between us, the coffeemaker finished brewing our coffee. I got up filled two mugs and we toasted them.

"To us, bro. To us," Tony remarked.

"To Terrance," I amended.

A rain came, and the dust of our lives was washed away forever. Our former glories were flooded with future uncertainty and the party had indeed been over for some time. We now walk in the spirit of knowing what happened and pondering to ourselves how we all wished it was different. But there is beauty in a breakdown, I suppose, and each new dawn would propel us forward towards unknowing. We finished our coffee and stared out the window at the wild rainstorm that was swallowing us into a hurricane.

What was waiting for us on the other side? Part of me wanted to know, part of me did not. The rain was music, and the roaring wind a ghost. Love what you have, before another rain comes again.

ACKNOWLEDGMENTS

For Jose
It's that simple. You are my world.
You are art, baby. I am continually impressed by you.

For Eddie Munks
Those "If you were a hot dog would you eat yourself" cracks to
the teachers at Xaverian High School were fucking hilarious. I
still think about all the times you said it. And how annoyed
they would get. I miss you, brother. I just wish I could have
been there for you.
Forever young, my guy. Much love in heaven.

For Benny Ether
Our friendship is a fine wine, brother.
Better and stronger with time.
May we cure other's wounds one poem at a time.

For my family
Ma, Dad, Mike, Kat, Benny, Anne, and Tomas.
Love you all. My heart is full. About to explode.

For my publisher, Tara at Raw Earth Ink
You do stunning work for my novels. And I could not be more
appreciative of all your efforts and time for my work. Thank
you!

For the real villain, Tatyana
Your monstrous and inappropriate behavior has inspired me
more than you will ever know.

www.ingramcontent.com/pod-product-compliance
Lightning Source LLC
Chambersburg PA
CBHW020632250626
47154CB00008B/2639